BOOK

THE ENDLESS KNIGHT

T.C. EDGE

Table of Contents

1

A Changing World

Wrapped up in a warm winter coat, a cool breeze hits the only exposed skin on my face and sends a shiver down my spine. I look down from the summit of the rooftop, watching the world shiver too. But it isn't the cold mountain air that causes it. It's a deep, collective shiver of fear.

Around me, the streets of the plateau of Petram bustle with activity. I sit on that rooftop and look out as people come shuffling through into the city, the gate and external walls heavily manned by over a hundred vigilant guards.

The mountain pass, too, has seen its security strengthened in the last day or two, beyond the levels of the preceding months. Because now, it's not a secret enemy we're dealing with. It's not some small force looking to destabilise things and gain revenge for the past. Now, we're looking at the reversal of power across the nation. If we aren't able to stop this turning tide, we'll all be washed away.

The landscape has changed abruptly. Not just politically, or militarily, but literally. Across the regions, and mainly along the coast, once prosperous cities have been partially decimated. For miles and miles, the lands burn, swarming with the enemy soldiers built up over many years in the shadows.

But above all of that, the great capital city of Eden has been destroyed.

Now, Petram is the only major safe haven we have. As with two decades before, when the regions were controlled by Augustus Knight, and the Deadlands were held by the rebels, the same structure is beginning to form. Here, in this great mountain fortress, we will figure out a plan to end this civil conflict before it consumes us all.

That, of course, is easier said than done. No one expected the Baron to destroy Eden, to rip it apart from within and send it sinking into the depths of the ocean. And if the Baron can manage that, then perhaps he truly is willing to bring the entire world to its knees, to spread the fire of destruction from coast to coast.

To fulfil the legacy of his long dead master. To burn it all down and then rebuild from the ashes…

I think, as I sit there, about the terrible sight that has been lingering in my thoughts ever since we witnessed it upon that boat. As the paltry few who managed to escape from the city drifted away on the waves, watching in horror as the great sea city twisted and crumbled into the churning surf.

It will remain like that now, an old relic filled with thousands, tens of thousands, of bodies, entombed within it as it sits like an iceberg, only its contorted tip peeking up above the water.

Right now, many may still be alive inside it, imprisoned within the metal walls with no way of escape. Waiting there in the darkness, praying for someone to come to their rescue, for an operation to begin that will see them cut free and saved.

It will never happen. Anyone still there will never leave that place. They will slowly die of thirst or drown as the water gradually rises, or see the air in their trap begin to run out, starving them of oxygen. I think of those who were caught in the explosions as my father and I escaped the city. Of those who were burned before my eyes, or crushed by some falling debris.

Perhaps, in the end, they were the lucky ones.

Their deaths were mostly quick, sending them to the next world in the blink of an eye. Those that remain will see their final days and hours pass by with the hope that they'll be saved. A hope that, by now, will have faded and grown weak. They must know now that they'll die where they are, sealed in darkness forever.

I've dwelt on the thought since we drifted away on the water. The idea of hope, helpless hope. These poor souls, locked in their metal prison, hoping until their last breath that someone will come and save them. Such a thing must be torture.

Now, the same feeling pervades the lands. That feeling of hope that spreads among the people, fading with the passing of the days. It's a hope that the heroes will stand tall and rise again, that evil will be repelled. That the spreading darkness will once more be driven back.

I hold onto the same hope. Right now, there's no alternative, no other option but to believe that we have the strength to defeat this evil. That the heroes of the past like Link and Athena, Cyra and Drake, will be able to muster their full power and take the fight back to those who work, night and day, to crush us.

I swivel my eyes back to the great wall of the mountain, at the arches that give passage into the main chamber. Inside, we're all gathered now. All of us who escaped the terror of Eden are now safe. Drake is in there, still being treated for his many wounds. Vesuvia, injured during the defence of Mercator, has now re-joined her sister, her leg tightly fitted inside a cast. Many others from the regions have already begun to drift this way, the mountain beginning to swell once again with the infirm and injured, with those with no homes or lands remaining to defend after the Baron's sudden and sickening assault across the regions.

The last couple of days have seen our concerns for extended family and friends grow too. My mother's brother, Carson, and sister, Cassie, have safely joined us, along with their families. My father's brothers and parents, however, remain in Agricola where they dwell, drawing up arms to defend their farms from any invaders.

Over the years, I've spent little time with my uncles and aunts and grandparents on my father's side. However, the little I know of them tells me that they will muster their full strength where they live, and defend themselves from anyone foolish enough to come calling. Across those lands, many have tasted war before. They know exactly what's coming their way.

Ajax has fewer worries to distract him, his own extended family limited to a sister on his father's side who is on her way here with her husband and daughter. Velia and Vesuvia, meanwhile, tell me that their mother will stay where she is with her people. That far to the West, they're safe enough from the fighting.

For now, at least…

The theme is the same across the country: the world is on high alert. Now, the cloak has been swiftly slung from the shoulders of the regions, and the chaos of war has descended. And this time, it may be even bloodier than the last.

As I sit on the rooftop on my own, contemplating the state of the world, I find my fingers drifting into the pocket of my thick winter jacket. They grasp a small notepad, and draw it out, and once more I open it up and read the words so clearly emblazoned in Professor Lane's hand.

The other source comes from Cyra Drayton…

I've read those words so many times now in quiet, private moments. Trying to make sense of it all. Trying to reconcile their meaning for myself…for my mother.

Her genes, her DNA, her blood; all run through the veins of the most powerful of the Seekers. Half

Knight, half Cyra, with his grey-blue eyes and black-blond hair, his complexion cold like Knight's but carrying a reminiscence of my mother along with it.

I knew, the first time I saw him up close during battle, that there was something I recognised in his expression, something familiar. I couldn't put my finger on it until I read those words. Now, they make so much sense.

Further excavations into Professor Lane's notepad have revealed a little more. Back before the War of the Regions, Augustus Knight always had a special interest in my mother, in her truly extraordinary powers of foresight. She always believed that his aim was to use those powers to extend his own rule and influence, to craft her into his most powerful servant.

And yet, his goal was even more nefarious: to use her DNA, and his own, to develop clones more powerful than either of them. His ultimate goal, perhaps, was to extend his grip beyond the boundaries of our nation, and to stretch his shadow far and wide over the entire world.

And these clones would be at the forefront of his conquest.

In the end, his death put paid to that, but he continues to live on through his unnatural progeny, the destruction of our way of life now the task. And yet, it appears that this unique clone, this mix of Knight and my mother, has been earmarked for a special purpose, Professor Lane discovering something else that she never had a chance to elaborate on.

Unfortunately, that's where the clues end, the Professor's good work cut short by the crumbling city that trapped her within its vice, ending her long life of service. She'll never get a chance to conclude her work, to make any further discoveries. Now, it's down to us to find out just what the Baron's next plot will be.

As I sit there, thumbing through the notepad once more in search of more clues, I hear the sound of a door creaking open behind me. Instinctively, I shut the book and slip it back into my pocket, turning to see the face of my father emerge through the door to the rooftop.

I sigh a breath of relief at the sight of him. So far, he's the only other person who knows about the notepad. The only other person who knows the true identity of the prime Seeker.

"I thought I might find you up here," he says, pacing towards me. His eyes drift down to my hand, safely hidden inside my pocket as it clutches the book. "Found anything else?" he asks, clearly noting the distorted shape of the fabric.

I shake my head as he nears me.

"Not much. Just that this main Seeker has a special purpose of some kind."

"A special purpose?" he asks, taking a seat beside me on the rooftop.

I shrug. "I don't know what it means."

"So, Professor Lane doesn't explain it?"

"I guess she didn't get a chance," I say.

He goes quiet for a moment, her death still so fresh, and spreads his eyes to the busy streets below.

"You haven't told Ajax anything, have you?" he asks eventually.

"Nothing, dad," I reply. "What about mum…doesn't she deserve to know?"

He turns his eyes back to mine.

"It's not about deserving, Theo. I'm afraid of how your mother will take it, and we need her at her strongest right now. If she comes face to face with this boy, it will be better if she doesn't know what he really is to her."

I turn my eyes back to the world below, but he draws them straight back to his.

"The same is true of you, Theo," he says, fixing me with a steady stare. "This boy is a science experiment gone wrong, and nothing more. Don't go thinking beyond that. There is nothing of your mother, of your real mother, in him…"

"But…there is," I counter. "He's half her, dad."

"No, he's not. All he has are her building blocks, but that isn't who or what your mother is. Your mother has been shaped by her experiences, by the life she's led. Those are things that go beyond DNA and genes."

"But maybe…"

"No, no maybes, nothing. Maybes will only lead to weakness. If you encounter this boy again, you have to look at him as if you never read Professor Lane's words. He is your enemy, Theo. And he needs to be destroyed. Do you understand?"

"I guess so," I say.

"No," he says firmly. "No guessing. In war, you don't guess…you know. Now answer me again. Do you understand?"

I harden my eyes and look right into his, dull blue under the grey clouds above. "Yes," I say. "I understand."

"Good," he says, patting his bionic hand on my shoulder. "Now, tell me how the others are feeling?"

He doesn't need to explain to me who the others are. I know he's talking about Ajax and Velia, in particular. Vesuvia, with her serious leg injury, is out of action for now. As a tightly knit group, and a powerful one, Jackson knows all too well that our mental state is crucial right now.

"Ajax is good," I say. "He's itching to get back into battle, as far as I can tell." I see my father smiling at my words. They're the sort he wants to hear.

"And Velia?"

"It's harder for her," I say. "She's worried about her sister."

"Shouldn't that be the other way around," asks Jackson, frowning. "Vesuvia is safe in the mountain…but when the time comes, it'll be Velia going to battle."

"Yeah, I know. But, she's just like that I guess. It's the twin thing. And I can tell she's worried about her mother too, and her people."

"Yes, I can understand that. But, if they want to stay where they are, that's their right. People are passionate about their lands, and their homes. Many will give their lives to defend them."

He knows that well enough. More than most, my father has people to worry about out there, his entire family unwilling to leave their farms over in Agricola. As yet, the war hasn't reached the borders of the region. I'm sure that it will soon enough.

We talk for a little while longer, discussing the current lay of the land. Right now, however, I know that we're in consolidation mode, everyone still just trying to get their bearings after the Baron's recent and coordinated assaults. But one thing is most certainly clear: the fabric of the nation is changing fast, and the fight for power, and control, is going to be a brutal one.

As we talk, the streets below rumble with a bustle of activity. From the mountain pass, people continue to come, vetted as they enter through the grand gates of the outer wall. Soldiers remain highly vigilant, always watching closely, trained to detect anything suspicious up here in the great mountain stronghold. City officials and administrators guide people to their correct abodes, the vast caverns within the high peaks once more beginning to fill with those looking to escape the war below.

Leeta, of course, has once more found her calling. Two decades ago she was here, helping go direct matters and organise things inside the city. Now, after twenty years of peace, she's back, scurrying from place to place in service of Markus, the city Master.

It's odd how fast everything can shift. Only weeks ago, when we escaped the Baron's compound and the perils of the desert, Petram was quiet and subdued. Now, with the outbreak of war, it's grown hurried and hectic, the people preparing again for the inevitable terrors that accompany such times.

Some will have come from the Deadlands, fearing perhaps that their lands are about to be besieged as they were before. Others, however, will have spread here from the regions, their towns and cities already subjected to the fighting, seeking refuge now in the only place they can think of. And with so many of the leaders from across the regions now lying entombed within the carcass of Eden, Petram is one of the only places left where proper leadership can be found.

Next to me, my father can't linger too long. There's too much to do, and not enough time to do it. He stands, and looks down at me, and extends out his bionic arm. I take the metal hand and feel him easily drag me to my feet.

"I've got to get back to work," he says. "And *you've* got a meeting to get to…"

I frown. "What meeting?" I ask.

He smiles. "Your grandfather has asked to speak

with you."

2
Drake Awakes

As my father disappears away into the crowded streets, I turn my attention to the high arches leading into the central chamber of the city. Battling through the force of city residents, refugees, officials, and soldiers, I work my way through the cold and towards the entrance to the mountain.

Inside, the indoor city ahead has also morphed since my last visit. In fact, it's more akin to the first time I came here, many months ago, when the world was at first mourning, and then celebrating, the life of Troy, the recently deceased city Master.

Then, the interior was filled with revellers toasting their great leader, partying until dawn as they forgot their troubles for one night only. In the following months, fear grew once more, the people afraid of what might be brewing in the darkness. Now, the new devilry came stepped into the light, and the city has changed once more.

Still cloaked in fear, it's busier than I've ever seen it. Business is being shut down, the central chamber now given over to the housing, feeding, and nursing of the people. Everywhere, new residents are being given temporary dwellings, some lucky enough to gets room in spare buildings, others forced to move into deeper chambers where short term settlement camps are being erected.

Those that live here permanently have been more than willing to give over any spare space they have to the refugees. Some invite distant family members and old friends to stay with them. Others welcome strangers with open arms. The well known hospitality of Petram is being put to the test, and is passing with flying colours.

I make my way through the wide central street, the relentless footfall of the people muddying the path, and set my sights on a passage at the back of the chamber. As I go, my mind rushes with thoughts of my grandfather. The last time I saw him, he was badly cut up and bruised from the torture he suffered at the hands of the Baron's men, chained to the wall in the deep recesses of the facility hidden beneath The Titan's Hand.

Since then, I haven't had a chance to speak with him, the doctors working to patch him up and bring him back to life. Only yesterday, having just arrived back in the city, did I hear that he would be OK, and that his wounds were largely superficial.

With so much on my mind, however, I've barely had a chance to think about him. Until now, at least.

I hurry my step as I progress through the chamber, a few eyes wandering towards me as I go. I suppose they must know me by now, know that I'm son to Cyra Drayton and Jackson Kane, know what I can do. Not so long ago, I'd have revelled in such celebrity. Now, it's merely a second thought that pulses to the front of my head only briefly, before fading away once more.

I have no use for fame anymore. Those childish, selfish thoughts have long since evaporated from my mind, my only motivation now on making sure that those I care about, and the people at large, stay safe and unharmed in a free world.

That is my purpose. That is my duty. Anything else that happens is merely a by-product.

As I go, however, one name does cause me to turn and take notice.

Bear's Bane...

I look to see a couple of scruffy looking men staring at me with popping eyes as I march past them. Their cloth is poor, and makes it clear they're from the Deadlands. They must have seen me at the Watcher Wars weeks ago, and know me only by my gladiator name.

I can't help but smile to myself as fleeting memories of my time in the games materialise in my mind. It's where all this started, really. Where my path, and Ajax's path, converged with that of the Baron's, and the twins'.

And from that convergence, war has sprouted.

They whisper between themselves as I turn back and march on, leaving them ogling me as I pass. Others do the same, perhaps more of those who know me from the fighting pits. Here, as the city swells with Deadlands dwellers and regional people alike, I suppose that's not unexpected.

Soon enough, however, I'm reaching a quieter portion at the back of the chamber, and heading down a more narrow passage away from the throng. Ahead of me, the rudimentary city hospital lies in wait, a place I last visited when Link was battling through major surgery.

Drake, thankfully, isn't so badly injured.

I feel an excitement brewing as I quicken my step and turn towards the hospital chamber. At the main doorway, I find a couple of well-equipped guards protecting the entrance. Blocking my path in, they stop me with suspicious eyes and ask why I'm there.

I tell them I'm Theo Kane, grandson of the President, and am allowed immediate entry. I suspect that they already knew all of that, but am happy for the vigilance. At times like this, you can't be too careful.

I pass by the surgery room where Link was seen to, and set my eyes on another. Fixed into the rock walls, a wooden doorway awaits with the words 'Recovery 2' stamped across it. A couple of doctors and nurses pass by, nodding respectfully at me as I lift my hand to knock. Clearly, they know exactly who I am.

My knuckles rap on the door, and I wait for the grizzled voice of my grandfather to respond. It comes after a few seconds, deeper and more throaty than usual and partially muffled by the door.

"Come in," comes the call.

I twist the handle and enter, shutting the door

lightly behind me. Ahead, lying in a hospital bed and surrounded by equipment, I see Drake watching me with a smile. My eyes quickly scan the myriad of beeping monitors around him with a frown.

"It's just precautionary," he tells me, his voice gruff from lack of recent use. "Come in, Theo, and give your grandfather a hug."

I move towards him and take a grip of his body. When I release him, he holds me near for a moment and inspects my face.

"You've grown up," he says. "I hear you've done some wonderful things for us…"

I shrug as a way of not taking credit.

"Don't be modest, Theo," he says. "Truly, you and Ajax, and the twins…there's no counting how many lives you've saved."

I find the praise unexpectedly hard to accept. Again, I merely nod and stay quiet, looking over his body at the many bandages covering his flesh. Clearly, the concern in my eyes is obvious.

"Don't worry," he says. "Like I said, all this is precautionary. I'll be back on my feet in no time…just like Link."

"Good," I say quietly. "We need you, grandfather."

He smiles at me. "You've been getting along just fine without me."

I huff. "You think? Eden was destroyed…tens of thousands are dead…"

"And many more have been saved because of you, and your mother, and your friends. Don't second-guess the positive part you've played in this, Theo. I know that's hard, with such devastation following you where you go, but it's true. Without you, those who were saved from the city may never have been rescued. Things could be a whole lot worse."

"It doesn't feel like it," I mumble.

"Look at me, Theo," he orders.

My eyes rise to his. There's nothing in them that shows any doubt at all. Only a complete conviction in what he believes. I've missed those eyes, missed that look, missed his direction and wisdom. It's good to have him back.

"We have a war to fight here," he says. "Looking back isn't part of the deal. Turn your eyes forward, and know that what you've all done is give us this chance to fight again. I can't thank you enough for that. And now, it's time I did my part too."

He invites me to sit, and I do so. Then, the question that's lingered in my mind for some time rises to my lips.

"What happened out there…to you and Link?"

He frowns. "Link didn't tell you?"

"His memory is frail," I say. "He doesn't remember much."

"Well, I'm sure you've all put it together by now," he says. "Suffice to say, we were ambushed by a superior force and all went to hell. They managed to snare me in a net, but not Link. I called for him to escape and get help. That's when I felt the butt of the gun on the back of my head. Next thing I know, I was waking up where you found me."

"In the facility?"

"Yes. Although, I had no idea where I was at first…"

"And, it was the Seekers that ambushed you?"

"I suppose so," he says. "We didn't know who, or what, they were, of course. It's thanks to you that we do. They came with a force of soldiers. We were overwhelmed pretty quickly."

"Yeah…that's not surprising. I guess you heard about what happened on Eden?"

"I did. Your mother told me a little while ago. It's all a lot to take on board, I have to be honest. Four clones of Augustus Knight is something I'd never have seen coming."

I open my mouth to correct him, to tell him it's not four Knights, it's actually three and a half, with half of his daughter thrown in for good measure. But before the words come from my mouth, the cautionary words of Jackson echo in my mind and pull me back.

"You have something to say?" asks Drake.

I hesitate briefly. "Just…that they're strong, grandfather. One of them, in particular…"

He eyes me closely, reading me as only the most powerful Watchers can. I get the sense that he's working something out, but he doesn't push it.

Instead, I quickly move the conversation along with a further question.

"You said you didn't know where you were at first," I say quickly. "How did you work it out?"

"I didn't, really," he says. "There was a man, a doctor whose job was to tend to my wounds and keep me alive and lucid. He didn't seem so bad, and eventually I managed to get a few truths out of him."

"Like what?"

"Well, where I was, for a start. It was obvious he wasn't in on the full plot, but he seemed to know that Eden was the main target. I suppose he thought nothing of telling me, given my predicament there. I mean, who would I have told?"

He laughs faintly, still capable of seeing the light side of things as he's always seemed to. Yet behind his eyes there's a growing darkness, and when he next speaks, his words have deepened.

"There's more to come," he warns. "I know about everything that you've discovered, and I know what I heard down there in that torture cell. But above all that, I feel it inside me, somewhere deep down right in the pit of my stomach. Our world, Theo, is under siege…and it's even worse than last time."

His words haunt me, and so does the sudden look in his eye. There's a depth of concern there that transcends mere worry for family and friends and local lands. His eyes tells of a threat that will consume us all, person after person, town after town, all burning under this new reign of terror.

In my pocket, my fingers fiddle with Professor Lane's notepad. I want to reach in and pull it out, reveal its latest secrets to him.

But I don't. I will not betray my father's wishes. When the time comes, he can reveal the truth.

Instead, I simply ask: "Did you hear anything about a special purpose for the Seekers…for one in particular?"

I don't see the reaction I hope for, but only get a frown and shake of the head.

"Nothing," he says. "Is there something you know that you're not telling me, Theo?"

Once more, his powers of deduction begin to work overtime. I shake my head and retreat, mumbling something about needing to get back to Ajax and the girls.

He watches me silently as I move towards the door, stopping to tell him how good it is to have him back.

He smiles at me, and returns the compliment as my fingers reach for the door handle and twist it down.

And before I walk through, I ask him one more question.

"Why did they torture you?" I enquire. "What did they want to know?"

His eyes narrow, and the smile fades from his face. And slowly, his head swivels from side to side.

"Nothing," he says, coldly. "They never even asked me any questions…"

3
A Broken Spell

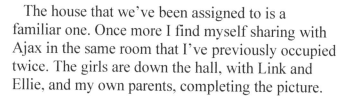

The house that we've been assigned to is a familiar one. Once more I find myself sharing with Ajax in the same room that I've previously occupied twice. The girls are down the hall, with Link and Ellie, and my own parents, completing the picture.

The chamber, however, isn't quite like it was before. Previously, it's appeared to me as a private residential chamber for some of the city's high profile residents, with most houses inside being only sparsely filled by wealthy and important individuals and families. Now, though, every spare room has been occupied, with the central square of the chamber housing a temporary command post. Inside, the city's various administrative necessities are managed, with Leeta taking up a regular post there in the service of Markus.

I always imagined that, during war, it was all about the soldiers and military leaders. But really, seeing Petram in this state has opened my eyes. People like Leeta are equally important in making sure things run smoothly. Sanitation, health and safety, rationing, housing, and many more tasks are essential to ensure that the place continues to function during this time of crisis.

Leeta, by the looks of things, was born for this.

Within the chamber, many of the higher profile escapees of Eden have been housed. Senators and Governors and Mayors and other officials who we managed to extricate from the clutches of the Baron. Down here, they'll be heavily guarded and protected, essential figures in helping to bring the country back to life once this mess has been cleaned up.

Some were full time residents of Eden, the Senators mostly. Having seen their beloved city destroyed, they generally sit in quiet contemplation, still shell shocked from the assault. Others, however, were in the city by invite of the traitorous President Alber, a man who doesn't even come close to deserving that title. They had come for his false coronation, a pawn in the Baron's game, his task only to allow the enemy easy access into the city in order to see to its destruction.

He was a blind fool, and didn't see through the Baron's lies, thinking that he'd remain as President under the new regime. Like the rest of us, it never crossed his mind that the city would be torn down around him. Unlike us, however, he never got a chance to consider the implications of his treason. A bullet to the head saw to that.

The men and women who were drawn into the spider's web, however, were never supposed to escape it. Now, the remaining regional Governors and officials from the various cities across the nation are impotent, unable to return to the places they love for fear that they'll be struck down and killed. Many wish to, desperate to pass back across the skeleton of Knight's Wall and into the regions, to gather up their people and see to their safety. But they can't.

Right now, all they can do is sit tight and try to manage things as best they can from here, try to help organise and make sense of all this chaos. And all the while, their cities and homes burn, black pillars of smoke constantly pouring fumes into the sky. Across the regions, the heavens have grown dark, filled with a smog of death that even the brightest sun cannot pierce.

It's hectic in that chamber, as it is across the city. I make my way down the passage, passing through the security checkpoints as I go, and work my way into my own accommodation, tucked up against the towering rock wall. I move inside and find that there's a rare quiet in the air, the chorus of noise from outside muffled by the heavy wooden door.

It's no surprise to find the place in this state. Jackson, Cyra, Ellie, and Link all have endless amounts of work to do, the latter most likely down in the training room, seeing to the rehabilitation of his fabled powers. They'll only ever come here to eat and sleep, allowing only a few short hours for such things each day.

The rest of us have yet to be assigned any duties, having only just returned to the city after escaping from Eden. As I walk in, I see a flickering light through a door to the left, hanging ajar. I push it open and move into the sitting room, the low flames of a fire bringing a warmth to the space.

Sitting on a comfortable sofa, I see Velia alone. It takes her a moment to notice my entrance, her mind clearly elsewhere. She looks up, and her sombre expression lights up with a smile, the fire catching in her big hazel eyes and reflecting off her sultry brown hair.

"Where are the others?" I ask, moving to sit on an armchair opposite her.

Her eyes gesture to the ceiling.

"Vesuvia's resting. Ajax is with her."

Her eyes linger for a second as they look up, before dropping back down again. It must be strange for Velia to now be sharing her sister with Ajax. All their lives, it's just been the two of them against the world. Now, Vesuvia and Ajax's mutual affections have become known, the two spending plenty of time together as she rests and recovers from her wounds.

"Are you OK?" I ask Velia, her solemn disposition clear for me to see.

She nods and raises a fresh smile.

"Where have you been?"

I briefly tell her about my day up until now, spending time on the roof, wandering through the city. I've needed that time alone, just to get my head around things, not wanting to worry about someone catching me flicking through Professor Lane's notepad. Then I speak about my brief meeting with Drake, and see her eyes light up at the name.

"You spoke with him? How is he?"

"He's doing well, his injuries are nothing like Link's."

"So he'll be back up and running soon?"

"That's what he tells me. When he's back, and Link's full health has returned, I think we'll have a fighting chance."

Her eyes narrow, and I see a flash of rare negativity spread across her face.

"You think so?" she asks, her tone more dampened by doubt than usual. "We all saw what those Seekers could do…especially that one who injured Athena and cut down those Watchers…"

Once again, the image of the mixed DNA clone flashes in my mind. It was he who called a close to our battle outside the hanger on Eden, he who broke down our rear-guard action and bested Athena in battle. Before that time, myself and Velia were beginning to work out our own opponent's fighting style. After, however, we were all swiftly defeated.

"We did better than I expected, though," I say. "Imagine a full strength Link, Athena, Cyra, Drake…and me and you and Ajax and Athena's two best Watchers. All of us together would be a pretty good team."

She shrugs, her body language refusing to give up on that deflated, negative demeanour. It's unlike her, but I know what's brought it on: the injury to her sister, which is still playing on her mind. Without her by her side, I know she doesn't feel whole, like half of a single person, her flank exposed.

"And Vesuvia too," I make sure to add. "When she's better, obviously."

"Maybe," is all she gives me. "But the way they just took out most of Athena's Watchers...it was brutal, like they were nothing."

I step up from my armchair and move towards her in the flickering light. Her head remains low as I drop beside her on the sofa.

"Velia, it sounds horrible to say it, but those Watchers *were* nothing to the Seekers."

My words draw a frown over her eyes, an element of shock within the hazel at the callousness of my words. But that's not how they're intended.

"What I mean," I say, explaining myself, "is that they had no chance against them. Most of Athena's Watchers have limited gifts and abilities. They were cut down easily because they were the weakest of us. The rest of us held our own."

"Until we didn't," she says. "Holding our own is good and all, but it makes no difference if we can't win. What's the point in just holding out, only to be defeated? The way they fought together, it was like they were fighting as one. I've never seen anything like that."

"And when we fought them separately," I counter, "we were almost getting the upper hand. Had Link and Drake been there, who knows what could have happened."

I'm trying to imbue some positivity into her, to

bring back the Velia I'm used to. To a degree, it works, her shaking head turning to a weak nod, her expression telling of some agreement. It's not much, but it's a start at least. Right now, negativity isn't welcome here. That's what Drake, or Jackson would say. And when they're not around, it's up to me to take on that mantle, to help lift those up who are beginning to falter.

We sit by the fire, and talk for a little while longer, trying to move onto other things. I'm reminded of when we were last here, when the two of us sat here, late at night, trying to bring some light into our lives, to shoo away the darkness, if only briefly.

So we do the same as the evening descends, my own aim to make her smile as much as possible, even laugh. When I finally achieve that goal, the sweetness of her giggle brings a warm smile to my own face, and I feel an urge to lean in a little closer to her, get a little nearer. I find my eyes lingering on her lips, soft and pink, her white teeth shining behind as her smile brightens the dim room.

For a split second, I forget all my worries in that moment. Forget the concerns for those I care about. Forget about the Baron and the Seekers. Forget about the war. For that single, fleeting moment, I think only of Velia, this beautiful, tough, passionate girl before me.

And just as I creep closer, wanting that moment to strengthen into another, into something greater, a voice sounds behind me, breaking the spell.

"You're back…"

It's so sudden I almost jump out of my skin, the room coming back into stark contrast as I swivel around and see Ajax peering around the door frame.

He looks at me, now right up close to Velia on the sofa, with a glint in his eye and one corner of his mouth curved into a grin.

"Sorry...I'm not interrupting am I?"

"No, no, not at all," says Velia hurriedly. She sounds like she was just as embedded in that spell as me.

"You sure? I can, um, come back later if you want."

"No, seriously, AJ, we were just talking," I say.

He shrugs and steps further into the room.

"Alright, I believe you."

"How's my sis doing up there?" asks Velia, keen to swiftly move onto another subject.

"She's just sleeping," says Ajax. "I heard some laughing, so thought I'd get in on the joke. What have you guys been up to?"

"Not much, just chatting," I say. "I saw Drake earlier. He's getting better fast."

"That's awesome, Theo. We need his leadership right now. I mean, your dad's done a great job, don't get me wrong, but Drake's led armies before."

"Yeah, and he's got that foresight," I add. "Seriously, it was so good seeing him back. I felt sure he was dead for all those weeks before we found him."

"Yeah, and the Baron made a big mistake not making that happen. It might come back to haunt him."

As we speak, the sound of commotion outside begins to grow closer to the door. Then, suddenly, a fresh burst of voices rumbles into the house, the sound of Cyra and Ellie and Leeta bustling inside. I hear Leeta and Cyra move off into the kitchen, as Ellie's eyes swing into the room.

"Hey kids," she says. "Leeta's cooking up her famous beef stew. You want to come help set the table?"

She frames it as an offer, but really it's an order. As our school Principal back home, she's used to that.

Despite everything that's going on, I know that our parents, our mothers in particular, want to ensure that some semblance of normality is maintained. Dinnertime is one such opportunity, so just like back on Eden, we help set the table in the kitchen and offer to aid Leeta with the cooking.

I do consider that, perhaps, it's better to have someone else perform the job, given how many other things they have to do, but don't bring it up. Truth be told, doing something as relatively mundane and unimportant as cooking and preparing dinner is probably welcome respite for all of us.

Back on Eden, of course, the world hadn't quite come to the verge of collapse as it is now. Mostly, life was going on as normal, with the threat of violence simmering in the background. Now, it's come to the boil, and yet our parents still consider it important to maintain this particular custom.

Dinnertime on Eden was also something I welcomed; an opportunity to sit down and pick my father's brain in particular. That evening, however, he doesn't materialise, my mother telling me that he's too busy participating in war meetings with Markus and the various leaders of the war effort.

Link, however, does appear, fresh from a day of training and meetings of his own. He looks stronger than he did the day before, his wounds quickly healing and his full powers returning in force. It's an extremely comforting and rousing sight, and helps to give the rest of us strength too, particularly Ajax.

And, right now, it's just what we need after the last few days we've had. Some good, home cooked food, the company of friends and family, and the unnerving positivity of the likes of Leeta and, to a lesser extent, Ellie.

At a time like this, it's the little things that make you realise just what you're fighting for.

4

State of Play

It's not until the following morning that I see my father again. He enters my room after a brief and sharp bout of knocking, and sends his eyes over Ajax and me as we groggily sit up in our beds.

"We are holding a meeting in the Master's chamber to update you all on the current state of affairs across the country. Meet me downstairs in five minutes," he says.

As quick as he entered, he's gone, his footsteps taking him off down the corridor. A check of my watch informs me that it's still only a little past dawn, regular hours perhaps not such a fixture at a time like this. As quickly as possible, Ajax and I dress and head downstairs to find Ellie and Cyra awaiting us. Moments later, Velia appears from the top of the stairs as well, alone once more and without her sister.

"Vesuvia not coming?" I ask her with a whisper.

"She's still weak," she tells me. "I'll update her later."

Given her current state of health, it's also possible that she simply didn't get the invite. Whether a Watcher or not, a serious injury like she sustained is enough to take anyone out of the game.

We head off together up towards the main chamber, the command post in the square of our residential chamber already growing busy. I see Leeta already there, getting on with her many tasks, busily working with her team.

Link, I learn, will meet us there. According to Ellie, he woke early to get some further rehabilitation work in before the meet. Trust Link to do such a thing. Most people who'd suffered such injuries would be getting as much rest as possible. Link, meanwhile, prefers to spend every spare minute he has recuperating his abilities, pushing his body right to the limit.

I hope that he doesn't suffer any sort of burnout. When I bring the concern to Ajax, he merely shakes his head and declares that his father knows just what he's doing. I have absolutely no basis to counter than argument.

Through the main chamber we go, led along by Jackson as we sweep through the city, drawing many early morning eyes with us as we march. They look at us and see action, wondering what plans we're cooking up to save them all from the spreading shadow. Right now, I'm wondering exactly the same thing.

Soon, we're at the entrance to the passage that leads to the chamber of the city Master, given to the discussion of war just as it was two decades ago. As it was then, all designs for our cause will begin in there, all major plans drawn up by the brains trust of

Petram in that cosy chamber. I look upon Jackson and Cyra and Ellie with confidence, knowing that they've been through all of this before.

Now, it's the turn of the younger generation to join in and help in the fight.

Many guards line the passage, maintaining a constant vigil over their leader. We pass through the corridor as the rocky walls turn smooth and flat, the mountain neatly morphing until its appearance resembles that of a man-made building. We reach the heavy wooden doors and pass straight through into Markus's war room, finding many others already there awaiting us, Link among them.

I scan the room immediately and see many familiar faces. Markus himself stands around the central table, already in discussion with several others whose faces I recognise. One, I know to be General Trent, commander at Fort Warden and head of the Eden military forces. Another is General Proctor, commander of the forces of Petram. Others are Senators and Governors from Eden who either escaped the destruction of the capital or were absent from the city when the fighting began. By the looks of it, half the luminaries from across the nation still on our side have congregated here.

Athena, too, is present, standing beside Link with her two Watchers. I think of how many others she's already lost, and whether she has any remaining. The eyes of some of Markus's personal guard suggest she does, several more having been left behind to protect the city when she went on her hunt.

As we enter, bringing the room to its full complement, Markus's eyes draw up to us and order for the doors to be shut. The many voices in the room hush, all eyes swivelling towards us. Then, Markus's voice brings them back to him.

"Good morning, everyone," he begins. "I've gathered you all here to bring you up to speed on exactly what's happening across the country as we speak. Some of you will be up to date, others won't. Suffice to say that right now, things are developing quickly, and we need to be ready to act fast in response."

His eyes sweep across the room as he addresses us, before stopping on my father.

"Jackson, would you start. Bring us up to date on the health of our President...our *true* President."

My father quickly informs those who don't know that Drake is currently awake and doing well. That his wounds are largely superficial and his mind is just as sharp as it was.

"He'll be right here with us in no time at all," he concludes, bringing a short round of applause as he does.

There's not a single person in this room that doesn't have the deepest respect for my grandfather, of the things he's done. Having him back up and running will be an enormous boon to our cause.

"That is excellent news," says Markus, currently running the show in his stead. "However, all good news is tempered with the bad. As of right now, there's plenty of the latter."

The mood quickly darkens. I listen to him intently, desperate to hear what's happening out there that I don't already know.

"We have had reports coming in over the last two days. Ever since Eden was destroyed, the regions have been under siege. The Baron's forces are spreading through the lands, giving those they meet a single choice…silver or lead."

"Silver or lead?" asks Ellie. "You mean, join or die?"

"Essentially, yes," says Markus. "The Baron is working to build his forces further, and create a new world order. We have a young man here today who can bear witness to this."

He swings him arm over to the left, and for the first time I see a young man, cowed and timid amid such esteemed company, ruggedly dressed and weary looking.

"This is Elton, a young man from the small town of Ship's Haven on the North-eastern coast. He's travelled here overnight to tell us his story. Please, Elton, step forward."

Nervously, the young man moves ahead of the watching eyes of a room full of Generals, Senators, Governors, and Watchers, many of them legends of the past and present. He's hardly able to make eye contact with anyone as he speaks, his voice brittle and nervous.

"My town…we were attacked," he begins slowly.

"We'd heard about Eden, and the fighting. But we never expected it to come to us. They rounded us up like cattle and pointed their guns at us. They…they asked us if we wanted silver or lead, like the Master says…"

His eyes begin to water as he speaks, his body trembling. Standing nearby, my mother steps to his side and gently puts her palm to his back.

"It's OK, Elton," she says softly. "Take your time."

He looks at her in wonder, her presence giving him strength. His voice firms up, and he continues.

"They explained that if we took silver, we'd join them, and live prosperous lives. But if we didn't, we'd be shot and killed right there on the spot. It wasn't much of a choice. But some…some refused the man, maybe they didn't believe him. They were killed right there in front of me."

"And those who said silver?" asks Jackson.

"They were put into a truck and taken off. I…I don't know where…"

"The same thing is happening everywhere," cuts in Markus. "Right now, we don't know what the Baron will do with these people, but none will get the prosperous life he promises. Other reports have come in, telling of people going willingly. It's well known that not everyone has been happy with the current regime. Droves of people are joining his ranks without needing to be threatened."

"Any you, Elton," says my father, turning all eyes

back to the young man. "How did you escape?"

He shakes his head. "I didn't, sir. I…was let go."

"Let go?"

"Yes. They told me to come here, stand before you like this, to tell you my story. They want you to know what they're doing."

"And who was it who told you this?"

"I don't know. I didn't see his face. He was wearing a…a cloak, and his face was in shadow."

He doesn't need to continue. We all know who he's talking about.

Markus steps to his side.

"Thank you, Elton, for having the strength to come here," he says. "But you're safe now. Rest, and eat. You will be well looked after.

"Well done…you did well," I can hear Cyra whisper to him as he's led towards the door. It opens, and I see a young city official waiting outside to take him off. When the door shuts, the conversation resumes, Markus once more taking the floor.

"News of the Baron's sadistic choice is starting to spread through the regions. As of now, people are fleeing their homes before they're found, escaping into the wilderness where they think they'll be safe. Many are coming across to the Deadlands. Already, we've had a few reports of dead bodies being found out there, killed by the heat. We can expect many others to be ill prepared for what greets them in the wasteland. And yet, still they come…"

"And the city continues to fill," adds in Jackson. "We have only so much space and provisions to house them, but they know Petram to be our only impenetrable fortress. When the going gets tough, this is where the people flock to."

"Indeed. We who experienced the last war know what it's like to see this city swell. However, the playing field is very different from last time. We have our own standing army here, and spread across the Deadlands. General Proctor, would you fill us in."

Now, all eyes move to the man in charge of the forces of Petram. He's typically grizzled and gruff for a military man from these parts, someone who's never tasted the air of Eden, his life spent in the desert and mountains. With a mane of warm brown hair and searching brown eyes, he looks every bit the predator, stalking the floor as he begins to speak.

"Our forces are spread across the Deadlands at their posts. If given the order, they are ready to rally and march to battle. Unlike across Knight's Wall, my men are completely loyal to our cause…"

It's a veiled insult to the forces of Eden. Already, some have defected willingly, their own commanders part of the Baron's plan from the beginning.

"General Trent," says Markus, calling out the leading military figure from the regions. "Perhaps you'd like to fill us in on your own movements."

Older, taller, and quieter than his counterpart, the wiry figure of General Trent turns his keen eyes to General Proctor.

"Your point is taken, General," he says, his voice precise and measured. "But none of us foresaw what Baron Reinhold was up to. He was a resident of these lands, and yet his plot slipped under all of our noses. Now isn't the time for pointing fingers. It is the time for action."

General Proctor bows his head respectfully at his words, as Trent continues.

"Regarding our military movements, we're doing all we can to protect the major cities and larger populations. Over the last couple of days, our entire military force has been mobilised, with all our bases, including Fort Warden, emptied out. We are doing what we can, but it's a losing battle. We don't have the manpower to cover all settlements, and have no means of predicting where and when the Baron's men will turn up next. Currently, ladies and gentlemen, we are losing this fight…"

Markus's eyes swivel to Athena, watching proceedings quietly until this point.

"We may have some means of prediction, General Trent," he says. "The one advantage we have are our Watchers, many of whom are highly trained and experienced. The Baron has his Seekers, yes, but they are young and there are only four. Athena…"

Now Athena takes the stage, her face a typical snarl and eyes like that of a fox. Her arm, injured only days ago on Eden, sits in a sling, weak but on the mend.

"Thank you, Markus. Yes, from what we can gather, the Baron has no Watchers outside of his little force of clones. They're powerful and can see deep into the Void, but their ability to search and decipher the future in their visions may be a weakness. Here, we have certain individuals who have supreme gifts in such arts, Cyra in particular. We will make it a priority to find out where any fresh assaults will dawn. By the sounds of it, the Seekers are splitting up as they comb the country. Together, they are extremely powerful. Individually, however, they are vulnerable. We have to make it our goal to take them out, one by one."

I look across at the Watchers in the room. Link, Ajax, Velia, Athena's two loyal servants. Mostly, however, my eyes greet my mother, her full powers returning. If anyone can see far into the future, it's her.

"Good," says Markus. "I want all of you working closely together on this, and want regular updates. Be sure to keep Drake in the loop. I'm merely keeping his seat warm…when he's fully recovered, he'll be leading this cause."

I've always liked Markus, and that sort of comment is exactly why. He was once Drake's right hand man during the War of the Regions, and despite now being the city Master, continues to defer to him. Frankly, there's no one better out there to be guiding our path than my grandfather, and we all know it.

For a little while longer, the meeting continues. Other voices are heard, offering insight into what they've discovered, or fleshing out some of the latest rumours about enemy movements. Many in the room, however, have little to contribute, here largely as a courtesy due to their positions in the major cities and regions being discussed. We are, after all, talking about their fates of their people, and they have a right to know what's happening to them.

Naturally, of course, the current location of Baron Reinhold and the Cabal is of primary concern. It's Link who brings the question to the table, his voice joining the fray for the first time.

"He's back in hiding, as far as we can gather," answers Jackson. "Directing matters from some unknown location. I doubt he'd peek his head out right now, not unless his Seekers are there to protect him. However, we do know that a large force has been gathering along the ravaged coastline, taking up positions in Piscator and Mercator. It appears he's making them his central command post, using the area as a base of operations from which his men can strike out."

"So he could be there?" asks Link eagerly.

"Could be, but we have no definitive proof. His need for overall subterfuge is gone. Now, his forces are out in the open. Just not him…"

"And the Cabal?" asks Cyra. "What about his allies. Lord Kendrik, Count Lopez, and the rest?"

"They, too, haven't been seen. I assume, like us, he's keeping himself and his most trusted supporters tucked away somewhere. He'll use his pawns to do his bidding. And their numbers are growing…"

"Yes, we have already given up the fight along that stretch of coast," says General Trent. "We have to be smart about our choices, and they have control of those lands and cities now."

"Then we continue to consolidate for now," says Markus. "They caught us off guard, but the playing field is starting to even out. With any luck, the Baron will have shown all his cards and won't have any more tricks up his sleeve."

I doubt that's the case, but don't say anything. The Baron has shown himself well capable of tripping us up, time and again. As far as I can see it, the playing field isn't level. It's very much in his favour.

The meeting concludes soon after, the morning still young as we move back down the passage and into the main chamber. Before we go our separate ways, Athena gathers us Watchers together and reiterates our orders.

"We all need to be looking for any fresh attack," she says.

Personally, I don't much like the sound of it. We spent half our time on Eden looking for where the next attack might take place, a frustrating process at the best of times. Now, it looks like that process is going to start all over again.

Yet, I know that it's not really about saving a few people in some regional town. It's not about making sure they don't have to suffer the choice of silver or lead. No, this is about squaring up against the Seekers once more, getting one alone and outnumbering him. If we can do that, the likes of Link and Athena and Cyra can surely break them down.

"You know what they look like," continues my old mentor. "You know how they smell and sound. Look for them, night and day. Never let them drift too far from your mind, and we'll find them, we'll see them coming. And then, together, we'll hunt them down."

And with those words, the hectic morning of greetings and meetings and top secret information finally concludes. And from the green woods of Lignum, and my quiet little life, to the high passes of Petram, I find myself right at the centre of a civil war, in the heart of a collaborative effort to stop darkness from spreading across the lands.

And like Leeta helping to run the city over in that command post, I know that I'm born for this too.

Right here, right now, is exactly where I'm meant to be.

5

The Guardians of Liberty

I begin to suffer a sense of déjà vu as the following days come and go. Tasked once more with hunting down signs of any major attacks, the true curse of being a Watcher unfolds before me more profoundly than it ever has before.

With war spreading fast, death and destruction is never far from my mind. Often, it's just as it was when Ajax and I first trained here under Athena before the Watcher Wars, when our powers were first developed. During that time, I'd see murders and accidents happening down in the mountain passes and deserts below, never able to spot anything specific enough to help me stop them.

Now, with so many escaping the fight across the regions, I see the unforgiving tundra swallowing people up as they cross the wasteland. Right before my eyes as I sleep or meditate, they die of thirst or get sucked into quicksand or pass out from the unrelenting heat that they will never have experienced before.

I know, now, just how desperate things can get down there, how things can turn calamitous in the space of only a few hours for those unused to the perils below. Now, desperate to flee the fighting, people are willingly putting themselves into harm's way, choosing the lesser of two evils as they leave their homes behind. It's a sign of their despair that they're willing to go to such lengths, many dying as they succumb to one hazard or another.

The numbers of the dead rise by the hour, going far beyond anything I've yet seen. It creates so much fog in my head, my visions clouded and indistinct as I see one accident or death after another, watch as innocent people get sucked from this world in terrible fashion.

Ajax and Velia appear to be having the same problem, Vesuvia too. She may not be able to fight right now, but she can search her visions as she rests and recuperates. Together, we gather in the twins' room with Cyra, who once more offers us the wisdom she's accumulated.

"You need to do as Athena told you," she says. "Think only of these Seekers. Search for them, and nothing else. There is nothing we can do for individuals and families crossing the Deadlands. That is a task for someone else. Our job is to find our main enemy. Think of them, and them alone."

It's a harsh mentality, but a necessary one. I've learned plenty of times now that seeing a person die or get injured in a vision is very rarely enough. That the vast majority will never be saved, the accident occurring in an unknown place and at an unknown time. It's the true curse we bear, watching these people die with no means of saving them. And at times like this, our minds are continually assaulted.

We all agree to work harder, though, and to do just as Athena and Cyra say. My mother's words, in particular, echo within me, her proficiency at such things exceeding all others. I know that she's already been seeing signs of major attacks hundreds of miles away in the regions, the landscape and architecture making it clear of the general area in which they're taking place. Few, if any, of us can see that far and maintain that clarity. And yet even she tells us she hasn't seen a Seeker as yet.

Of course, for me, filling my head with thoughts of the Seekers isn't too difficult. They've been dominating my thoughts for a while now, one in particular. He lingers in there almost constantly, his image emblazoned before my eyes, his grey-blue eyes glinting behind his hood.

Never is he far from my thoughts, this boy who is half built from my mother. I think of how the Baron called Augustus Knight the Seekers' father once before, when we met in the training room beneath his compound. If that's the case, then Cyra is this boy's mother...

And I am his brother.

More and more, I grow desperate to tell someone about it, to talk about it. I look at my mother each time I see her, feeling more guilty by the day that she doesn't know. I itch to let it slip to Ajax or Velia when we share private moments together, when they ask what I'm thinking about as I go quiet, not knowing what thoughts are in my head. Each time, I brush it off and dodge the question, but they can both tell that something is up.

Worst of all, I barely see my father at all. He's the only other one who knows, the only person I can talk to, and yet rarely does he appear in the house. Working all hours he can, he doesn't even come for dinner, returning late and leaving early in the morning before I get a chance to talk.

One night, several days after the meeting, I creep out of bed once I know Ajax is asleep, and head downstairs into the sitting room. I wait by the dying fire, listening for footsteps outside the door, my head and body weary as I struggle to stay awake.

The creaking of the door signals my father's return. I hear him move in towards the kitchen to grab some food before setting off for a brief slumber, and catch him before he can go.

"Theo, what are you doing up this late?" he asks.

"I need to speak with you," I tell him. "It's eating me up, dad, this Seeker…I need to talk about it."

I can tell he's weary, and this is the last thing he needs right now. And yet, still, he leads me back into the sitting room and we take a seat.

"Speak, son," he says.

Frankly, I don't even know what to say. Only that it's been on my mind recently and I've been itching to spread the word a bit more.

He shakes his head as I speak, then cuts in with a firm: "No."

"But…"

"No, Theo. I told you before, and nothing's

changed…we need your mother focused on her job, and the same goes for everyone else. If anyone knew that this clone was half made up of your mother, then it might impact their behaviour in battle. We know full well just how ruthless he'll be, and we need to be the same. We can afford to be nothing else."

It's the same thing he's told me before, and I'm not surprised that nothing's changed. Given how much he's got on his plate, he probably hasn't thought about it much. I, on the other hand, have been obsessing.

"You said you understood when we talked about this before, Theo. Now, I'm going to make you go one step further. You need to promise me you won't mention it to anyone."

He fixes me with that stare of his that demands compliance.

I take a breath and have no choice but to nod my head.

"Yes, sir."

"Say it."

"I…I promise I won't say anything," I say.

He nods.

"Good. Now get this off your mind, OK. It's doing you no good at all, and we need you strong. Imagine if everyone else knew, and they were all feeling the same as you. Would that be a good thing, or a bad thing, during this time of war?"

"Bad," I admit, conceding to his wisdom.

"Precisely. Now, it's late, and I really need to get some sleep. That's the thing about wars...they're not kind on anyone's schedule."

He smiles at me and stands, before swiftly slipping from the room.

The exchange didn't exactly go as I'd hoped, and yet no better than expected. Frankly, when you're at the centre of running a war, this particular concern must seem fairly minor to my father. Still, though, just getting it off my chest and hearing him reassert his strong opinion on the matter helps to assuage my doubts.

For now, at least.

Outside of the city, the world continues to rush along at a frenzied pace. Already, many of the Petram soldiers stationed around the Deadlands are being mobilised and brought to the mountain passes. With so many refugees still swarming in, their numbers are essential in helping to ensure law and order is kept, and in protecting the people from any would-be threats.

Right now, however, an attack anywhere beyond the ruins of Knight's Wall isn't being expected. The Baron's grip certainly can't extend that far without overreaching and making him vulnerable. So, as more people come, and the city fills, large camps are set up down in the valleys below to cater to the civilians and Petram army alike.

The Eden forces, meanwhile, continue to offer as

much support as they can across the regions. Mostly, the coastline has been given up, and reports have come in that the other sea cities have succumbed, the soldiers stationed there fighting to the last man with no real means of escape.

Yet the entire picture remains hazy, and we have no accurate way of determining the size and scale of the Baron's operation. As his mercenary army continues to spread, gathering people to their cause, it's impossible to know how many are joining, and how many are being killed. Mostly, however, people are evacuating before they're discovered, choosing to go one way or the other: those loyal to us going into hiding, or passing Knight's Wall and continuing on towards the Deadlands; those disaffected with the current regime choosing to willingly join forces with the usurper and would-be leader.

Slowly, the grand picture forms, telling of the changing shape of the nation. People running scared and hiding where they can, groups of mercenaries spreading far and wide, our own soldiers defending the people, holding down the fort at certain towns and cities across the country where their concentrations are high enough to fight on.

Mostly, the fighting remains locked relatively close to the coast, the further regions like Agricola still yet to be touched. My extended family on my fathers' side remain there, passing him information as they gather all those able to fight and form their own vigilante force. The same appears to be happening elsewhere: those unwilling to run and hide are gathering arms, organising themselves into their own groups to defend their homelands.

Such spirit is what this country, and this regime, is built on. A never say die attitude that pervades great swathes of the population so tired of being subjugated. They will not run from the Baron's men. They will not risk the perils of the Deadlands in an attempt to find shelter from the storm. They will stand tall, and face it head on, and collectively tell the Baron that they're not afraid, that the evil of Augustus Knight has been banished from their lands, never to return.

And soon enough, a name begins to spread from town to town, settlement to settlement, a name taken on by these protectors of the nation.

The Guardians of Liberty, they call themselves. Regular people, unwilling to yield, unwilling to run.

Willing to fight

Willing to die.

6

A Fond Farewell

The emergence of this new force gives everyone cause for optimism. Once more, I find myself invited to a war meeting in order to hear further updates and provide any of my own.

Standing in the Master's chamber, all of the Watchers, starting with Athena, give details of their recent visions. Around us, the two Generals stand, along with Markus, Jackson, and a few other military personnel. A few politicians remain, but most of those who were gathered here before are absent, their presence seemingly doing little but adding unnecessary bodies and voices to this particular meeting.

Mostly, our testimonies are fairly disappointing. At the moment, with so much going on across the country, what we're seeing is muddied and opaque, visions shifting from one to the next as they fight for attention in our thoughts.

It doesn't help, also, that certain major cities continue to be focal points of the fighting towards the Eastern coastline, our forces and the Baron's locked in a stalemate. Such a large scale battle only serves to blur smaller visions, diverting our attentions away from minor skirmishes elsewhere, of which the Seekers may be playing their part.

Currently, we can be certain that they're not involved in the main fighting. Not only have we heard no reports from our own men of their presence there, but the simple fact that the fighting is evenly matched is testament to their absence. Were they to turn up, they'd quickly decimate our men, who'd have little defence against their powers.

That, of course, is what makes us all so curious. It's Ellie who brings the point up, saying what many of us are thinking.

"It's diversionary," she says. "The Baron is maintaining the fight to cloud our visions. He doesn't care if he loses men, just that it's hindering us, and allowing his Seekers to work in secret."

"And who knows whatever else he's cooking up," growls Link. "The fighting suits him while he continues to plot and scheme. What about the secret base at The Titan's Hand," he asks, turning to Jackson. "Have we learned anything?"

This is all news to me. I look to my father, who takes a breath and shakes his head.

"I've lost contact with them," he says.

"You've what?" asks Link.

"Earlier this morning, our transmissions were severed. I'm sending another party out to ascertain what happened…but I think we can all guess."

"They were attacked," says Cyra. It isn't a question. And it's not speculation. The look in her eye suggests she knows.

"You didn't see anything, did you?" asks Jackson.

"Flashes, maybe. I saw a facility being burned, soldiers being killed, but I didn't know where. It must be The Titan's Hand."

"Well, why didn't you say anything?" asks Markus.

"Because I wasn't sure where it was," she reiterates. "And, in any case, I wasn't aware that a force had been sent there," she adds, looking at Jackson.

"Yes, well I thought it prudent to discover what else we could find there."

"And clearly they didn't like it," says Link. "They're covering their tracks over something."

"The special purpose…" I whisper.

My father's eyes glance at me, demanding I stay quiet. The others, unfortunately, hear me too.

"What special purpose?" asks Link.

"Oh…um, nothing really. Just…Professor Lane, before she died, she said something about a special purpose…for the Seekers."

I bend the truth, not telling them about the notebook, and not telling them that the special purpose appears to be intended for one Seeker in particular. Still, it's enough to brew up a fresh bout of speculation.

We debate it briefly, but no one has any idea what it might mean. All the while, Jackson peers at me, urging me to keep my mouth shut and not mention anything else.

In the end, we press on, other more important things to consider.

"So we can safely assume that the base beneath The Titan's Hand has been taken if not destroyed," says General Trent.

"Most likely the latter," says Markus. "They have no further use for the base, and if it did hold any secrets, they'd want to wipe them out and not give us a chance to take the base back. The men we sent will be dead. I'd suggest you recall the others you sent."

Jackson shakes his head. "We might as well make sure. I'll instruct them to scout from a distance and then return. I doubt that the Baron's men will stick around there once the job's been done."

"OK," says Markus. "Now let's move on."

The conversation turns to the rare good news that's been coming in, that of The Guardians of Liberty, whose force is developing by the minute it would seem.

"We have heard reports from dozens of towns and settlements where people are refusing to leave," says General Trent. "They're setting up defences and sending off those who can't fight for their own safety. We need to be willing to aid the young and old and infirm as they flee. We can't have any more dying as they cross the Deadlands."

"My men are on it," says General Proctor. "We have a force of several hundred patrolmen out there as we speak, combing the lands and guiding people here. They're using scanner equipment to see through the sandstorms and are ready to help anyone who needs them."

"And the camps down in the valleys?" asks Athena. "Are they being managed?"

"Yes, everything is in order. We can cater to thousands, tens of thousands if needs be. However, the more civilians we have to care for, the more recruits we'll need for the job. It's a waste of resources using my soldiers to babysit the people."

"I agree," says Markus. "We need to have a fighting force ready and waiting to march at the drop of a hat. If the Baron swells his full force, we have to be prepared to meet him. As it stands, we need more aid."

The chamber goes silent for a few brief moments. Despite all those who are currently taking up arms against the Baron, we still don't know exactly where we stand. Estimates of his own numbers appear to be growing daily, bolstered by the defectors.

It's Velia's quiet voice that breaks the silence. Rarely during any of these gatherings does she speak, her confidence and bravado reduced amid such company.

Coyly, she offers her opinion.

"What about those in the West?" she asks. "They're not exactly loyal to Eden, but they hate the Baron as much as anyone."

"You mean the far reaches of the Deadlands?"

asks Markus. "The Western coast?"

She nods, growing in confidence as everyone stops and gives her the floor.

"For my entire life, the Baron's drugs have been poisoning our lands. Maybe that was part of his plan all along, to weaken us so we'd have no means to fight or defend ourselves. But there are brave people there who would be happy to see him get his comeuppance."

"Are you sure about that?" asks Markus. "The Westerners keep to themselves mostly. They don't care about what happens across the wall, or even here in Petram. They're detached from this."

"But they won't be soon. The shadow of the Baron will spread. They've suffered under his rule before. They won't want the entire country to share that fate."

I look at Velia with pride. Pride in her passion, and the faith she has in her people and the lands she comes from. All her life she's built up her own powers so that, one day, she could take the Baron down. And while all of this is new to me, she's been fighting this battle for many years.

"She's right," says Athena, herself hailing from these lands. "I have travelled West many times over the years. They've suffered the subjugation of the Baron for a long time. Perhaps they will join us."

"Then go," says Markus. "Go and make sure they do." His eyes swing to Velia, and across to Athena. "Velia, these are your people. And Athena, from

West to East, the people know what you can do. Go, together, and see what you can muster."

Velia's eyes light with the fire of purpose, and she nods assertively.

"I'll do whatever it takes," she says.

The plan is formed for Athena to accompany Velia West, leaving the following morning. That night, my mind finds it difficult to lose its grip on her, thoughts of her safety an ever present threat. I know that they're illogical, and that there's nowhere safer right now than the West, and in the company of Athena no less, but still I can't help it. Since we met, I've seen her every day, fought side by side with her on many occasions, and shared quiet moments with her that have been a light in the ever growing darkness.

Truly, I don't want to see her go.

That evening, however, it's with her sister that she spends most of her time. She'll no doubt see their mother again, passing on any messages Vesuvia might want to give her. And while my thoughts are on her leaving, hers will be on leaving her sister, or seeing her mother, or returning to her home.

So, I choose not to bother her or seek her attention. I merely get on with my own tasks, and take up my position in the sitting room as the night grows late, searching aimlessly for the Seekers we've been ordered to hunt.

The fire flickers as I sit there alone, my yes shut as I attempt to track down something that we might use. But nothing comes to me except the normal images of death and war, the fighting so far away as to be difficult to decipher.

It's one of the problems, really. Here, in Petram, we're so far from the regions that our visions are rarely distinct. Only Cyra appears able to regularly watch from this distance, the rest of us having limited success. If we want to clarify our visions, we may need to move closer to the action. And in doing so, open ourselves up to the threat of the Seekers.

Perhaps that's the Baron's plan. Maybe he's still a step or two ahead, drawing us out, luring us closer. Maybe the Seekers have better foresight than we think. Maybe we'll all move towards the regions, and be ambushed just like Drake and Link were, or how we were on Eden outside the hanger. On multiple occasions, they've seen us coming. There's no reason to think they won't do so again.

As I sit there, my mind fills with thoughts of them, and a few distant flashes of battle greet me. They're typically hazy, far off lands suffering great turmoil. But within them, one sight flashes clearer; a face my mind has lingered on so often.

Standing before me in a quiet, deserted town, I see the hooded figure of the prime Seeker. I drift forward towards him, and he doesn't move, and blurred words flurry through my mind, as if we're in conversation, talking through water. And then, just as I near, a knock at the door drags me back into the room.

I'm pulled out of the vision and back into the quiet

sitting room, the orange flames of the fire growing small, the house completely silent. I look up, and through a widening crack in the door see Velia standing.

"I'm not disturbing you, am I?" she asks softly.

"No…not at all," I cough, the sight of the Seeker fading to the back of my mind. "How, um, how's Vesuvia?"

"Disappointed," she says, moving to sit beside me. "She wants to come too, but she knows she can't really."

"I guess she'd like to see your mum?"

"Yeah, she misses her a lot. But it's more than that. She wants to do something, to help. It's not easy for her being laid up like she is."

"I can imagine," I say. "You all set to leave, though?"

She nods, keeping her hazel eyes on mine.

"I won't be gone long," she says, as if knowing it's what I want to hear.

I smile and her face reflects the look. And for a few moments, we just sit together in silence, as we have a number of times before.

Suddenly, however, I don't know what to say. In my head I work through a few things to ask her, but they all just sound stupid, so instead I say nothing. And the longer it goes, the more my thoughts drift, the sight of the Seeker appearing before my eyes once more.

I'm torn from the spell by the feel of Velia's body sliding a little closer to mine. And in the dim light, I turn to see her eyes looking at me, a light dancing inside them. They drift up my face and stop on my blue eyes as she begins to lean in a little further.

I find myself gulping as she advances, the tip of her tongue gently running over her bottom lip. My gaze drops to them, soft and inviting and coming ever closer. And in my chest, my heart begins to thud as fast as it would during battle, a strange feeling of nerves flooding through me.

Her eyes drift shut as she gets closer, and mine naturally follow. And in the sudden darkness, I feel her warm lips close on mine. For a few moments, they lock together, before being suddenly cast apart once more. Cool air rushes where her lips no longer dwell, and I open my eyes to see her leaning away once again.

"I've wanted to do that for a while," she whispers. "I just thought…since I'm going away and all…"

"Me too," I say. "Me too.'

A smile climbs up her face again, and the tough warrior I know momentarily melts into a giddy girl. Then, she composes herself, and stands up ahead of me.

"I guess…I'll see you when I get back?"

"Can't wait," I say, trying to sound cool and calm while inside my heart still paces hard.

Again, she smiles, before stepping away towards the door. And leaving me behind, I allow myself a bigger grin than perhaps I should, given all that's happening in the world. But in this room, it seems, little moments of joy can be had.

And for me, that was a really special one.

7

A Rare Perception

The following morning, I wake to the knowledge that Velia and Athena will have already left the city. When I go downstairs, the kitchen is empty but for Ajax and Vesuvia, the two sitting at the table eating breakfast in quiet conversation.

The others are absent, which isn't unusual. Link, like Jackson, doesn't spend much time in the house. Cyra and Ellie, too, have duties to attend to outside of their orders to search their visions. For the rest of us, our only prerogative is to do just that, and the relative quiet of the house is the best place to perform that task.

It's rare to see Vesuvia out of her room, however, especially in the morning. She looks upset, the skin around her eyes a little red, Ajax doing his best to comfort her. Like his father, he's a brutal looking young man, but with a sensitive core. There's a protective streak that runs through him that makes him ferociously loyal to those he cares for. Vesuvia is very much in that bracket now, and I can tell that seeing her upset is a real distraction for him.

The cause of her current state of sadness, of course, is seeing her sister depart, doubled with the thought that she won't get to see her home or mother. If it stings me to see Velia leaving, it must be on a whole other level for her, the twins barely spending more than an hour or two apart their entire lives. It's the sort of bond that someone like me just cannot fathom. The closest I have, perhaps, is my friendship with Ajax. But whilst we've been as close as brothers for years, we still have independent streaks that demand the occasional bout of alone time.

The girls, meanwhile, are lost without each other. And this particular break up, short term though it will be, is much harder on Vesuvia.

As I enter the room, however, she stiffens herself up and tries to shield the redness around her eyes from my view. Playing along, I pretend not to notice, and despite feeling low that morning myself, try to add a spring to my step as I wander in.

"You're up early," is all I say.

"I'm taking her down to see the doctor," says Ajax, speaking for her. "He's going to take a look at her leg, see how it's healing."

"Oh, that's good," I say. "How is it feeling, Vesuvia?"

She coughs to expel the final cobwebs of emotion from her voice before speaking.

"Better," she says. "Hopefully I'll be able to start rehab soon."

"That's good news. Be good to have you back on the team," I say with a smile.

We eat in silence after that, before Ajax helps

Vesuvia out of the house and towards the medical chamber away through the city. Once more, I'm left alone in our residence with nothing to do but focus on the theme of death and chaos that continues to spread across the country.

I feel weak that morning, though, and I don't like it. There's a sense inside me that our band of Watchers are growing more disparate, that we're not all on the same page at the moment, or working together to the same ends.

Velia and Athena are gone. Link is in training and rehab. Ajax is perpetually distracted by Vesuvia, while she's distracted by her leg and her sister and a whole host of things.

My mother and Ellie, meanwhile, have begun to grow more connected to the war effort, just as they were during the last war. Their status as heroes and respected leaders is important in helping to manage the people at such a time of crisis. I know that they're spending as much time as they can searching their visions too, but their attentions are certainly being drawn in several directions.

In fact, I get the feeling that it's only me who's actually committing to this task, and this task alone. I stay in the house, alone in the sitting room or any quiet space I can find, and work to try to hunt down any sight of major attacks. And even on a day like this, when I'm feeling low, I don't allow myself any time or space to wallow. I return to the job at hand, and enter a state of meditation, and within that state, hunt down the one face that I'm so desperate to find.

For me, more than the rest, this is a single task that I alone can perform. Because really, I'm the only one who knows the true nature of this particular Seeker. Only my father joins me on that, and yet he doesn't have the powers that I do, the ability to track him down. For him, there are bigger fish to fry, and more important things to do.

For me, there's nothing more important right now than finding this boy.

I see the same vision again that day, among many others. Searching the future for hours on end, eventually his face appears before me, just as it did before. There he is, standing in an abandoned, dilapidated town, waiting for me as I approach.

Once more, however, the vision quickly fades, morphing into something else, taken over by the sight of death and fire at some unknown location.

I grit my teeth and try to seek him out again, but it's no use. And for the rest of the day, my mind fills with terrible, and yet useless sights, visions of war that I can do nothing with, alter in no way at all. I feel impotent, witnessing such atrocities and yet unable to stop them. Most of the time, being a Watcher is a truly thankless task.

More regular meetings are held now, down in the Master's chamber. Each time the congregation of attendees is slightly different, but always made up of the same core group of war leaders. They happen daily, with the first one that day missing out on Velia and Athena. The following day, General Proctor is absent, his leadership needed down in the valleys. On the third day since Velia and Athena's departure, I notice that we have a full compliment of our remaining Watchers, but that a couple of the more regular Senators who attend aren't with us.

It's a constantly changing landscape, the duties of the leaders often a double tap on their time, pulling them in multiple directions at once. However, the content of the meetings maintains the same structure, with each attendee giving reports on matters under their surveillance, helping to ensure that we're all kept up to date on everything that's going on across the country.

Of course, my single duty is to report on my visions, which has become an increasingly frustrating matter by the day. For the last couple of days, I've said nothing of the Seeker, not wanting to mention it until I see a little more and can put it into greater context.

That day, however, it's drawn from my lips by the appearance of a fresh face to the group. Although, really, fresh isn't the best description of the grizzled visage of the man who walks in that afternoon.

Standing around the table, with Markus at the centre of the picture, the meeting has barely gotten underway when the door knocks loudly. We turn, and a soldier appears in the doorway.

"Sir, we have a late arrival," he says.

He steps back and, in his place, the unshaven face of Drake appears, looking like he's come directly from the hospital.

"Drake!" says Markus. "We…we weren't expecting you."

The reaction of the rest is immediate. As he comes in, each person lines up to greet him warmly, shaking hands and hugging him where appropriate. I look particularly on the faces of my main allies and see great joy, and relief, almost, that he's come to re-join us.

I hug him in a manly fashion when I get my turn, before he wanders over to the side of the room, set back a little from the table.

Markus moves from the table's head.

"I've been keeping it warm for you, Drake. Please…take my spot."

Drake shakes his head. "No, Markus, you're the Master of this city and have been doing a fine job. I'm merely here to watch for now, and catch up on things. Please, continue…"

"Of course. If that's your wish."

As Drake settles in towards the side of the room, surveying matters, the meeting continues. Reports are given by Generals Proctor and Trent regarding the state of affairs down in the valleys and across the regions. Jackson offers his own take on the current stalemate that continues to rage towards the Eastern coast, and notes that The Guardians of Liberty's numbers continue to grow.

When it comes time for the Watchers to give their reports, the same things are heard as have been for the last few days: their visions continue to be scattered and clouded, much like my own.

I'm the last to give my testimony, and buoyed by the presence of Drake, and perhaps wishing to offer something positive amid the apparent lack of progress we're making, I mention the vision of the Seeker. The others listen carefully as I describe what I've seen, and the usual questions of 'where' and 'when' the vision takes place follow.

Of course, I have nothing to say on that matter. Their hopeful eyes turn sour when I admit that it's all very brief and unclear, and that it may even be that it's little more than a fabrication in my mind, a sort of daydream that I wish to come true.

Jackson offers me a knowing look when I tell them how obsessive I've become about finding these Seekers, knowing where that obsession comes from.

"I guess," I conclude, "it could just be a manifestation, and not a vision…it's getting harder to tell these days with so much going on. My mind is cluttered and clouded."

I notice the others nodding, all seemingly suffering from the same affliction. When Cyra speaks, however, we all listen.

"I don't think so," she announces. "Not if you've seen the same thing several times. Keep looking, Theo, and bring us something more."

Other than my vision of the Seeker, only Cyra herself appears to have witnessed anything that we can use. Two days ago, she spoke about a town in our home region of Lignum being burnt to a crisp. Given her knowledge of the area, she was able to pinpoint where it was. Only this morning, it emerged that that attack had occurred overnight, making it clear that the Baron's forces were still spreading out from the coast. It touches a nerve, knowing that my home region is now being dragged into the war. And while certain parts have been abandoned, others will be protected by local Guardians, set to die for their homes if they must. It pains me that we can't be there to help protect them.

So, right there in that meeting, I bring my concerns to the table, suggesting that we're not having the impact we should whilst hiding in this mountain.

"No one except mum can see that far," I say. "Not with any clarity anyway. We should move and set up camp nearer to the regions, maybe around Knight's Wall. Then we'll be able to see everything much clearer."

It's obvious that this is a debate that others have had as well, both privately with themselves and between one another. Consequently, a few give the thought their support, Link and Ajax among them.

"Theo's right," says Link. "We are strong enough now to decamp and go out there to help. There's no sense in staying here."

"But there is," says Jackson, "for now at least. As we know, the major fighting is still limited and contained around and near the coast. And other than Theo's vision of a single Seeker, none have been sighted. The rise of The Guardians has also set the Baron onto the back foot. Other than some minor skirmishes, like what Cyra saw, the spread of the Baron's men has been slowed. It's obvious he's consolidating, and we need to do the same."

"But why?" asks Link. "If what you say is true, Jackson, and we have him on the ropes, then isn't now the time to attack, and take the fight to him?"

"No," comes Cyra's voice. "If we set out like that, we show our own hand too early. The Seekers might see us coming, and band together to try to wipe us out. And if that happens, our armies will have little defence against them and the Baron's forces."

"And who's to say they'll wipe us out?" grunts Link, seemingly insulted by the suggestion. "When Athena returns, and with Drake on the mend, we'll have the strength to defeat them."

"Perhaps," says Cyra, "but perhaps not. You're yet to face them in battle, Link, not properly anyway. They're unlike any Watcher we've encountered before…they're nothing like those you hunted after the war."

"Then what? We just wait?" asks Link.

"We wait," says Jackson. "If you're right, and we have the strength to defeat them, then it'll only be with our full complement. That means waiting for Athena and Velia to return, and giving Drake enough time to fully recover. Only then do we have a chance. But right now, we sit tight."

At the mention of Drake, my eyes swing over to

him, sitting quietly in the corner and almost forgotten amid the debate. He watches proceedings calmly, soaking it all up, not bringing his own voice or opinions to the party. Not, at least, until he's invited to do so.

"And you, Drake, what do you make of this?" asks Link.

He takes a long breath, considering things for a time. Like Link, Drake is very much a man of action, and yet doesn't have the same hot streak. He's measured, a fine strategist, and is always able to see the bigger picture.

"Both options are valid," he says calmly, "but the debate is mute until, as you say, Athena and Velia return, and I fully recover. Both will take more time, and I think the prudent move right now is to stay here, and see how things play out."

"And in the meantime, let people die?" asks Link flatly.

"Yes," answers Drake immediately. "Such is war, Link. You know it all too well. It's clear you're itching for a fight, and you'll get it sooner or later. But for now, leaving this place could prove our undoing. We cannot be reckless. Things are too finely balanced for that."

As always, Drake's words command total obedience, putting the debate to bed without the need for the Generals, or Markus, or anyone else to even offer an opinion.

And, right there, it's clear to all of us that we have

our President, our leader, back at the helm.

When the meeting ends, however, and I prepare to shuffle off out of the room, his voice calls from behind me.

"Theo, would you stay for a moment. I'd like a word."

The rest leave, with only Markus remaining. Promptly, Drake also asks that he give us some privacy, which he does without hesitation despite this being part of his own chambers.

As the door shuts, I find myself alone with my grandfather, his keen eyes searching mine as he peers at me.

"What is it you want to talk about, grandfather?" I ask him.

He looks at me a few moments longer, and then simply says: "You're keeping something back, Theo. I was watching you as you spoke. There's something you're not telling everyone..."

My heart begins to thud. I feel as if I've been caught out, put on the spot. My reaction is to frown and shake my head, but Drake is wise enough to see right through that.

As I mumble a few words, telling him I don't know what he's talking about, he inspects me further in a manner that suggests he's reading me like a book.

Then, suddenly, he says: "It's about the Seeker. The one from your vision. The Seeker with the special purpose."

Again, I continue to play dumb, but in my head all I can think of now is the boy, this pseudo brother of mine, the most powerful of our foes. He appears before my eyes again, that familiar look of my mother hidden amid the cold countenance of Augustus Knight.

And as he swamps my thoughts once more, Drake's voice filters into the room.

"Cyra…" he whispers. "This boy…he isn't just a clone of Knight is he? There's a lot more to him than that…"

There's no surprise in his eyes. Only the clear sense that he's putting the pieces together, figuring things out for himself. The look on my face gives him what he wants; there's no way for me to lie to him anymore.

Instead, I merely nod.

"How did you come to learn this?" he queries.

"Professor Lane. She worked it out from the file, and wrote it in a notebook. She gave it to me before she died."

"And this special purpose is for this boy, this mixed clone?"

Again, I nod.

"Your father knows too, doesn't he? He…he asked you not to say anything."

I look at him, still amazed by his intuition, his ability to work things out just by peering into someone's eyes, into their mind. I tell him 'yes' with a look in my eyes.

"You doubt it, Theo, but you shouldn't. Jackson is right. No one else should know about this."

"You agree with him?" I ask, surprised.

"Your father has a mind for these things, an ability to not let emotion cloud his judgement. If others knew, it might impact how they behave to this boy. That cannot happen, Theo..."

"I know that now," I say. "I...I haven't mentioned it to anyone else."

"I know you haven't. And I know that it's a difficult thing to bear. But you're strong, and there's something at play here that might work in our favour."

"I...I don't understand."

His eyes drift off, looking into the middle distance.

"This Seeker, his special purpose...perhaps it could work for us," he says lightly, half speaking to himself.

"Grandfather," I say, pulling his eyes back to me. "What do you mean?"

His gaze swings back around, a renewed light in his eyes, something brewing within.

"Just that you need to keep searching this vision, Theo. You need to find out where, and more importantly, when, it takes place."

"But why?"

He fixes me with a calm stare, and lays his wrinkled and worn hands on my shoulders.

"Because sooner or later, you're going to be standing there ahead of this boy. And when you do, you're going to be going alone…"

8
Seeking a Seeker

That evening, as we eat dinner around the table with half the seats empty, I find my mother peering at me just as her own father did hours before.

I shield my eyes from hers, however, in a bid to keep her off the scent. Given her many years of suppressing her powers, she hasn't quite learnt to develop the ability to read eyes and minds quite like Drake can, and to a lesser extent Link and Athena. And yet, she's got that motherly instinct that she knows I'm hiding something.

She doesn't ask me, however, if that's the case. She merely questions what Drake wanted to see me about after the meeting.

"Nothing, really," I say as casually as possible as I stir my soup. "Just about how things are going here with everyone."

She accepts the lie without further questioning, although I suspect she knows that it's not the truth. Still, she chooses to back away, perhaps knowing that anything she can ask me, she can ask Drake too to corroborate my story. Thankfully, we figured that this might happen before we parted, and formed the lie together.

The only others at the table are Ellie, Leeta, and

Ajax. Link and Jackson, as with most nights, are off seeing to other things, while Vesuvia continues to seek the solitude of her room. Half way through the meal, Ajax departs with a tray of food for the patient, while the rest is portioned off for Jackson and Link for when they return. Drake, meanwhile, will take up residence within the Master's chambers with Markus, provided with his own quarters off from the main war room, a place afforded to the President of Eden on official visits.

Naturally, that title is going to have to change, given that Eden is no more.

As Ajax departs, I'm left with only our mothers and Leeta, three veterans of wartime life. Leeta, despite her growing years, has a work ethic to match the best, up at dawn and not resting until the final chores in the house have been completed. She spends all day managing the city, and all night managing the house, cooking the most delicious dinners as she goes. In many ways, she's the glue that keeps all of this together, her face rarely lacking a smile, her attitude perpetually positive.

I sit quietly for the rest of the meal as they talk as old friends do, speaking of the old days and how all of this is so familiar. When my mother was first taken to Eden, it was Leeta who accompanied her, with Ellie joining along the way. It's so weird for me to imagine it all, my mum and Ellie as kids, Leeta twenty or so years younger, leading them both into the centre of the world where they were to become Watchers.

It didn't take long for war to break out back then,

just as it hasn't now. Within months of leaving their homes, the two were embarking on a quest to help save the nation. Now, the exact same thing has happened to Ajax and me, the world shifting so dramatically, so quickly, that it's barely recognisable to what it was.

It's as if history is repeating itself, the same heroes fighting against the same, lingering evil. The world once more embroiled in a civil war that could go either way.

In the end, only time will inform us as to which. As Drake said earlier, things are finely balanced, and should we tip just a little, one way or the other, we might all go tumbling into the void forever.

I sleep alone in the room shared between Ajax and me that night.

"I'm going to stay close to Vesuvia," he tells me. "You know, with Velia gone, someone should be there in case she needs them."

I nod along, unsurprised by it all. And while I can understand, it disappoints me a little that his focus is so divided, his mind torn between her and his duty.

He leaves before I can raise any concerns, my own attention undeviating. Right now, I have tunnel vision, and while there are other things on my mind, I don't let them in, don't let them settle. I've learned, by now, that I'm strongest when I commit to a single thing; whether searching for a face in a vision, or doing battle with a foe, maintaining a single and total focus on my quarry is essential.

Ajax, perhaps, isn't quite so proficient at that as I am, so easily distracted as he can be by those he cares for. We saw it on Eden, as Link lay in his coma, Ajax's concern for his father dominating his thoughts and actions. And now, we're seeing something similar again, Vesuvia taking up too much of his time.

It frustrates me, but in the end, I don't think there's much else he can do right now. Here, so far from the action, we're being wasted. And all we can do is sit tight.

But for me, I have my orders, and I'm going to see them through. So, that night, I draw myself back into the sea of visions that swarm into my mind, seeing one horror after another as I search for what I most desire.

And within that world, the Seeker appears again, and I focus ever harder. More clues appear, the world around me taking shape. I seem to be somewhere in no man's land, not far from Knight's Wall. The shape of the mountains dominate the distance, old relics of the wall remaining at their base. The day is growing on, evening starting to fall as the sun begins to set and the light fades. I try to make out something in the town to identify it, but there's nothing at all, only strewn rubble and the rusted husks of cars, old remnants of battles fought years ago.

It's all so non descript, one of a hundred possible places littered across the stretch of no man's land behind Knight's Wall. When I'm pulled from the vision, and I wake that morning, I know that I'll probably never know exactly where it is.

That day, I go to see Drake to seek his advice. He listens as I describe what I saw, the two of us trying to figure it out together in secret. Recently, I appear to be keeping a lot of those; first with my dad, and now with my grandfather. I'll be glad when all this cloak and dagger stuff is over.

Still, Drake comes to the same conclusion as me, agreeing that the town could be any and that, unless I get lucky and see an old town name or street sign, I'll probably never know where it is.

But there's something in his eye that suggests he's got a plan, a twinkle there that I like the look of.

"So, what shall I do?" I ask him.

He smiles at me and says: "Look to the sky, Theo. You said it was early evening, yes?"

I nod.

"Good. Find the moon, and she'll tell you what you need to know."

He ends the conversation there, his time once more growing valuable as he heads to another meeting. Slightly cryptic as always, I follow his advice, heading quickly back to the house and finding a quite spot to myself.

Once more, I go through the well worn routine, and search for the face of the prime Seeker. And once more, I wade through a river of horrors before I get there, my mind getting twisted and bent by the sight of blood and fire and death. But by now, it's little but a blur as I siphon through it all, my ability to search the future growing stronger by the day.

My obsession has given life to that power, my strange connection with this clone feeding and fuelling my gifts. So consumed am I by it, that I'm able to re-enter the vision almost every time I try. And it doesn't matter how much horror I have to see to get there, I will never stop until I do.

It comes again, the image forming: the Seeker, hooded and still; the town, run down and empty; the sky, clear of clouds, the first signs of starlight appearing in the heavens as the sun drops.

But it's not the stars that I seek, it's the moon. Keeping that thought in mind, and nothing else, I feel my eyes begin to sway upwards across the sky, and there, faint as the light fades, the glow of the moon appears before me.

I look close, and take note of its shape: half of it visible on the left, the right side still hidden in shadow.

There's nothing else to see. There's nothing else I need. And in that moment, the vision fades out once more.

Excitedly, I return to Drake, rushing down the passage towards the Master's chamber. The guards let me pass as I go, and I knock hard on the chamber door before they can do anything to stop me.

It's Markus who greets me. By the looks of things, I've interrupted a meeting, several other dignitaries inside with various maps and documents spread out over the central table. I scan the room as he asks:

"Theo, what's the matter?"

There, among the small gathering, I see Drake. His eyes widen at the sight of me, and he comes straight over.

"It's OK, Markus, I can take this from here."

Markus peers at the two of us and nods, as Drake comes through the door, shutting it lightly behind him.

As I prepare to speak, he leads me a little way down the passage away from the nearest guards. Then, with a harsh whisper, he says: "What did you see?"

"The moon," I say hurriedly. "I saw the moon."

"And it's shape?"

I nod. "The left side was visible, the right was in shadow."

"Split right down the middle?"

I nod again.

"OK, come with me."

He leads me straight up the passage, through the main city chamber, and out of the high arches onto the plateau. Outside, the air is cool and the sky dark, a few puffy clouds still drifting overhead on the wind.

Immediately, he looks up, and from behind a slowly moving cloud, the bright light of the moon emerges, casting a cool glow down into the mountainside. I look at it, and see that it's similar to what I saw in my vision, the only difference being the curve of light stretching further to the right, eating into the shadow on that half.

"What does it mean?" I ask.

"Six days ago," says my grandfather, staring up, "the moon was full. Now, as you can see, it's waning, entering the last quarter."

"So..." I ask, a little confused.

"So, Theo, we have little time to lose. The moon you saw will appear in two nights time. That is when you will come face to face with this Seeker."

"But...grandfather, I don't know where?! How can I meet him if I don't know where he is?"

He smiles and shakes his head.

"It doesn't matter, my boy. What matters more is *when*. This meeting is set, and it *will* happen. Wherever you are in two nights time, that's where the Seeker will be."

I take a breath, and feel a sudden bolt strike through me. Not quite a bolt of fear, nor one of excitement. Somewhere in between perhaps, a mixture of the two.

Drake holds his eyes on me, watching me react to the realisation.

"So, I'm leaving?" I ask.

He nods. "Yes, you're leaving. And we have no time to waste."

Once more, he leads me on, this time returning

back into the city and down the passage we came from. In through the door we go, the meeting still in progress. Mercifully, my father isn't present, nor anyone else who might consider my interruption suspicious.

"Drake, anything I should know about?" asks Markus as my grandfather leads me in.

Drake shakes his head. "Not right now, Markus. I'll be back with you in a moment."

He continues across the war room, and towards another door, partially hidden in the rock. Inside are his own quarters, a comfortable bedroom and living space only for him. He moves towards a wardrobe, opens it up, and pulls out a bag from a drawer.

He comes back towards me, and hands me the bag.

"Tomorrow morning," he whispers, "more recruits are being gathered to help down in the valleys. Our soldiers are being stretched thin, and we need all the help we can get. Use it as cover to get down there undetected. From there, you can get to the desert floor and cross towards Knight's Wall. It's important that no one knows you're leaving the city. We don't want any rumours going around."

"But the people know my face now. How will I get down there without them seeing me?"

"Look in the bag," he says.

I open up the little sack, and pull out a flimsy piece of plastic. Holding it up, it resembles a mask.

"This…is going to help me?" I ask, a little

unconvinced.

Drake smiles. "It's a morph mask, Theo. Tomorrow, before you join the recruits, put it on, and I can assure you than no one will recognise you."

"I guess I'll have to take your word for it," I say, putting the mask back into the bag. As I do, I notice that there's another one inside. "There are two…" I say.

I look up and he smiles. "You never know," he says. "A second might come in handy."

9

Volunteers

That night, I don't concern myself with my visions. Instead, I sit in a state of nervous contemplation, thankful now that Ajax has decided to uproot himself and park over in Vesuvia's room.

In the lonely silence, I prepare myself for the journey I'm about to embark on, packing a bag to take along for the ride. Inside, my trusty hunting knife awaits, now usurped by the extendable dagger given to me by Athena, but still holding a strong sentimental value for me.

Along with both weapons, my bear claw necklace nestles comfortably into a side pocket, another memento that has served to define me in recent months. From it came my name at the Watcher Wars – *Bear's Bane* – a name that many in the city know me by now.

Most certainly, word of my recent adventures has spread around the place, my face and names – both real and warrior – being well known across the city and world beyond. No longer am I merely the son of legends: I am joining them on that top step, my deeds written alongside theirs in the annals of time.

Many months ago, I'd dreamt of such a thing

taking place, of hearing my name spoken by strangers with such reverence and wonder. Now, it's nothing but a side thought, a welcome bonus among the more serious issues the world is facing.

And, right now, my celebrity is perhaps more of a burden. Because, as Drake told me, getting out of the city unseen and unknown is a top priority.

I hardly sleep that night as I prepare to leave, for the first time heading off into uncharted territory alone. For anyone else, going head to head with this Seeker without aid would seem like almost certain suicide. After all, this boy may be the most powerful of all of us, lifted above even the likes of Athena and Link. And yet, despite the obvious deficit in our training and powers, I don't feel as if this encounter will be my last.

Something inside tells me that I won't be dying by this Seeker's hand. That my journey isn't set to end yet.

Drake must think the same. Were my life to be under threat, would he really send me out there with no support? Surely, right now, if we know the Seeker is going to be there on his own, it would be best to summon all of our Watchers and take him out? At least, that's what others would say. I can hear my father, in particular, spouting those words right now in my head.

Clearly, however, Drake assumes that there's something else at play here, something that I, we, need to see through. Those are my orders. And that is what I'll do.

Dawn rises swiftly after only brief bouts of sleep. During such days of war, it's common for many to rise at such unholy hours, sleep given short thrift when there's so much to be done. Soon enough, a gathering of volunteers will be appearing at the entrance to the main chamber, set to head down into the valleys to help with the war effort. Their remit: to help with the management of the refugee and support camps, and to help comb the Deadlands for those still trying to flee the fighting across the regions.

At a time when all movements are being carefully monitored, they will act as the perfect cover for me to sneak my way out of the city and beyond. To break free of the shackles of Petram, and set my sights on my destiny beyond.

So, as dawn shuffles into early morning, I creep to the doorway and listen intently for movement. Already, the sound of voices and activity can be heard out on the landing and into the kitchen below, all of the adults in the house quick to get on with their days. In only a few minutes, they'll all be out the door, heading off on their separate paths and leaving me alone to begin journeying on mine.

So, I wait, and listen, until the house goes quiet once again, before creeping out onto the landing and checking the coast is clear. Looking down the corridor, I see that all doors have been left open except one; only Ajax and Vesuvia remain asleep.

I move down the stairs and into the kitchen, before grabbing some bread and tinned beans to take with me on the journey. They join the rest of my meagre possessions in my bag, replacing a couple that are removed.

Firstly, for good luck, I pull out my necklace and hang it around my neck, tucking it under my shirt to best conceal it. Then, my fingers grip the soft, jelly-like morph mask given to me by Drake. I move over to the window and look out to see that the square beyond the house is already starting to grow with life. However, it's the reflection in the glass that most interests me, my face staring back as I gently place the mask over my skin.

Before my eyes, I see my features change as the strange material grips at my flesh, morphing the shape of my nose and chin and cheeks, adding a little padding here or taking away some there. For a few moments, it undulates and ripples over my face before setting firm, leaving me with a completely different appearance. I look at myself for a few moments of quiet astonishment, gently touching at my new face, before letting my eyes drift through the windowpane once again and out into the square.

Within the command post, I see Leeta at work, others continuing to join as a new day begins. Secretly, and as quietly as I can, I open the door to the house and step out, keeping my head low so as not to draw attention from anyone. Mostly, it's Leeta's gaze I want to avoid.

Staying as inconspicuous as possible, I begin making my way towards the passage that leads to the main chamber. A few eyes wash over me as I go, but it's nothing but my own paranoia that gives birth to any suggestion that they know I'm up to something. Each merely look at me, and then look away again, getting on with more pressing business.

By the time I've reached the main chamber, getting little attention from the guards, I'm feeling far more comfortable in my new skin. Around me, the waking world doesn't give me the same looks as I've come to expect. No longer am I the budding celebrity and hero. Now, I'm just another kid from the regions or the Deadlands, come here to hide away from the war and escape the fighting.

I wander down the streets, just one of the people now, and see the gathering I'm here to join over by the large archways that lead out towards the plateau. There are a few already there, assembling around a couple of women with electronic tablets. I move over to join them, and see that the people are giving their names as part of a roll call.

One of the clerks looks up at me as I get closer.

"Good morning, young man. Are you here to join up?"

I nod. "Yes, ma'am, I want to help wherever I can."

I feel a pinch of guilt at my phoney enthusiasm, knowing that they'll assign me to a duty that I won't be seeing through. It's not something I like to do, letting people down. But I have to remind myself that my purpose goes far beyond this.

"OK, excellent. What's your name?"

"Brandon Trimble, ma'am."

She taps my name into the tablet, before peering

back up at me.

"Do you parents know you're here, Brandon?" she asks me.

I shake my head and continue to build the lie.

"They, um...they died. That's why I'm here. That's why I want to help."

My words are enough to get a comforting hand on the arm and words of consolation from her. It sounds like she's had to deliver the same to many people before.

The questioning doesn't extend beyond that, though. All she says is: "Well, we'll be delighted to have you with us, Brandon," before telling me to wait here while others arrive, and that we'll be moving down to the valleys in the next half hour or so.

First stage of my plan complete, I decide to wander down the streets of the central chamber for a little while, enjoying the sudden anonymity I've been granted. The place continues to come to life as the minutes pass, the burgeoning business of the city largely suspended in favour of the war effort. Now, many places of work have been given over for the cause, being used to house newcomers to the city and providing shelter to those who need it most.

Still, some places operate at they once did, the entire city not strangled by the conflict. Here, life will continue to go on as it can't elsewhere, the mountain fortress safe from attack and the only place where some semblance of normality can continue.

I pass by a few stalls that still operate in the merchant sector, not moving too far from the archways for fear of being left behind. I browse through the place, wandering casually here and there, looking on as the group of volunteers continues to swell.

Soon enough, I'm about to make my way back, strolling up the streets towards them. And, as I do, I feel a heavy hand come down on my shoulder, twisting me around and into a quiet side alley.

In the shadows, I see the scarred face of Ajax staring at me, his dark brown eyes peering curiously at my face. It takes me a moment to remember that I'm wearing the morph mask, making his interruption all the more unusual.

"What the hell are you doing?" he growls at me.

I take a moment to wonder just how he knows it's me. For a second, I play dumb, before coming to the conclusion he won't be fooled.

"I know it's you, Theo," he says. "Where'd you get the mask?"

"How…" I ask.

His eyes glance down to my necklace.

"The bear claws," he says. "And I know your clothes, and your walk, and your shape. Hell, Theo, you're my best friend…of course I know it's you."

Jeez. I didn't think I was so easy to spot.

"Now what's going on? Tell me…"

"I'm just having a stroll," I lie. "I'm sick of people knowing who I am all the time."

He clearly doesn't believe it for a second.

"And I guess you just found the mask lying around the house, right?"

He inspects me closely, like his father might, seemingly trying his hardest to read my new face. It's my eyes, however, that he looks at most intently, those which haven't been altered by the mask.

"You're leaving, aren't you?" he asks me. "I know you've been shady recently. You've got a plan going on. Tell me."

I glance past the alley and down the street at the volunteers. By the looks of things, a final count is being done, suggesting they're about to leave. Ajax's gaze follows mine, before returning with a frown.

"You're sneaking down to the valleys? Why?"

"I have to," I say, before quickly trying to move past him without further explanation. His strong arms stop me, holding me back.

"That's not good enough. Just tell me!" he whispers harshly.

I take a breath, and watch as the volunteers continue to get marked off. I notice the eyes of the clerk who took my details searching the assembly, perhaps noticing my absence. In a moment they'll consider me a lost cause and go without me. I try again to move past Ajax, but have no chance of doing so. And, something inside me doesn't want to.

Then, I think of my bag, of the second mask inside. And of Drake's words last night.

You never know, he'd told me. *A second might come in handy.*

Did he foresee this too…

With Ajax's eyes glaring, and the crowd beyond beginning to leave, I have no choice but to give my friend what he wants.

"I'm going to meet the prime Seeker," I say.

His eyes widen and bulge. "What! Are you mad!? How…"

"I have no time to explain right now," I say. "I've got to go, AJ."

For a third and final time, I try to move past him. And again, I know he won't let me, even less so now.

"You're not going alone," he says.

Already, I feel my hand dipping into my bag as he talks, trying to lecture me on how foolish I'm being.

"You'll be killed," he announces. "You've been so secretive lately. Tell me what's going on…"

"I will, AJ. But not now."

My hand comes out of my bag, the second mask gripped between my fingers.

"Drake knew you'd come after me," I say. "He knew you'd be coming too."

I pass the mask to him, and he stares down at it.

"Put it on, AJ, because our train is leaving the station."

And, with a final push, I brush past him and begin marching towards the crowd, hurrying to catch up. And when I reach the back, and turn my eyes around, I see Ajax's towering frame rushing to follow.

Only now, he's lost his scars.

And has a completely new face.

"Ah, Brandon, there you are."

Reaching the back of the pack, the eyes of the clerk find me.

"Sorry, I got caught up with something," I say, as she comes over and ticks me off the list. Her eyes then rise to Ajax as he joins, and I have to stifle a laugh at the new face he's bringing along with him. "And who's this?" she asks.

"Er, this is my friend…Gerard," I say. "He wants to join up too."

"Um, OK, the more the merrier really," says the clerk. "Good morning Gerard, can I have your second name please?"

Ajax was never brilliant at thinking on the spot. For a second I see his mind turning inside out, searching for a name, before I'm forced to answer for him.

"It's Smith," I say, the most obvious name I can think of dancing into my head.

"Right, excellent. You're all signed up, Gerard. There are trucks waiting beyond the walls to take us down to the valley. Find any spot you like, and get comfortable."

She passes a warm smile to us before moving back towards the front of the group, and we make our way over the plateau and towards the perimeter wall. Ahead, the gate is beginning to grind open, revealing a convoy of buses waiting beyond.

"Gerard...*really*?" asks Ajax as we walk.

I shrug. "It's all I could think of. Anyway, it doesn't matter. We're not sticking around with these people."

"Right, well, now's the time you tell me exactly what I'm getting myself into. You realise our parents are going to go spare knowing we've gone missing. And Vesuvia..."

"Don't worry," I say, calming him. "Drake knows what he's getting us into. "I'll explain everything on the bus, OK."

"Fine," he says. "I'll trust you, because I'm not having you go out there alone. But, for the record, I'm not exactly happy about this."

I look into his eyes, burning behind his funny new face, and can't help but laugh at the disconnect.

"Noted," is all I say, before quickening my step to escape his blazing gaze.

As we climb onto our bus, we make sure to find ourselves a spare two seats to get some privacy. When the convoy begins rumbling, accompanied by a military escort, the noise of the many loud engines and grinding tyres is enough to hide our conversation. As others engage in their own discussions around us, I quickly catch Ajax up on exactly what's been going on.

The only thing I leave out is the true identity of the prime Seeker. That, for now, is something I will not reveal, keen as I am to remain loyal to my father's wishes as much as I can.

Of course, it appears that, once more, Drake has taken the lead as my main co-conspirator, Jackson relegated into second position behind him. Personally, I'm looking forward to the day when we can all catch up onto the same page again. All this cloak and dagger stuff, all this sneaking around, it's starting to take its toll on me.

Having Ajax alongside me, however, is a real boon. As I tell him what's been happening, I begin to feel the weight being lifted, some of the burden passed to him.

Still, he clearly doesn't completely agree with the plan.

"So, let me get this straight," he whispers. "We're heading into the regions, where war is raging, to meet the most powerful Watcher in the world. A boy who wants nothing more than to kill us, and who was, I might add, bred for exactly that! And, we're doing all this alone…without bringing along the most powerful Watcher on our side… my dad? Am I right so far?"

"Pretty concise, yep," I say nonchalantly.

"And…the big question, really, is…WHY?! Why aren't we getting every damn Watcher we have and taking the guy out? If we took him out now, we'd take out the others no problem…"

"Because that's not what Drake wants, and it's not what I want."

"Well why not? What do you think you're gonna do, have a cosy little chat with him? I just don't get it, Theo. He's the enemy, isn't he?"

"Yeah, but maybe…I don't know. Look, my vision had me alone with him. That's how we have to play it out."

"Right, and what about me? Am I in your vision?"

I shake my head.

"Well then, maybe you don't know what you're seeing. Maybe the other three Seekers are gonna come pouring out of the woodwork and kill us both. Jeez, Theo, I thought you had a proper plan here."

"Just trust me, OK. And, if you can't do that, trust Drake. Remember the Watcher Wars? He knew we needed to be there, and look what happened. He's got a sense for this, AJ, that we can't see and don't understand. But I trust him, and so should you."

My words seem to break down his doubts a little bit. At the least, they're enough to quieten him and bring him a little more onto my side.

"Fine," he says, eventually. "I'll play this out. But if we die because of this, then I'm gonna be pretty damn annoyed!"

"Fair enough," I say, patting him on the back. "Good to have you on board."

He grunts with displeasure, as the bus winds down the mountain, the valleys below growing clearer and more verdant. I turn my eyes to the window, not wanting to continue the debate for now, and watch as the world changes and the high mountains rise as we descend to their foundations. And there, in the sprawling basin between the ragged peaks, the sight of hundreds of tents and huts appear, and thousands of tiny people littered among them. And beyond, another camp, this one filled with military colours, thousands of soldiers from the Deadlands and regions gathering here for an assault and the protection of the mountain passes.

I see sprawling fields of vehicles too, both for civilians and the military, used by the people to get here. Army jeeps and tanks and other armoured cars and artillery units. I even see aircraft, too, set aside along an airfield, the numbers of men and machinery in far greater concentrations than I've ever witnessed before.

In the bus, I notice that everything has gone silent now, but for the growling engines and grinding tyres. All voices have dropped, all conversations ended as the volunteers look out in wonder at the world below. And, to my great relief, the sight appears enough to distract Ajax too, his eyes staring as they search the plains beneath us, his lips hanging a little open and murmuring words of wonder.

As we continue down, my mind turns to the next task of getting away. Spying the shape of the clerk, sat down at the front of the bus, I stand and make my way towards her. Her eyes rise to mine as I appear.

"Hi, ma'am," I say, drawing her attention from the window. "I was just wondering…my friend and I want to help on the Deadlands, looking for stragglers. Can we do that?"

"Well, you look a bit young, Brandon. How old are you? Can you drive?"

"We're both 18," I lie, "and can both drive. It's just, we know the lands really well, and would be more useful out there than helping in the camps."

"You're 18?"

"Yes," I say, nodding.

She seems slightly doubtful, owing to the more youthful complexions our morph marks have given us, smoothing our lines and scars and adding a bit more puppy fat here and there. Without them, I doubt she'd have any such concerns. Nevertheless, our large frames appear sufficient to convince her, both of us much larger than the average man.

"OK, Brandon, I don't see why not. If you know the lands, you'll know it's dangerous out there, but I'll put you down on the list. There will be a briefing when we reach the valleys that will take you through everything you'll need to know."

"Thank you," I say, before returning to my seat.

When I sit back down, Ajax quizzes me on what happened.

"Just making sure we get a car down to the Deadlands," I say. "We have to get across the wall by tomorrow night, remember. There's no time to mess about here."

Ajax doesn't ask anything more. I'm getting a sense of buyer's remorse from him already, a feeling that he's regretting coming along. If I know my friend like I think I do, however, I know that he'll come around soon enough.

Before too long, the path is levelling out and we're crunching over the rocky ground that signals the beginning of the open plains of the valley floor. Here it's still cool, the valley way up in the mountains and above the desert floor. Ahead, the sprawling sea of tents and troops and trucks await, our little convoy coming to a stop at the main entrance to the temporary mountain base.

We're ordered out, and are quickly separated into two groups: one intended for helping in the camp; the other for the more perilous task of searching the Deadlands for travellers in need of our help. Ajax and I join the second, a smaller bunch of hardy folk, all of us ordered into a large tent for the briefing the clerk mentioned.

I'm grateful by how efficient it all is, the morning still yet to turn to afternoon as we're hastily taken through things by the team leader, a Major named Vilius from the Petram army. He tells us briefly of the perils we'll face, before we're paired up and given radios used to call anything in. Ajax and I are thankfully put together, and we're all led out into the vehicle field to be assigned our cars. Then, we're all passed maps and targeted areas that each of us are permitted to visit, certain zones that need to be covered before we return each night. By the looks of things, some more seasoned 'searchers', as they call our breed, are allowed to stay at particular safe zones further field. All newbies, however, need to merely stick to their specific search fields before returning each night, where they will make camp right here in the valley base.

It's a well co-ordinated operation, but one that Ajax and I aren't actually going to be part of. I just have to hope that the area we're meant to canvass isn't going to reveal someone who might need our help. Help that will never come.

Because, as soon as we get behind the wheel, and begin grinding away down to the desert floor in our rusted old jeep, the orders of the Major go right out of the window. Starting in a large convoy, as soon as the red desert appears before us at the base of the mountains, we spread out and go off in our separate ways.

In only minutes, cars are being swallowed up by the dust spat up by their tyres, or disappearing behind chunks of rock, churning through the tundra in a bid to find any poor soul lost in the unforgiving wilderness.

The heat is immediate, that suffocating, brutal blanket of warmth that wraps itself around you and doesn't let up. Right now, as the heat of the day begins to build, and after so long spent in the mountain air of Petram, or the manufactured cool of Eden, I feel my body quickly react, sweat pouring from pores, my throat drying as fast as it can be wetted by water.

And for a little while, as we set our path ahead to the East and pray the car doesn't fail in the heat, we do little talking. A grumpiness settles inside the car, neither of us willing to draw attention to it and choosing instead to just sit and stare at the endless red and orange that now dominates our view.

The only distraction in the car becomes the radio, crackling occasionally as people report in their findings. After a little while, I turn it off, and toss it into the back seat, turning my mind from those behind us, and setting it only on those ahead.

I take the wheel first, driving for several hours, before Ajax offers to take over. It's a sign that he's coming round, that he's in this with me now. So I accept, and we stop to swap seats, before continuing along our path.

"You sure we're going the right way?" he asks me, following my directions. "Do you know which town we have to go to...beyond Knight's Wall?"

"Yes," I say, giving him a little white lie.

Frankly, to tell him 'no, I have no idea which town', would be counterproductive right now. Really, I don't have the energy to explain to him at the moment that whatever town we end up in, that'll be the town we'll find the Seeker.

I have to trust Drake on that matter, despite having my own doubts about it. Because right now, we're acting on faith alone. Faith that my visions aren't playing tricks on me. Faith that this Seeker will, in fact, be alone himself, and Ajax and I won't perish at his hand. Faith that we're going to get something out of this mission, that Drake's cryptic foresight is going to turn out to yield some reward.

It's a lot to put down to faith, really. A lot to put down to hope.

But, at a time like this, with our backs against the wall, it's not an opportunity we can pass up.

11
Quarrels in the Heat

We drive until the sun goes down. And then we drive some more.

The air cools, but not drastically so, not after spending our days in the mountains. Everything is relative and the night air down here on the desert floor is still like a furnace compared to that of Petram.

Still, we find that it's cooler outside of the car than in, and so set about locating an area of rocks on which to sleep. Thankfully, I came prepared, partially at least. I never expected to have a companion on this trip, and so brought along a single fold out mat that I intended to sleep on.

Given Ajax's chagrin, I offer it to him. Being stubborn as a mule, he refuses to accept. Unfortunately, I'm similarly inclined, so the mat spends the duration of the evening unused.

Instead, we use the many clothes we've shed in order to form our own little beds. Having come from the mountain, we have plenty of layers to spare, and with no need for a covering, are able to manufacture suitably comfortable nests for the night.

I suspect both of our sleeps with be short, though.

Not only is the heat tricky to master, but the sun is set to rise early, bringing a harsh yellow light to our eyes in a matter of hours. Thankfully, we've grown used to waking early, and still have a long way to go, so that's not really a problem that concerns me.

In the end, I drift off with thoughts of the following day dominating my mind, and the Seeker's face the central focus of it all. Mercifully, however, my mind is too busy to discover any local visions of terrible things, and so I fall asleep and wake up with only thoughts of the Seeker in my head.

The following morning, we continue our journey, spying the sight of refugees on occasion as we go. The sight of swirling dust usually gives them away, a car or two, or even the odd small convoy moving West across the Deadlands in search of safer places to wait out the war.

Settlements appear here and there too, many of them deserted. It's hard to tell, sometimes, whether they've only recently been abandoned or have been like that for years. Out here, many such places exist, relics of a past age when these lands were less harsh and hostile to human sensibilities, when the lands were better suited to farming and cultivation. Now, so much of the world sits barren and unused, the changing nature of the climate and seasons bringing an end to the old way of life that once endured here.

Still, we don't encounter too much, whether old towns or people, given the vastness of the landscape we cross. Soon, however, the world begins to give away signs that we're progressing, the distant horizon telling of the mountains that help to block the regions from the Deadlands, once supported by Knight's Wall.

As we move closer, I feel my body beginning to swell with nerves and anticipation. With each passing minute, the day is growing older, quickly summoning the night to continue in its stead. Soon enough, the moon will make its appearance, barely visible at first as the sun's rays continue to dominate. And then, as the light fades, I'll see that half moon, and know that my vision is growing ever closer to completion, to becoming reality.

So on we go, rumbling closer until the scarred earth of Knight's Wall appears, little areas still yet to be dismantled. Not too far away, somewhere to the North, the old remains of the Baron's base, hidden beneath The Titan's Hand, may still be burning, still spewing up a cloud of black ash. I turn my gaze in that direction, but know we're too far South to see it.

It's an odd feeling, when we cross over the skeleton of the wall, officially leaving the Deadlands behind. Knowing that, not too far away, the regions are engulfed in fighting, tens of thousands of soldiers battling for territory and supremacy across the land. But not here, not in no man's land.

Here, the country has remained largely empty for years, mile upon mile of relics, lonely towns once filled with people, once prosperous. For many years, this entire stretch of land was a battleground between the regions and the rebels, long before my parents joined the cause and fought in the War of the Regions.

I wonder, sometimes, whether this nation will ever see the back of war. Whether these bouts of peace will ever stretch into something more meaningful. Whether this wanton killing will ever end.

As my mind wanders, Ajax's voice pulls me back into the world.

"Which way then?" he asks, sitting behind the wheel, looking left and right and ahead, at an old crossroad still lingering in the dirt.

"Er…" I say, taking a moment to think. I have no idea, of course, which way to go. Whatever way I choose will be right.

"Are you sure you know?" he asks, the car chugging at a standstill. "What's the name of this town?"

"Um…"

Once more, my mind deserts me, still wandering and wavering.

"Theo, you *do* know where we're going, right?"

"Straight on," I say quickly. "Just…go straight on."

He looks at me curiously before putting the car back in gear and continuing on. We stretch away from the remains of Knight's Wall, moving further into no man's land, moving through the dirty scrubland as I search for the nearest town.

Soon, we're approaching one, small and barely

standing. It doesn't look right, not big enough for the site from my visions.

"This is?" asks Ajax, growing suspicious.

"No," I say assertively, trying to get him back onside.

On we go, as I turn my eyes back to the path ahead, and around at the open landscape. Behind us, the blocks of craggy hills rise up to the heavens, giving me something to go by. I think again of the vision, of the shape of the mountains that framed the horizon, and know that we're not yet far enough from them, that they're too close and clear.

We drive further down the ancient, cracked road, trees and old shacks and cars peppered here and there, until the distance to the mountains seems right. I ask Ajax to stop, and get out of the car to take a proper look around. Climbing onto the roof, I give myself a better view of the area, and note that we need to move Northwards a little from here.

Ajax looks at me with some measure of ambiguity as I stumble my way to our destination. When we get back in the car, he comes out and says it.

"You don't know where you're going, do you?" he asks blankly.

"I'll get us there," I say confidently.

"Where, exactly? This is like a wild goose chase."

"To where we need to be, AJ. Wherever we end up, that's where we need to be. Drake told me that himself."

I see him roll his eyes and shake his head as he continues on, turning the car left and heading North. We pass by another couple of settlements that don't seem right, and each time he gives a little sigh that begins to grate on me.

It annoys me to think that he doesn't trust me, and that he doesn't trust my grandfather. Does he think I've come out here for my damned health?!

"You don't have to make that stupid little noise each time," I say, unable to hold in my irritation.

"What noise?"

"That little sigh. For God's sake, AJ, cut me some slack here. I'm trying, alright."

"Yeah, trying to get us killed. I should turn around and drive back."

"Since when did you become such a coward?"

"Excuse me?!" he asks, skidding the car to a stop off the track, and turning his eyes to me.

"You're spending all your time with Vesuvia these days," I shout, unable to hold it in any more, "and not doing your damn duty. And, finally, you get a chance to do some good, and you're moaning and doubting every damn thing I do. If you wanna go, then go, I'll walk the rest of the way on my own..."

I get out of the car, swinging my bag onto my back as I go, and begin marching down the track. I'm stamping so hard I barely see him coming, but react just quick enough as he comes charging at me from behind.

118

He moves to tackle me to the ground, but I'm swift enough to sidestep him, pushing him along so his momentum carries him into a thorn bush. Roaring, he bursts free of the leaves, little cuts inflicted on his skin from the thorns, and comes at me again.

He swings at me, hard, a fire roaring inside his eyes.

"You think you're more special than me…" he calls, fists flying. "You always did!"

I manage to hold back the storm, dodging the blows, but don't fight back. He's wild and panting, his focus incomplete, his emotions getting the better of him. Yet still, his natural gifts come forth, his arms moving faster, his large body looming ahead of me as I try to hold him back.

Eventually, he manages to sneak through my defences. I see the attack coming, but it's too strong and I can't stop it, his fist moving through my palm and connecting with the left side of my face. My skull rattles and I move backwards, hitting the earth. And as I do, I spy the shape of a familiar town right ahead.

"Stop!" I shout, holding my arms up as he comes down on me.

He follows the look of my eyes, and sees the same town.

"That's it," I pant, his heavy body holding me down. "I'm sure about it. That's the place…"

He takes a deep breath, and heaves his weight off

me. For a moment, I stay down, before his hand comes out. I take it, and he pulls me to my feet so that we're standing face to face.

"This is stupid, AJ," I say. "I'm sorry for what I said. I…I didn't mean it."

Another large exhale of air pours out of him as he nods and locks eyes with mine.

"I guess I'm sorry too. I just…I get the feeling you're not telling me everything, that I'm not being kept in the loop."

"I know. I think we've just been on different paths these last couple of weeks," I say, trying to get around the question. "But we're here now. And we need to stand together. You're my best friend, Ajax. And I need you."

"Don't get soft on me, mate," he says, a smile creeping onto his face. "Now come on, let's check out this town."

Leaving the car off the side of the road, we wander down into the town, and I feel an instant recognition for the place. I move to the middle of the central square, and take a look around, and note the old frames of long dead cars, and the strewn rubble of buildings littering the floor. I turn to look left, and see the mountains in the distance, and the little remains of Knight's Wall below. And then, my chin tilts up, and my eyes scan the sky, and there I see the faint sign of the moon beginning to appear, so faint behind the remaining light of the sun.

But it's there.

I turn to Ajax, who watches on at me with hopeful eyes, our morph masks long since discarded and left in the car.

"This the place?" he asks.

I nod at him. "This is the place."

12

AK1

There's a general sense of awkwardness between Ajax and I as we sit in the ruins of an old house, looking out into the square. The light is slowly beginning to change, its brightness fading a touch, the warm oncoming hues of sunset just starting to approach.

I know, soon enough, I'm going to have to step out there and wait for the Seeker. I know, now, for certain that he will appear. And I know, too, that Ajax needs to stay here, hidden from view, and allow the scene to play out before him.

What I don't know, of course, is what will happen. All I've seen is the two of us here, at this place and at this time. What happens beyond that initial meeting is subject to doubt. I just have to hope that my instincts, and Drake's, prove correct.

Still, as we sit and wait, I find a question bubbling to the tip of my tongue, something that I never knew Ajax felt.

"Did you mean what you said back there?" I ask. "That I think I'm more special than you?"

He doesn't answer for a second, clearly figuring out the right response as he fidgets with his feet. And yet, the delay is enough for me to know there's some truth to it at least.

"Sometimes," he admits candidly. "I don't know, it's just an impression I've gotten in recent years. Maybe it's just your desire for adventure, to be known. You've always wanted that a bit more than me, I think."

"But that doesn't mean I think I'm more special than you. Really, I hate the idea that you think that. I've always thought *you* were stronger than *me*…"

"No," he says, cutting in. "That's not what I mean. It's not about strength, or power. It's about you wanting to be a legend, like your parents. It's as if you've thought that's your right, you know."

"I don't think it's my right. Just my duty, I guess."

"Well, maybe you were right," he says. "I mean, everything we've done, everything we've been through…most of it's been through you. You've been more important to all of this than me. I guess, maybe I'm just being jealous."

"You shouldn't be. We've been side by side on everything so far. We've done everything together. We're a team, AJ, and that'll never change."

"I know. It's just this war. We left looking for adventure. I never expected this, Theo."

"Nor did I. But everything that's happened so far has told me one thing: we were born for this, both of us. Athena's always talking about believing in yourself, right, and having confidence in your abilities. Well, we should have confidence in ours. We should be proud of ours."

"Yeah, I've just felt a bit side-tracked lately."

"Because of Vesuvia?"

He nods quietly.

"I care about her, Theo."

"I know you do. And I think you two are great together. But right now, we've got a war to fight. That's where our heads need to be at."

"And what about you? Velia and you seem to be getting along well."

Her face flashes across my eyes. I won't admit it, not when I'm trying to be so stoic and strong, but I miss her already. I can understand exactly where Ajax is coming from. If it were Velia injured in that room, and I wasn't having any luck with my visions, maybe I'd be doing exactly the same.

"I like her," I tell him. "We…we kissed the other night."

"You kissed?!"

I shrug and try to act cool about it. Really, though, memories of that kiss are flooding my mind when they shouldn't be. I need to keep my head in the game here.

"Yeah, before she left. So, I get where you're coming from, AJ, I really do."

"But right now you need to focus," he says. His eyes move to the sky, taking in the changing light. "You think he's on his way here now?"

"I hope so. It would be a shame to come all this

way for nothing, right?" The slight tickle of nerves in my voice must be obvious.

"Yeah," he says. "Let's just hope he doesn't get violent. You know, do what he was born and bred for."

"I'm hoping that there's something else in him," I say. "And if not, well…we tried, right?"

"Yeah, they can put that on my headstone. 'He died doing something foolish. But, hey, he tried…'" His eyes dart on me sarcastically, but I know that it's what he's truly feeling.

And there's a growing part of me that's feeling the same.

"Anyway, you'd better get out there," he says. "I'll be here, Theo. I'll be right here."

I look at him and feel happy for his support, for his friendship. If anyone was foolish, it was me, thinking I could come here alone, come here without by best friend.

"I'm glad you're here," I say quietly, our eyes locking for a few moments. And then, I turn, and step out of the house and into the open square.

I pace forward, feeling the clock ticking down in my head. The light is close now, so close to being how I remember it. I scan the sky and see the moon, growing clearer, more bright. It hovers in the heavens, gently moving into position. Any time now, the boy will appear.

As my heart pounds, and my breathing grows deeper, I shut my eyes and try to calm myself.

Slowly but surely I get a grip of my functions, focusing hard on maintaining my poise. Holding my head down, I count to ten behind my eyelids. And then, on ten, I open them wide and stare straight forwards.

A figure looms before.

Cloaked and hooded and shrouded in shadow. Only a dozen metres away he stands, silently entering the square as I held my eyes closed.

I look at him, and the vision locks in time, passing the threshold into reality. And for a good few moments, I merely indulge in it, bathe in it, watching the Seeker before me as he stands like a statue.

I sense it has to be me to make the first move. I take a step forwards, closing the gap a little. As I go, I open up my desert jacket, and reveal that I have no gun, my knives left over in the house with Ajax.

"I'm unarmed," I say loudly, hoping for him to do the same.

He doesn't. He merely stands there, watching me approach, giving nothing at all away.

I cover more ground, and creep a little closer.

"Have you come alone?" I ask.

I look closely for movement, and see the slightest nod of his head. Then, from behind his hood, his voice growls.

"How did you know I'd come here?" he asks.

"A vision," I answer. "And you?"

"Something…drew me here. I don't understand why."

"A connection," I say. "There's a connection between us…"

"There's nothing between us," comes his voice, cutting like a sharp knife. There's hatred in it, so pure and deep, something he's been taught his entire life.

I don't answer. Countering his claim might force him to attack. Instead, I draw back, keeping my voice calm as if I'm dealing with a hungry tiger.

"Do you…do you have a name?" I ask tentatively.

His head shakes. Then he answers. His voice is still simmering with heat, just off the boil.

"No name. A designation. They call me AK1."

AK1, I think. *That must be short for Augustus Knight 1. The first of the clones…*

"The initials of your father," I say quietly.

He doesn't answer.

I take a breath, and move another step closer to him. Beneath his hood, I can see that his face is tight, his jaw stiff and lips locked together. And his grey eyes, just about visible under the shadow, flash with that sign of blue.

I take a chance, creeping towards the reason I'm here.

"And what about your mother?" I ask.

I see his chin lift a little, casting more light over

his face. He stares at me, and I see a frown knotted over his eyes, narrow and intense.

"I have no mother," he says. "You know what I am…"

"I do," I say. "I think I know more than you do."

Those words cause a reaction in him. It's as if he's heard such sentiment his entire life, heard others speaking of him in such a way. As if he's nothing but a weapon, a blunt object without any emotions or use beyond chaos and war. As if he's not a real person at all.

But he is. And so those words cause him to stir, suddenly bursting forth from his standing start. With a couple of paces, he comes straight at me, marching on across the gritty earth as the moonlight continues to grow in the sky.

I instinctively lean back, but hold myself firm and don't move. Instead, I let my hands hang by my sides, showing him I'm not here to fight. I add my words in an attempt to halt him.

"I'm not going to fight you, AK1," I say, but they do nothing to stop him.

Reaching me, I see his face clearer than ever, tangled into a web of confusion. Confusion, perhaps, that he's felt his entire life. His fist lifts and I sense an attack coming, but maintain my position, not holding up my arms in defence.

I see some doubt behind his hood, his fist stopping momentarily as I whisper again.

"I didn't come to fight," I say. "And I know you

didn't either."

Again, my words need to be carefully chosen. Clearly, telling him what he thinks or feels, or how he acts isn't the right course of action.

"You have no idea why I came!" he barks, suddenly sending his fist flying at me.

I shut my eyes and brace for impact, sensing his tough knuckles coming straight for me. Before they can hit, however, I feel another presence, another body, intervening and stopping the blow.

I open my eyes back up and see Ajax right there beside me, his large paw wrapped around the Seeker's fist just in front of my face. For a split second, no one moves. And then, like a volcano, the young clone explodes.

He tears his fist back out of Ajax's grip so fiercely he nearly takes my friend's hand with it.

"You're trying to trap me!" he roars, pouring straight back in towards us.

Ahead of me, the world fills with white as his fists surge, flying from all angles. I have no choice now but to lift my hands and try to defend myself, Ajax doing the same. We stand together, as we have so often, deploying a stance of defence as we try to weather the storm of flying limbs.

Yet this boy is beyond anything we've faced. Beyond the threat posed by Athena when we trained with her in Petram. Faster, stronger, more accurate with his blows.

And yet, we too have grown stronger as the days

and weeks have passed. Those early days were the first of our training. In the last few months, our powers have grown exponentially, our abilities creeping up towards those of the legends of the past.

And so, for a few minutes, we hold our own, fighting off the boy and keeping him at bay, stopping his most perilous and powerful blows as we try to subdue him.

He uses only his fists to attack, no weapon coming forward. But it's not the same for Ajax. From his belt, I see him bringing forth his extendable spear, a quick click of the button shooting the blade from one end.

In the midst of battle, the Seeker's eyes light at the sight of shining metal, and his anger and power seems to rise up another notch. He turns his full attention to Ajax, attacking with a thunderous combination as my friend attempts to put the blade into his gut.

"NO!" I shout, trying to hold Ajax's arm back and knock away the spear.

Yet the clone needs no help from me. He quickly penetrates Ajax's defence, and hooks a fist right across his jaw. It's enough to send him straight to the turf, his eyes rolling back in his head and body crumbling like a house of sand beaten down by the surf.

I stand back and look upon my friend, a sight that would usually cause a stir in me to avenge his beat down. But not this time.

This time, I take a step back, and let my arms fall by my side again as AK1's eyes surge back up to mine. His hood now hangs down the back of his neck, flicked back during the fighting, his full face revealed to me. He's breathing hard, his eyes glowing with flame, his nose and lips contorted into a grimace of hate and anger and confusion.

"Why did you do that?!" he growls at me. "Why did you try to knock away his weapon?!"

"Because we're not here to fight," I repeat, my eyes wide and holding no lies.

"THEN WHY!" he shouts. "WHY ARE YOU HERE!?"

He comes at me again, his burning anger unrestrained, but I refuse to react. Reaching out, he takes my collar with his hands and presses me to the ground, pushing me against the earth again and again.

"WHY DID YOU COME! WHY!"

His fingers creep over my throat, starting to cut off my air supply. I see his entire face burning with confusion and unsuppressed rage, his eyes so savage they could kill.

I take a grip of his hands, and summon my full strength, pulling his wrists back and giving me space to breath. And with my breath, I shout out to him: "Because you're more than you think you are…you've been lied to your entire life! You're…you're like my brother, AK…"

His hands weaken. His eyes stare. His body lifts

from mine, stepping up and back.

He looks at me for a long while as I cough and regain my breath. There's something inside him that says he knows, that says my words make sense. That the connection between us is real, and he knows it.

Slowly, I stand, the night now growing dark. From behind, a heavy burst of thunder comes crashing, a storm brewing in the distance. Thick black clouds spread across the sky, moving closer as we stand in silence.

"Your father...Augustus Knight...is dead," I say, regaining my breath. "But there's another half to you, another half that's still alive."

His eyes grow intense, his head begins to shake. Everything he knows is being tested and denied.

"Cyra...my mother...you have half of her in you too. And that makes us brothers..."

The shaking of his head grows more acute. The grimace on his face stiffens further.

"You're lying to me...why are you lying to me!"

He takes another step forward threateningly, an internal battle raging, wanting to attack but somehow holding himself back.

"I'm not lying, AK1. The Baron is just using you, all of you. But you...you in particular. He has a special purpose for you. You're just a pawn in his game, just a weapon..."

"NO! I'M MORE!" he shouts.

"I know you are," I say, stepping back again as he pulses forwards. "You are to me…but not to him."

The sky bursts with a bright tongue of lightning. Another crack of thunder rumbles through the air.

Still, the clone shakes his head, his eyes darting here and there now, bewildered and confused.

"You're wrong," he says, quieter now, more introspective. "You're wrong…"

He steps back, and from above, rain begins to pour and flood, the heavens opening as the storm gathers. Obscured by the darkness and the sudden deluge, I look at the Seeker and see the doubt in his eyes. Yet they don't meet mine, they don't look at me again.

With another loud burst of lighting and thunder, he flicks on his heels, his sodden cloak flowing behind him, and begins rushing off away from me, away through the town square. I watch on for a second as he disappears into the darkness, feeling an urge to shout out after him, to follow.

But I don't.

I just stand, and stare, and feel the cool splash of the rain as it dances on my face, the light swirl of wind as it caresses my skin.

And then, from below, I hear a voice, croaking from the dirt.

"He's half…Cyra?"

I look down and see Ajax staring up at me. His eyes are like the Seeker's, confused and lost.

I nod, and turn back to the darkness.

"And that's exactly why we came," I say.

13
The Valleys Swell

"It all makes so much sense now," says Ajax, his voice half drowned by the thundering storm.

We're sitting inside the house again, rain bombarding the roof and dripping down through gaps in the ceiling. Outside, through the broken down walls and smashed up windows, the wind howls and whistles, and the black sky intermittently flashes with shards of lightning, bringing the baritone voice of thunder along with it.

"He looks different to the others," continues Ajax. "The blue in his eyes, the brighter colour to his hair. I can see Cyra in him now…I can see *you*."

He looks at me, still coming to terms with it. Peering at me in a strange way.

Then, he speaks again. "How long have you known?" he asks.

"Since we escaped Eden," I say. "Professor Lane…she left us a notebook with some more details from the file. The others, they're just Knight, through and through. But this one…he's got half my mother inside him."

"AK1," whispers Ajax. "I could hear it all from

here. I understand it now, why you've been seeing him in your visions, why you wanted to come here. I get it, Theo. He's different from the others."

"There's something more in him," I say. "He's conflicted…"

"Who else knows about him?"

"My father, he's known from the start…"

"And Drake, I'm guessing?" he asks. "Anyone else?"

I shake my head.

He frowns. "Not your mother?"

"Dad warned me not to tell her. He thinks it will weaken her. He didn't want anyone else knowing."

"And Drake agrees?"

"Yeah. No one else needs the distraction right now. But only Drake knows I'm here, and knowing him, he's probably worked out that you've come with me. We need to get back, tell him what's happened."

I make a move to stand, but Ajax pulls me back down.

"Not tonight. Let's rest. We can leave at sunrise, once the storm has passed."

I nod, and settle back into the chair, my mind still working overtime. Ajax begins shuffling around in my bag, pulling out some tinned food and bread and bottles of water, preparing a little picnic right there in that crumbling old house.

We talk a little more as we eat, my stomach suddenly informing me that I have a voracious appetite. Ajax has plenty more questions regarding the Seeker, ones I'm happy to answer if I can. It's nice to have him back on the same page as me, my partner in crime back at my side.

"So, what's this special purpose?" he asks me as he munches on a piece of bread.

I shrug, gulping down some water. "Professor Lane never elaborated. We have no idea."

"And he doesn't either. The kid seemed lost, you know, like he didn't know what or who he was."

"Yeah, he's lived in a lie his whole life. I feel sorry for him, really. I mean, Augustus Knight made *himself* evil…he built all that over decades. These clones aren't like that. Just because they have his genes, it doesn't make them evil too. No one's born that way."

"But that's how they've been bred," says Ajax. "To hate us, to kill us, to wreak havoc. That's all they know."

"Yeah, but not this one. This one's confused and conflicted. That's why I wanted to come here. I wanted to look into his eyes and see the truth."

"And the truth is?"

"That he's been kept in the dark his entire life, groomed for something that he doesn't even know about. Now, the truth is trickling into his mind, and he's going to want to find out more."

"Yeah, and so do I," remarks Ajax. "You sure

there's nothing else in the Professor's notebook?"

"Trust me," I say, nodding, "I've combed that thing a hundred times. There's no code or anything cryptic that I'm missing. I guess she didn't have a chance to work out anything more before she…you know."

"Such a shame. I never met her, but she sounds like a good woman."

"She was," I say with a smile, thinking of the old Professor. "She meant a lot to my dad. He's not used to losing people like my mum is, not in the same way."

"It's something we all need to get our heads around, though. At times like this, anyone can fall."

I nod in agreement. It's a fact we know all too well. As yet, we've suffered the near loss of both Link and Drake, for a time fearing the worst for both of them. In the end, they came back from the dead. But those lingering scars remain, those fears that loved ones will be lost.

It's a fear that all people hold in war, the inevitability of death part and parcel of the game. In the end, you can only do so much to prevent it. And no matter what you do, luck and fortune, or lack thereof, will always play the staring role.

We sleep that night in fits and starts, talking late before finally getting some rest as the storm begins to abate. When we wake, the sky has brightened, little drops of rain still dripping down from the ceiling and forming little puddles on the floor.

We're quick to rise, though, gathering up our things and hastily moving out of the town and down the path towards the car, still awaiting us where we skidded to a stop the previous day. We climb in, and I pray we don't suffer some malfunction like we did when crossing the Deadlands after escaping the Baron's compound. Thankfully, the old jeep grumbles to life, coughing out a little smoke as we steer it back in the opposite direction.

We speed up the track as quickly as we can, turning towards the wall and Deadlands beyond, setting our path back from where we came. As with any journey, the return leg appears to go much faster, knowing our course as we now do.

The hours filter by fast as we take it in turns to do the driving, covering the earth with a speed that brings us closer to the mountains as the night begins to fall.

We press on through the dark, our pace now limited as any pitfalls ahead disappear into the blackness. In the end, we slow to a crawl, a covering of dark cloud blocking out the light of the stars and moon. Yet on we go, refusing to stop and sleep as we grind through the endless night.

As we go, a few lights appear in the darkness, dots of orange specking the horizon. Remaining vigilant, we steer clear of them, debating what they might be. Coming around a portion of rock that blocks our path ahead, our question is answered: they're the lights of campfires, set by those crossing the desert in pursuit of a safe haven.

More appear as we go, the world peppered with them. And as the dark fades and dawn rises, we see cars and carriages moving, and people walking, some alone, others in small groups or larger convoys.

And the nearer we get to the foot of the mountains, the more of them appear, all flocking to the camp in the valleys. And down from the mountains, the cars of the 'searchers' come, moving out to offer their aid. The job we signed up for only a couple of days ago, and which we couldn't see through.

We have other things on our mind, though, our sights set on Petram right at the summit of the mountains in the high passes. We reach the road up through the low hills, rising up into the valleys, and soon come around the corner to witness the staggering sight of the giant camps set up in the lofty plains.

We drive on, and the early morning light brings into stark contrast the surge of activity going on in the military camp.

Everywhere, soldiers from the Petram army are being mobilised, vehicles being checked and fitted and sorted into formation. Men and women in uniform work busily, weapons being handed out and body armour being issued.

Such is the sight ahead that we stop and get out of the car, marvelling at the scale of it all. As a soldier walks by, I call out: "What the hell is happening here?"

He turns to me, hardly losing stride in his rush.
"War. We're going to war."

14

Pawns in the Game

The scale of the operation grows clearer as we continue to rise up the mountain. With Ajax behind the wheel, I'm able to get a good look down over the edge of the perilous cliff on the right of the mountain pass. Down in the plains, the sight of thousands of soldiers being mobilised draws the eye, as large a force of people as I've ever seen.

I never realised that Petram had such a military force at its disposal, spread far and wide across the Deadlands as they were.

"It's different from the Eden standing army," Ajax offers. "Those guys are full time professional soldiers. But a lot of those from the Deadlands are temporary, you know, only coming together when they need to."

"Where'd you hear that?" I ask.

"Vesuvia told me. Apparently there are well over ten thousand possible soldiers that Petram can call on."

"Lucky for the regions," I say. "The Eden army has been waning over the years. Peace has made them weak."

"Yeah, and a lot of those that are left have joined the Baron. Some soldiers have no loyalty to a cause. They just go where they're told, and do what they're ordered to. It doesn't matter who's holding the whip."

We fly up the mountain, soon entering the mist that hangs up in the high passes. Entering the soup, the view of the valleys below is swallowed up, giving me nothing to look at but the road ahead. Once more, the welcome chill of the mountain breathes life into the car, sweeping away some of the dust it's accumulated over days in the sand and rock.

It dawns on me that we've essentially stolen the vehicle, and should probably make sure it's returned at some point. Right now, though, I doubt too many people will kick up a fuss about it.

Soon, we're flattening out as we climb to the summit of the path. Ahead, through the swirling mist, the long tunnel through the mountain awaits, an impenetrable barrier to the plateau and city of stone beyond. Blocking the tunnel, the thick gate remains shut, a dozen soldiers manning the checkpoint.

Guns are quickly raised as we approach, a constant vigilance maintained. Truly, though, an enemy would have to be quite something to get to this point unscathed, the pathway below crawling as it is with our forces.

We roll up and come to a stop, and a soldier moves to the side window.

"What is your purpose here?" he asks, peering through at us.

"We're Ajax and Theo," says my friend. The names no longer need any explanation. "We have urgent business with President Drayton."

The man offers no additional questions or queries. Our faces, no longer requiring of morph masks, are famous enough now to give us free passage just about anywhere. He nods us through and we enter past the gate and into the long, dark tunnel, cruising through as fast as the old jeep will allow.

It coughs and chugs loudly, its voice echoing around the walls, as if it's calling for a break.

"Don't worry, old girl," I say, patting the dashboard. "We're nearly there."

Moments later, we're bursting back into the light, our presence called ahead by the tunnel checkpoint and the gate on the perimeter of the plateau opening up to allow us entry. We stop outside and get out of the car as the gate commander greets us.

"We weren't aware you were out of the city," he says.

"It was a top secret mission," is all I say, before pointing at the car. "That was part of the collection used by the Deadlands searchers. Can you please make sure it gets back to them."

The officer nods and sets about making it happen as we head straight into the city, our eyes set on a single path. And down it we go, moving along the smooth corridor leading to the Master's chambers and war room, the first port of call when searching for Drake.

As we approach, the guards outside the door tell us there's a meeting already in progress. They don't, however, prevent us from going straight through without knocking.

A series of familiar faces turn to us, our sudden intrusion clearly unexpected. The room is filled with the usual suspects, all presumably drawn together to direct and discuss the current goings on down in the valleys.

Ajax and I stand there, sweating and dirty, panting slightly as a short silence falls.

It's the man we've come to see who breaks it.

"Ah, Theo and Ajax, you're back…and just in time."

I scan the room and the expressions within it. The expected looks of suspicion are present, all glaring at us. Jackson and Cyra. Link and Ellie. Their sons have been gone for several days, disappearing without warning. Clearly, they want answers.

Yet, the countenance of Drake suggests otherwise. And his next words make it clear that he's already worked up the necessary excuses.

"For those of you unaware," he announces to the group. "I sent the two lads to the Deadlands for a couple of days to aid in the support of the refugees crossing the desert. By the looks of their clothes, they've been right in the thick of it. How was it, boys?"

Ajax and I are quick enough to catch on.

"Erm, yeah, pretty brutal down there," I say. "Lots of refugees coming in. But Major Vilius is running a tight ship."

I throw in the name of the Major in charge, hoping it will add some credence to my story. I look at my parents, who continue to look doubtful. Drake will have informed them of the lie early on. And, knowing them, they'll never have believed it.

Still, there are clearly other more pressing matters to get to, Drake taking the floor.

"Excellent, boys," he says. "And well done for getting back here so quickly. I trust you got my message OK?"

We both nod and say: "Yes, sir," as little smiles rise on our faces.

"Right, well, just to catch you up. We got word overnight that the war is spreading once more, and that the stalemate across and near the coast has been broken. The Baron's forces are appearing at various points across the map, attacking certain strongholds of The Guardians of Liberty. By now, the fighting is stretching right from Fossor in the North, to Agricola in the South. General Trent, would you take it from here."

"Of course, President Drayton," says the General. "The forces of Eden are on the back foot, and they cannot keep this tide at bay. I am coordinating with General Proctor and his men, and we are going to be bolstering our strength at the main areas of fighting.

The convoy will be leaving in a matter of hours. Ladies and gentlemen, Baron Reinhold has once more made his move. Soon enough, all the regions will be engulfed in this. We have no choice but to play our hand."

"And that means *all of us*," announces Link. "We can no longer sit and wait here in Petram. We have to set our Watchers free…"

He looks over Cyra and Drake, and then Ajax and me.

"I'm not sure how prudent that is."

It's Jackson who speaks, engaging with Link once more, as he so often has before.

"Prudent?" asks Link. "People are dying and you're talking about being *prudent*?"

"I have gotten word from some of my sources that the Seekers are once more at large," says my father. "We've had several sightings of them, and don't know where they'll appear next. We've had this debate before. If they lure our Watchers out, then it may all be over. We cannot fall into another trap."

"Jackson, with all due respect, you are *not* a Watcher. My full strength has returned, and I cannot sit here night and day, seeing people being killed in my visions, and do *nothing* about it. That is not how I am made. I grew up in Fossor, and I have lived in Lignum for twenty years. I will not let the people there, or anywhere else for that matter, die without doing anything to help…"

"And you think it's easy for the rest of us?" asks

Jackson. "You think your powers give you the right to act like a vigilante, acting judge, jury, and executioner. They don't, Link. I have my whole family fighting with The Guardians in Agricola but, much as I'd like to, I will not go out there with my own strike force to defend it unless by express command of this council. We have limited resources, and how they're managed is essential to our success. If you leave now, and are defeated by a Seeker, then you might just be dooming us all."

The two men stare at each other for a moment, going quiet. I can see both sides of the debate, understand both points of view. My heart agrees with Link. I want to be out there doing what I can. My head, however, sides with my father; right now, a single false move could sink us all.

"We're very different, Jackson," says Link eventually. "We always have been. I respect you, you know that, and I know you've done some great things. But I've spent my entire adult life saving lives, and I'm not about to stop now."

The room grows quiet again, as he turns and walks calmly to the door. I see Ajax staring at him as he goes, a weighty frown falling over his eyes.

"Dad..." he says.

Link doesn't turn. He opens the door, and begins moving away. Ajax calls again, but it's his mother who answers. She turns to Ajax, then to the group.

"I'll go after him," says Ellie. "I'll talk him round..."

She scuttles off, the door being shut by the soldiers behind her. A fresh silence swamps the room, until Markus's voice rises up.

"These are hard times for all of us," he says. "Link has always acted alone, and isn't a military man. His passion is something for us all to admire, and yet on this matter, Jackson is correct. We must stand together or not at all."

All those remaining in the room begin to nod in agreement. Only Ajax, to my side, looks on at the door forlornly.

"When we spoke on this matter before," says Drake, "we concluded that we'd need our full strength against these Seekers. As it stands, Athena and Velia remain in the West. They are having some success gathering more forces, men and women who we may end up counting on. Until they return, we must *all* stay here."

His eyes flash to mine, the irony of his words not lost on me. Because only days ago, he was instructing me to head towards the regions alone, to leave the city without any support and meet with the most dangerous foe we have. Drake, clearly, is willing to bend his own rules when needed.

There appears to be little more to say, the sting pulled from the tail of this particular gathering. At the moment, it's really the military commanders who rule the roost, their expertise and strategies designed to send countless soldiers out to their deaths, the pawns in this colossal game of chess.

And yet, I'm under no illusions about whether

that's right or wrong. In war, such lines are blurred, a single decision potentially costing the lives of hundreds, maybe thousands, of soldiers and civilians alike. A mistake, too, can be just as costly, and what might appear to be the right move could, in the long run, turn out to be the very thing that destroys us all.

Link, for example, might leave the city and fight the good fight, doing what he was born to do, saving hundreds of people. But then, out there with only normal men and women for support, he might run into a Seeker or two, who'd perhaps spied him in a vision mowing down the Baron's men.

He'd have no choice but to fight, so far from home, so far from the support we couldn't provide. And if he died, leaving us without our most powerful warrior, we'd be all the weaker for it. Who knows, maybe that would be the catalyst to signal the Baron's victory, the victory of evil, the victory of Knight.

Things are never so black and white in war. A valiant move by a hero like Link could doom us all. Or maybe he'd find a Seeker himself and take them out, giving us the upper hand? Maybe he'd go on a personal crusade of revenge, lighting the path for the rest of us to follow.

At the end of the day, it's all ifs, buts, and maybes. And for military men like Jackson, or Drake, or Markus or the two Generals, that's not good enough. They deal in strategy, in firm planning. That's how wars are fought.

The meeting concludes with a whimper, as the

commanders go off to continue coordinating the war effort. As everyone files out of the room, however, Drake calls out to Ajax and me.

"Boys, would you stick around a moment…"

I see Cyra looking on suspiciously.

"Nothing to worry about, Cyra," says Drake. "I just want an update on their time in the valleys…"

My mother looks far from convinced still, but is well used to her father's devious ways.

With Markus and Jackson in conversation across the room, Drake leads us through into his own quarters, shutting the door quietly to give us some privacy.

"It doesn't look like mum's buying the lie, grandfather," I say.

He shakes his head and offers a rueful smile. "She's not easy to deceive, and I don't exactly feel great about it. But let's not get into that. Tell me what happened. Did you find him? Did you talk?"

Ajax and I share a look.

"We did," I say. "He…he's conflicted, so full of rage. On another day he might have killed us."

"You fought him?"

"Briefly," says Ajax. "We lasted longer than I'd have expected, actually."

"But he didn't try to kill you?"

"No. There's something there, grandfather, a connection. I told him about mum, about who he

151

really is."

"And how did he take it?"

"Hard to say. He looked so confused and then just…ran away into the night. So, now what?"

"The seed is planted. Now, we have to let it grow…"

As we talk, a sudden rush of noise behind us breaks us from our quiet conversation. We all swing our heads around to see my father pouring through the doorway. He stares at us with narrow eyes, shutting the door firmly behind him.

"OK, Drake, this has gone on long enough," he says loudly. "I went with your lie about the boys being sent down to the Deadlands for a while, but I want a proper explanation now. Tell me what's going on."

His eyes turn to me, and mine go to my grandfather. Drake raises his eyebrows, and offers me a little nod.

"Theo…" says Jackson. "Explain yourself."

With my grandfather's approval, I bring my dad into the fold, quickly covering what he's missed and allowing Drake and Ajax to add in their own elaborations where appropriate. Within a few minutes, he's been concisely caught up. I wait in anticipation for his thoughts on the matter.

His first words don't fill me with much enthusiasm.

"Are you completely mad!" he says, looking to me

first and then up to Drake with wide, unbelieving eyes. "You'd let you grandson traipse across the country – a county which, by the way, is at *war* – and meet in secret with the most deadly damn Watcher in the world?!"

"*Let* isn't really the right word," I say, defending Drake. "I'd have gone anyway."

"Then you're all as foolish as each other."

"Except Ajax," I add. "He was pretty much dragged along by me."

"Fine, you *two* are as foolish as each other," Jackson says, staring at me and a placid-faced Drake. "You might have both been killed out there. What exactly did you hope to get out of this?!"

"To tell the Seeker about mum, and who he is."

"Oh for God's sake, Theo, we've been through this. This boy is your enemy, and being all palsy with him is only going to make things harder. Jesus..."

He begins pacing around the room, shaking his head and wiping his brow.

"Drake, I can't believe you allowed this," he exhales, still marching from side to side. "What were you thinking!"

"Jackson, calm down and take a breath," says Drake coolly. "What exactly do you think of me? Do you really think I'd have sent your son out there if I thought he'd be in danger? I must say, I'm insulted by the insinuation."

"Well, what is your excuse then?" asks Jackson, rounding on him.

"Firstly, I don't need an excuse, or to explain myself to you. I'll remind you of who you're addressing here, *Governor*. I have means and methods that go beyond what you can possibly understand or know. Theo's meeting with the Seeker was always going to happen, and it *had* to happen. And now, the boys are back, safe and sound, and have come bearing fruit."

"Fruit? Enlighten me…"

"I don't like your tone," bites Drake.

"With all respect, sir, this is my *son*…"

"And *my* grandson," cuts in Drake. "You do not hold a monopoly over caring for the boy. Yes, you are his father, but nevertheless, Theo is at the heart of this and he has an important role to play. This war is far bigger than any of us, and you need to take your emotion out of the game. We're soldiers here, all of us, and soldiers follow orders."

I watch the exchange like a game of tennis, my head swivelling from side to side as they spar. But enough's enough. Someone has to step in.

"I'm right here, by the way," I say loudly. "Stop talking about me as if I'm not in the damn room. Dad, I appreciate that you care, but grandfather's right. I had to go…it wasn't my choice or his or anyone else's. That vision was always going to take place, it was just fate."

Jackson takes a moment to himself, the heated

discussion cooling with my words. After several drawn out seconds, he begins nodding, and turns to Drake.

"I apologise, Drake," he says. "It's just been a hectic time recently, and this thing with Link…I don't mean to argue. It's just, this is news to me, and perhaps I need time to digest it."

"I understand, Jackson," says Drake. "We are all entitled to vent at times like this. Suffice to say, Theo and Ajax took a step forward the other night. Whatever you think of this Seeker, AK1, he may have a bigger part to play in this than we are currently aware of. We know from Professor Lane's notes that he has a special purpose. That purpose needs to be discovered."

"OK," says Jackson, adopting a formal military pose. "What is it that you need me to do?"

I look at him and know that Drake's words have had the desired effect. My father is, above all, a man who follows order and leaders. That's how he's lived his life, and barring the odd bout of insubordination, he'll always perform that duty.

Drake turns to him, and mimics Jackson's sudden posture, standing firm as he gives his order.

"I need you to find information on this purpose, this secret. I don't care what it takes, but we need to find out what the Baron is planning. They're clearly hiding something, and if my instincts are correct, these men will have made sure they've destroyed every last morsel of information we might find about their future plans."

"Their destruction of the base beneath The Titan's Hand is testament to that," suggests Jackson.

"Precisely," continues Drake. "There may have been something revealing in there, but we missed our shot. So we're going to have to get that information another way..."

Jackson starts to nod, pacing again around the room.

"With war spreading again," he says, "we might just have a chance. The Baron's focus will be diluted, and so will his attention. What we need are spies, people who can report to us from his own camp."

"Go on..." says Drake.

"The Baron is still offering the choice of silver or lead," continues my father, thinking fast, "and he's still gathering his army. We need some brave souls willing to join up and feed us information. If we can get an inside line, then we might just figure out where the Baron and the Cabal are hiding. If we can find them, we can find their secret."

"Good," says Drake, nodding. "I trust you to keep this one close to the chest, Jackson. And that goes for both of you too," he adds, looking to Ajax and me.

We nod, as Jackson answers. "I'll get on it immediately, sir. I have lots of well trained soldiers I can trust to see this through."

"And us?" I ask.

"Sit tight for now," says Drake. "You've both

been brilliant once again. I'm sure you'll be called upon before long."

And with that, yet another secret meeting comes to a close, something I'm becoming well versed in by now. Every week I seem to be embroiled in some sort of subterfuge, always operating under the radar.

But now, it's back to the waiting game.

And that's something I'm getting familiar with too.

15
A Secret Shared

The next days pass by without major incident, on a personal level at least. It's a funny thing to say, really, given how war now rages across so much of the land, but truly, here in the city there's little to tell of the terrors down below for the regular man.

For me, of course, it's different. Not only is my head a factory of visions right now, but I'm included in many of the meetings taking place in the war room. Not all, of course, but many. Some remain the domain only of the top echelon of command, those overseeing the specific actions of our military factions. My inclusion, mostly, is based upon my skills as a Watcher, my overall task still to hunt down signs of future attacks.

That particular duty is, however, becoming less of a priority. The simple fact is that, with war now engulfing so much of the country, new attacks have become the norm. And across our Eden soldiers, Petram soldiers, and The Guardians of Liberty militia group, we have enough men and women out there to give some forewarning of any major assault.

More to the point, any place with more than a few thousand, or even hundred, residents is well and truly expecting an attack at any point. Those who have chosen to run and hide are generally littered across the hills and woods and mountains of the regions, or hiding in old shacks or abandoned towns and cities; places where the enemy won't bother to look. That, of course, is if they haven't come here to the Deadlands, waiting for the war to pass as they hide somewhere across the sandy wilderness, or take up residence in the camps down in the valleys, or the city here itself.

The people who remain in their hometowns, however, are expecting a fight. Right now, our abilities to watch the future and search our visions are growing stale in this new arena of war.

What we can do, however, is continue the hunt for the Seekers. As the days pass, more sightings come in, more rumours suggesting that they're pressing on, working their way through populations of our soldiers with ease.

The news comes to us in a meeting, and my eyes turn to Link immediately. So far, Ellie has been true to her word to talk him around. Hearing that these Seekers are out there wreaking such havoc, however, looks like it might be the thing to push him over the edge.

He doesn't voice his concerns, though, knowing there will be no point. He just stares forward with a grimace until other news comes up, those clogs grinding and turning and leading him, perhaps, towards the decision to leave. Ellie, however, stays close to him, always working to cool him down. Ajax, too, tells me he speaks to him regularly, doing his best to make sure he stays on message.

"It would be helpful if he knew what the hell was going on," says Ajax, marching around the sitting room one evening. "We should tell him what's been happening. We should tell them all…"

I never thought it would happen, but now it's my turn to pull him off such an idea. So far, I've been desperate to keep the rest in the loop. Now, though, I've grown used to the secrecy, to the burden of carrying this knowledge. Being in cahoots with three others is certainly helpful in that regard.

So, like Ellie has with Link, I manage to talk Ajax down too.

"Fine," he agrees eventually, "but next time we have a secret meeting, I'm bringing this up with Jackson and Drake."

I smile and pat him on the shoulder. "Be my guest," I say, knowing how hard headed the two can be.

Naturally, though, my own concerns about the Seekers rise. When we do get a chance to talk, just the four of us, I ask whether there have been sightings of AK1. The answer from Jackson, of course, is that no one can tell the Seekers apart, not unless they get a really good look at them.

For some reason, I had it in mind that AK1 might hold back after our meeting, might suddenly doubt his place in the world, might withdraw and consider what he's doing. And then a fear strikes in me that the exact opposite might just be occurring. That instead of pacifying him, of stimulating the good part of him, I've merely enraged the evil that dwells inside him, cornered a dangerous animal and forced it to lash out.

Have we unknowingly unleashed him? Are we to blame for some of these massacres?

Those doubts linger for a time, but are quickly dismissed.

"We did only what we had to do," says Drake. "That meeting was set, and you attended. What happened, happened. There's no changing it now. Keep faith, Theo. We have no other choice."

I nod and feel some comfort from his words, but they're not enough to satisfy me for long. It's not that I necessarily think we've somehow spurred him on. It's more that, maybe after everything, I was wrong about him. That what part of my mother is in him, what light resides there, is never enough to quell the dark. That the blackness will always dominate the light, like the night sky only peppered with stars. Maybe I'm wasting my time on him. Maybe Jackson was right all along...

Still, his face is never far from the front of my mind. Memories of our meeting lingers there now, sometimes clear, sometimes cloudy, but always serving to obscure my true visions. My obsession has begun to consume me, preventing me from actively searching for new sightings.

He's the key, I find myself thinking. *For good or bad, he's the key...*

My thoughts continue to dwell on him, though, in some vague hope that I'll spy another meeting between us in my mind. But nothing fresh comes. Nothing new. Right now, with the world at war, the background noise is too loud to allow for any clarity in my visions. It's all just a jumbled blur of chaos and death, my mind too busy and hectic to truly focus on a single thought.

The days begin to blur, too. There appears little distinction between night and day now, little formality to the passing of the hours. Even the immutable custom of dinnertime begins to loosen up, the residents of the house rarely finding time to sit down and eat together. With so much going on, everyone finds their time stretched thin, moving from one thing to the next with barely a moment to stop and rest.

During those long days, I begin to feel restless, my innate desire for action bubbling to the surface. Often, I begin to turn to the side of Link, wanting to get out there and do something. It's a bitter pill to swallow, knowing that tens of thousands of people are out there, right now, fighting for their lives and families and homes, fighting for their country.

And here I am, sitting and waiting and hiding in this mountain. Hoping for some news to come, for some hint that the pieces are moving again.

Whenever I get a chance, I ask my father about his mission. He tells me little, keeping his cards close to his chest. All I know is that he's planted some of his soldiers in various spots as yet untaken by the Baron, waiting to be assimilated into our enemy's cause.

"We'll have news soon," he promises me, before hurrying off on another task.

News of Athena and Velia, too, is hardly forthcoming. By now they've been gone for well over a week, their mission to gather up forces in the West gaining traction but still incomplete. I begin to doubt whether it's going to be worth it, adding a few hundred, or even few thousand untrained men and women to the cause.

"Everything matters," Drake tells me after a meeting one day. "A single person can alter the course of a war. A single well placed gunshot, or a single piece of vital information...it can all turn the tide, one way or another. You never know what an individual might bring."

I understand the theory, but can't help but think that the only influential individuals in the West right now are Athena and Velia, the very people we sent out there. In my quieter moments, however, I realise that my thoughts on the matter are tainted by emotion. That it's my desire to have Velia back that's shaping my concerns. Truly, I never thought she'd be gone this long.

I never thought I'd miss her this much.

I shake the thought from my head and soldier on, though. Emotion, feeling...it all just serves to weaken you, makes decisions harder to judge from an objective standpoint. It's the very reason why Jackson and Drake don't want my mother to know of the existence of AK1.

Emotion and caring for others, a great virtue of my

mother in life, has nevertheless been her weakness in war. And, already, the same thing is moulding my thoughts, my knowledge of who this clone really is making me consider him less and less my enemy.

And yet, he's probably out there right now, killing our men, massacring women and children, little on the surface but an agent of evil.

But is it true evil that defines him? How can I judge a boy like that, grown in a lab, taught nothing but hate and death, bred to spread chaos across the land. Who knows what lies he's been fed, what reality he really lives in. A reality formed by the Baron, by the doctrine of Augustus Knight, by the terrible things he's been forced to see and do.

What if I were born into such a place, bred for such a purpose? How would I see the world, see my place within it? Would I question it, or merely act upon it, following through on the orders I'm given?

In the end, I wonder whether people are born to be evil, or merely bred to do evil things. And most of all, how far do you have to go before it's too late to turn back? How deep into the pit can you fall, before climbing back out again?

Such thoughts come to me more regularly now, the nature of good and evil something that grows more opaque in my mind, the grey between the black and white beginning to grow. One night, I find myself musing on it all in the kitchen, sitting alone at dinner as the rest continue to press on with their own lives.

I munch on some leftover stew from days past,

one of Leeta's favourites and one of the few meals she can spare the time to make these days. As I do, the door opens and the face of my mother appears, looking weary and drained.

"Mind if I join?" she asks with a little smile.

I quickly set about preparing her a bowl and pouring her a glass of fresh mountain water. She sits ahead of me on the long wooden table, the light dim and world quiet, and for a few minutes we sit and eat in silence. It's something we've done thousands of times before, sitting in a lonely kitchen, eating our dinner. And yet here, and now, the world is so very different.

I'm so very different.

I look at my mother, who's gone through all this before, and a question dribbles off my tongue in a whisper.

"How did you do it?" I ask.

She looks up from her bowl, and into my eyes, now filled with so much more memory, more wisdom, than ever before.

"What do you mean, darling?"

"This," I say, looking around. "War…everything. How did you get through it all?"

She reaches her hand across the table, and takes a grip of mine.

"With help, and support," she says. "It's caring for your loved ones that pulls your through."

"But…doesn't that make it harder?" I ask.

"Doesn't worrying about people make you weaker?"

"Weaker?" she says, frowning. "Oh no, Theo…it makes you stronger. What else are we fighting for if not each other? Without that, why would we fight at all?"

I nod and drop my eyes, thoughts of all those I care for drifting through my head. Before I know it, my mother's standing by my side, moving from the other end of the table, and pulling me into a hug. I didn't realise, but it's what I needed. And in that moment, I feel a wave of emotion pulse through me, tears threatening to build and drop from my eyes.

"You carry the weight of the world on your shoulders, my darling," whispers my mother. "What's really troubling you?"

I can't answer. I fear if I speak, my words will crack. I just shake my head, and steady my emotions, and feel like a son again, just a son to a mother.

"It's just harder than I thought it would be," I whisper eventually. "Everything's so big now…I feel lost sometimes."

She pulls away and sits beside me, looking into my eyes. Her own, big and blue, carry so much weight of their own. And yet, I see her as others do, when they see the great Cyra Drayton beside them, her presence giving them hope, making them believe.

For the first time, I see her like that too. She warms her face with a smile, vanquishing all the worries her countenance carries, and bringing some light to the room.

"You've been through a lot, just like I did. It's not easy being at the heart of something so grand, so important. It's not easy having the fate of so many resting on your shoulders."

"But how did you cope?"

"By standing together," she says. "By fighting for what I believed, and for those I cared about. It doesn't make you weak, Theo, it makes you strong. You'll realise that eventually."

In that moment, I want to tell her once more about everything that's being kept from her, want to reveal the truth of what's really on my mind. Maybe it's just selfishness, a desire to pass the burden to her shoulders, ease the weight that bears down on mine.

Or maybe it's something else; the ever present feeling that she deserves to know, that she, above all, should be part of all of this.

A battle rages inside me. I stare at her and then look away, and find her eyes boring into me, trying to seek out the truth. My mouth opens, and then closes, words forming in my mind but not being delivered by my lips. For what seems like an age, I fight the urge to reveal the truth, to betray the wishes of my father and grandfather.

And then, her soft voice drifts to my ears once again.

"It's OK," she whispers. "I know how hard it is being a soldier, following orders…*keeping secrets*."

My eyes flash up, widening a little. There's something in hers. Something that tells me she knows.

She smiles, and strokes her hand over my forehead, brushing away the blond hair.

"It's not your fault, Theo. It's no one's fault. This is just war, a cauldron of secrets and lies. I don't blame anyone."

"You…you know?" I whisper, searching her eyes.

She nods slowly, silently, her gaze never leaving mine.

"I saw you in my dreams, Theo. I saw you with the Seeker. I heard…I heard what you said."

"I…" I start, my voice preparing to rush.

She calms me with a hand to my cheek, and a shake of the head.

"It's OK," she whispers. "Really, it's OK. I know why Jack and my father wanted to keep this from me. I understand the way their minds work. And I understand yours too. I've seen enough to know what Augustus was capable of, Theo. He always had a special interest in me. Perhaps this was his goal all along…"

She turns introspective for a moment, memories of those past days washing likes gentle waves over her eyes. I look on in wonder, her control and understanding amazing me. She truly is something more than I ever knew, more than even the stories I heard and told suggested. There's a calm authority to her that these past weeks and months have revealed, something I never knew resided inside her.

"I wanted to tell you," I manage to say, before she can shut me down again.

She smiles and nods and strokes my cheek once more.

"I know you did, darling. But it's OK now. You've carried this for too long, you most of all. Now, you can share it with me. You're my son, Theo, and this boy...this boy is important to us both."

"AK1," I say. "He's known as AK1."

"I know," she says, nodding. "I've been seeing him from afar."

"You have? In your visions?"

"In my visions...and my dreams. He's out there now, searching..." she says, looking away into the middle distance.

"Searching for what?" I question, the thud of my heart growing stronger.

"For the truth, Theo," she answers. "He's searching for the truth."

16
Allies Divided

My father's head is low, drooping, his chin close to his chest. Drake, too, has a sheepish look splashed across his face. Both are finding it tricky to look my mother in the eye right now.

"I'm sorry, Cy," says Jackson quietly. "I thought it was for the best..."

"We both did," adds Drake. "We weren't sure how you'd take it."

Cyra steps closer towards them, and shakes her head.

"I understand, Jack...dad. I don't blame you for keeping the truth from me. I know you were just trying to protect me. But...there's no protecting me from myself, I guess. My visions have grown stronger. I couldn't help but see the truth."

We're in my grandfather's quarters, just off from the war room, once more engaging in a secret meeting beyond the knowledge of the rest of the council. I stand beside Ajax, watching on having introduced my mother to the room.

"She already knew?" asks Ajax with a whisper. "You didn't tell her yourself?"

I shake my head. "She saw it all," I say. "She's known for a while."

And for that, I'm truly happy. I don't have to feel guilty any more for keeping the secret from her, and I don't have to feel guilty for having revealed it. On both counts, I've been let off the hook.

And the relief is palpable.

"And...how do you feel about it all?" asks Drake carefully, peering now closely into his daughter's eyes.

"I feel like there's more to this boy than any of us know," she answers. "I've been watching him in my visions. What Theo told him has created a crack in his mind, and the light is beginning to shine in. He's hunting the truth, his mind is bent on it."

Jackson and Drake look at each other, then back at Cyra.

"You've seen all that way?" asks Drake. "Are you sure about this?"

"I have a connection with him," she answers calmly. "Theo has is too, that's why that vision of their meeting came so regularly. It's hard to describe, really. This is stronger than anything I've felt before, like I've got a special line into his mind. I can feel his confusion and anger...and fear."

"Fear?" says Jackson. "You can sense that?"

She nods. "The world he knows has been shaken. There are doubts in him now."

"And do you know where he is?" asks Drake.

"No," she answers. "But from what I can gather, he doesn't seem to be out there with the others. I'm seeing no pain or death around him. Only pain in himself."

Listening to my mother, I feel almost foolish for thinking my connection with him meant anything. Truly, their link is something else entirely, something more profound.

Jackson and Drake, too, carry the look of guilt with them. A regret, perhaps, that they didn't include my mother earlier, that they didn't trust her to handle it.

Yet now isn't the time for looking back. It's time we look forward.

In that room, over the next hour, we talk in quiet whispers, sharing the information that we were once keeping from each other. Cyra, for her part, does what she can to describe AK1's frame of mind in further detail. Jackson and Drake, meanwhile, catch my mother up on the secret initiative to infiltrate the Baron's camp with spies, ready to report back on the whereabouts of any of the top members of the Cabal.

To that end, there are updates that I'm keen to hear.

"I've got several soldiers who have gone dark," announces Jackson. "That can mean one of two things: either they've been caught and killed, or have put any transmissions on hold until they're in a position to call in."

"And how do they do that?" asks Cyra.

"They all have inbuilt communicators, grafted to their inner right wrist," says Jackson. "They're beneath the skin and activate on voice command, calibrated specifically to the user's voice."

"Can they be traced, discovered?" I ask.

"They can, but the technology is very new and it's doubtful whether the Baron's men will be aware of it. The communicator is about the size of a thumbprint, and invisible to the naked eye. They'd need a scanner of some kind to find it, and most won't pick up signatures that small."

"So…we're hoping that they're waiting for the right time to call in and update us?" asks Ajax.

"Precisely. Again, we'll just have to wait."

More waiting, more hoping. But now, we have Cyra's mind too, her direct line into AK1's mental state an essential thread that might help us to unravel this mess.

"Ajax, update us on your father."

The command from Drake brings Ajax's concerns to the fore, invited without having to be pushed onto anyone. Holding the floor, he passes on his doubts, those that we all share.

"He's struggling, sir," says Ajax. "More and more each day. Maybe…maybe it's best to include him? If he knew the bigger picture, perhaps he'd ease up?"

"Do you really believe that?" asks Drake.

"Whether he knows or not, Link can't contribute from here. I'm not sure it will do him any good."

"I'm not so sure," says Cyra. "Perhaps the entire council should be aware of this? What exactly is the reasoning for keeping things so tight?"

"Security," says Jackson, "and simplicity. We see no need to include anyone who cannot directly contribute to this. If we explain what we're doing, then we'll need to explain the very nature of this AK1. That will open up more questions that we don't have time to field right now. We don't need that attention on us."

"But why not Link, and Ellie? And maybe Markus?" asks Cyra. "We were all in this together once. We should stand together again."

"Cy, as far as I'm concerned, we have enough people involved. We have our core team now, and that's enough."

"Jackon's right," says Drake. "All will be revealed soon, I can assure you. But as it stands, until we hear any confirmation from Jackson's men, there's nothing to report. Is that clear?"

Drake, as always, issues the final command. And whether to the liking of those in the room or not, it's important that we obey.

Later that night, however, Ajax moans a little more about it, and I sit back and allow him to vent. His concern, really, isn't that his parents don't know; it's simply that he's afraid of what his father might do.

Whether it's connected or not is debatable. Personally, I'm more or less of the same thinking as my grandfather: whether Link knows or not, his desire to go and fight out there isn't going to change.

I just have to hope that we give him some good news soon. Something to chew on, to keep his mind on task.

The following day does bring news.

But it's not good.

By now, I've grown used to the general flow of the daily meetings, where we get updates on what's happening, and the Watchers pass on anything they've seen. Usually, such things occur in the afternoon at some point. That day, however, we're summoned early, the night bringing with it some awful reports.

Gathering in the war room of the Master's chambers, I look to see the usual maps set up over the table. Circles and ticks and crosses and other markings appear all over them, indicating the general state of play across the regions. That morning, those maps appear to be more tattooed than ever.

Heavy shoulders are slung, bodies weary and expressions sour as the reports are delivered. It's Markus who leads the charge, covering several places where our troops have been pushed back.

"It seems like the Baron ordered a sudden surge last night," he says with a heavy heart. "Many of the targets will be close to home for the people in this room."

I see his eyes flash around the chamber, stopping on certain people. Link is among them, smouldering as he awaits the news.

"Our Guardian stronghold in Lignum has been overrun," he announces after a brief pause. "Large swathes of woodland are being burned. I'm sorry," he says, looking again at Link and Ellie, Cyra and Jackson, Ajax and me. "Your homes have been destroyed. There's…there's nothing left in the area."

"No…" whispers Ajax.

"GOD DAMN IT!" shouts Link, smashing his fist on the desk with such force it cracks.

Some of the passive members of the council step back as a blast of anger radiates out of him.

"I should have been there," he growls, setting his eyes on Jackson. "I could have saved them…"

"You don't know that," says Drake. "The place was overrun, led by a Seeker. You might just have burnt with the rest of them."

Link's burning eyes turn to Drake, his words callous.

"I've had enough of this, of all of you. You're cowards!" he calls. "You fear these Seekers…these *boys*. I can tell you right now. I don't! Enough of this…ENOUGH!"

With those words, he turns and powers through

the door, smashing it back with force. Once again, Ellie has no choice but to rush after him, Ajax too. I try to hold him back, but know there will be no use.

As the sound of their footsteps echo down the corridor, Markus's voice rises again. I barely hear him, devastated as I am to learn about the loss of my home. I look at my mother, her own face riddled with sadness, her mouth closed tight. Slowly, she lifts her eyes to Markus, and mine follow as his voice forms in my head once more.

"It's not just Lignum," he says. "Word has just come that our power bases in Fossor, and Agricola, are under siege too…"

"Agricola?" asks Jackson sharply. "Has the stronghold been taken?!"

"The battle's still going on, Jackson," says Markus. "I…I'm sure they're safe."

My father's eyes widen and then fall, and Cyra moves to comfort him. Rarely does he allow his emotions to take centre stage. Now, they consume him, momentarily taking over. I can see the fear written across his face, fear that his parents, his brothers and their families, will be dead, defending their homeland as part of the militia.

"What…what are we doing to help?" he asks.

"There's little we can do," says General Trent calmly, in a manner befitting his role and rank. "You know how stretched out we are. We are fighting on all fronts, and have no men to spare."

"Then we make some difficult choices,"

commands Drake. "We determine what we can no longer keep, and let it go. With these Seekers at play, the Baron's men are running riot. There's little we can do to stop them. We must draw in our forces, we must retreat."

"Retreat?!" says General Proctor.

"I'm afraid we have no choice, General Proctor," says Drake firmly. "If we don't retreat now, we may not have an army left to fight with."

"Well then maybe Link is right," says Markus. "These Seekers are killing us! We need to stand toe to toe with them."

Coolly, Cyra's voice joins the conversation. It's not rushing like the others. It's calm, measured, her eyes turning back to the door, to the corridor beyond.

Looking out, away from us all, she merely says: "Whether right or wrong, Link's leaving. They'll be no keeping him here after this…"

Her words are prophetic.

Because as the argument rages on, and the minutes turn to hours, and the military commanders furiously debate their way to some solution, the door opens once more.

At first, no one sees her enter. No one except Cyra. Then, one by one, the voices die down, and we all fall silent and look upon Ellie, her face pained and eyes red.

No one needs to ask what's wrong.

"He's gone, hasn't he?" says Jackson.

She nods.

"I couldn't keep him back, not this time."

A strike of fear grips at me. Her tearful eyes turn to mine.

"Ajax…" is all I say.

Her chin dips and fresh tears fall.

And I know, right then, that Ajax has gone too.

17

The Road to War

I find Vesuvia inconsolable that night.

Her tough persona has melted with the departure of Ajax, her sister not present to help her through. She cries and cries as she lies in bed, her leg still wrapped up in a heavy cast, holding a blanket to her eyes to try to shield her pain.

I give her what comfort I can, but she won't accept it. So I speak words of confidence instead, telling her Ajax will be fine and Velia will be back soon. And all the while, my heart breaks that they're both missing too.

Downstairs, I know Cyra is doing the same for Ellie. From what I know, Link tried to persuade Ajax to stay, but he wouldn't have it. Wouldn't let his father go out there again, leaving him here with nothing to do but wait for word of his safety. In the end, Ellie couldn't prevent either from leaving, the guards stationed around the mountain too frightened of him to try the same.

I comfort myself with the thought that Ajax is with our most potent warrior. That he himself has grown so strong. Were the two to fight a Seeker, they might well overcome him. After what I've seen and done, that's something I truly believe.

That night, as the world descends into a new chaos, I begin to wonder why Jackson's men have gone dark. That maybe they, too, were caught up in the spreading violence, never to be heard from again. Already, our forces are retreating, moving back to our strongest bases of power deep into the mainland, consolidating what strength we have remaining and leaving other lands to the clutches of the Baron.

But losing land isn't the problem. Right now, it's the people that matter, those that still fight for us, side with us. The Baron isn't interested in holding territory, in controlling new lands. All he wants is the destruction of our people, of our way of life. And when the world stops burning, and the dust settles, he'll rebuilt a new one in the image of his master.

Right now, there are few rays of light in the growing dark. Few reasons to be cheerful or hopeful as the Baron's prophecy, Augustus Knight's legacy, continues to come true.

The world is burning. The people are dying. Each day that passes brings a fresh new tragedy, another massacre to add to the growing collection. We are becoming divided, our strongest warriors separated and drawn apart to the various corners of the land.

That might have been the entire aim after all.

In the aftermath of the attacks, word reaches me that two of my uncles have been killed. My heart breaks all over again when Cyra delivers the news.

"How's...how's dad?" I ask, half in shock.

She struggles to find an answer. When she does, all she can say is: "Focusing on his job."

Really, the question was stupid. My dad has always been fiercely close to his family. The deaths of two of his three brothers will be killing him inside.

The rest of them, at least, managed to make it out. Now, they're on their way to one of our final strongholds, Fort Warden, where many of our soldiers and militiamen and women have begun to gather. Well protected and armed, and currently set back from the fighting, it's just about the safest place across the regions right now.

That night, I see my father late in the evening and barely know what to say. I move in and silently hug him, and feel him grip me tighter than ever, his bionic hand pinching at my flesh.

But I don't speak any words. They're not needed right now. I just tell him how devastated I am with my actions, and the expression on my face. Because right now, there's no knowing who might be next to fall.

It seems that everything we do fails, that the Baron is always a step ahead of us, expecting anything we might try. His years of planning have given him a map of the future, a way of predicting what we'll do, how we'll react, to any move he makes.

How can you fight such an enemy? How can you do anything when he knows what path you'll take before you do so yourself. Any time we think we might be subverting his expectations, doing something he hasn't seen coming, we end up getting struck down again. When The Guardians began to rise up, and the statemate began, we thought it was all something he hadn't seen coming. But who knows now if that's true. Maybe he had anticipated it all, building up to strike out once more when we least expected it, hitting our strongholds and attacking the people and places we love the most.

He has no Watcher powers, but sometimes they're not needed. Time and clever planning can be just as effective, years of accumulated knowledge about all of us providing him with his own means of foreseeing the future. And with his Seekers by his side, who knows what else he's seeing, who knows what information they're feeding him. Perhaps they already know what we're going to do next. Perhaps they're planning their next assault based on actions we're yet to take.

When I think about it too much, it scrambles my mind. How you can make a plan based on things that are yet to happen, self-fulfilling that prophecy. Like when I went to meet AK1, and he came to me. We'd both seen it happen, knew it would happen, and so drew ourselves there. But what if we hadn't seen it? Would we have ended up there anyway? Would I have decided to randomly leave the city and make my way to no man's land, wait in a random, abandoned town in a hope that he'd appear?

Mostly, my visions involve seeing something

terrible happen. Things that will happen regardless of my actions, waiting to play out in the production line of time. Whether I see most visions or not, they will happen regardless, because I have no part to play in them.

But some, like when I saw my meeting with AK1, directly involve me. What if I had chosen not to go? What if he had done the same? Did I really have a choice in the matter, or would I have been drawn there anyway?

I could end up losing my mind thinking of such things, my thoughts going round and round like a carousel, always coming back to the same conclusion: that I am just another pawn in this game, the biggest game of all. A blip in the game of life, a tool in time used to fulfil a prophecy, to tie off a loose end.

And with such a conclusion comes another: that in the end, whichever side prevails, time doesn't care, the world doesn't care. We're all just notes in an endless chorus, one that will play forever.

Such a mentality, however, is a dangerous road to travel. In the end, if I truly think that, then why bother at all? Why keep fighting against the odds when we're all just going to be dust one day anyway? Whether we win or they do, we're all going to die, and this little war is going to be just another side note in the great game of time.

I let myself stew on such thoughts that evening, as I sit alone and contemplate it all. I allow myself the rare luxury of not caring for just a moment, giving me a cathartic release that, I know, will only be temporary.

Because when the dawn comes again, and the council decide on our next plan, I cannot let such negativity come with me to the war room. I cannot allow it to breed in me, and spread to the others. Right now, all we can do is keep fighting, keep believing, keep hoping that the tide will turn. And for my mother, and father, and friends and family, and everyone else who cowers under the growing darkness, I will do all I can to help hold back the spread of evil.

I may just be a blip in time. My friends and family may just be blips too. But they're blips that I love, blips that I'd die to save. And in the end, that's all the motivation I need.

Purged of my pessimism, I wake that morning with a renewed faith and hope. I go to the kitchen, and find the gloomy faces of Cyra and Ellie at breakfast. I go to my headmaster, and set my eyes on her, and simply say: "Everything's going to be OK. I know it. Link and Ajax will both be fine."

My words help her to raise a smile too, and I see my mother look on at me with pride. And at that moment, I realise how little moments can make all the difference. Just a word here, a hug there, a quiet moment of support and positivity in an otherwise bleak world. These are the things that matter. When added together, they can bring light to the dark, and set a faltering mind back on track.

"You seem chirpier today," remarks my mother,

her pride turning to curiosity.

"I guess I am," I say, nodding. "I have a feeling that today we'll get some good news."

"We need it," says Cyra, raising her eyebrows.

And when we get to the war room, my positivity is vindicated. The burden of the war hangs heavy over everyone, and yet there's something brewing that suggests a decision has been made, an agreement come to among our leaders.

"Link's departure has lit the way for us," says Drake, speaking to a full chamber of luminaries. "We have no choice now but to follow suit, and gather across the wall as he always suggested. We have held back for long enough, but now is the time to advance. As many of you will know, our forces are withdrawing from many areas known to be lost. We have tasted the bitterness of defeat, but only in battle. The war is yet to be won."

He looks to Markus, who continues in his stead.

"The plan is to empty the city of all remaining soldiers. We will bolster our armies across the wall with what we have here, gathering primarily at Fort Warden. Already, many of our forces have begun to accumulate there, waiting for orders. It's sufficiently far from any combat zones to be considered safe, for now at least, and we have spies all over the country watching for large troop movements. If they come at us, we'll know it."

"And what about the city?" asks Cyra. "Who will protect it?"

"We will leave a force of guards here for that purpose. I will hand over the running of the city to Leeta, who has been more or less fulfilling that role for us in recent weeks. She'll do a fine job with her support team, and will keep it running while we're gone."

I look over to see that Leeta is present for the first time, looking around a little sheepishly as all eyes are briefly drawn to her.

"The people will remain safe here, and in the valley camps below," continues Markus. "Those of us who fought in the last war will know the drill here. History is repeating itself, ladies and gentlemen. The regions beyond the wall are once more the arena of battle. And it's time we joined in."

I feel a pulse of energy move around the room. For some, that energy manifests as fear and nervousness. For others, it's a desire to get out there, finally, and do what we can. I'm certainly in the latter group.

Then, from the back of the room, a voice comes out from one of the Senators. "And what of Athena?" he asks.

I turn quickly back to Drake and see a smile rising on his face.

"Athena…is on the move," he says. "She's gathered a force of willing soldiers, and is currently travelling East across the Deadlands…"

"They're coming back?!" I find myself asking

loudly.

"Yes, Theo, they're coming back. And tomorrow, when we set off East, they'll be joining us."

I turn to my mother, and Ellie, and see them both smile.

Cyra looks down to me.

"I guess you were right," she says. "Good news indeed…"

18
Reunited

The Deadlands are sprawling.

Hundreds of vehicles, big and small, civilian and military, kick up a vast cloud of dust as they chug through the red desert. Petram has been emptied out, coughing up its final force of available soldiers to help with the war effort. The final stage is upon us.

As the colossal convoy grinds down from the mountains into the wasteland, I feel a growing excitement. We're moving, finally going to war. The main players are entering the game and, one way or another, for good or bad, it's going to come to an end.

Yet, aside from all that, my body swells with excitement for a very different reason. A much smaller reason. A more personal reason. But a reason that sets my heart pacing.

I'm about to see Velia again.

All this is alien to me; grand armies, giant battles, the fate of the world hanging in the balance. And yet this strange feeling inside is equally novel. Never before have I longed to see someone so much. Never before has a person's absence had such an impact on me.

Travelling at the head of the convoy, in a car

driven by my father, I watch the horizon with unblinking eyes, and harass anyone who'll listen with questions about Athena's current location.

In the end, it's the sight of billowing sand that answers, what appears like a sandstorm hanging over the surface of the earth. As we near it, however, the silhouettes of vehicles appear within the fog, emerging like spectres from a misty night. I look from left to right, and see dozens upon dozens of them, hundreds even, our two armies converging.

My eyes pop at the numbers.

"They've been busy," says Jackson, looking equally impressed.

They most certainly have. And right now, they're exactly what we need, a fresh force of bodies to help bolster our faltering ranks. And I wonder, as I look upon them, whether the Baron counted on them as well, whether his intricate plot assumed that those from the West would join our cause.

Soon, the two convoys are moving closer, and my eyes are scanning the front vehicles, searching for some sign of Athena...of Velia.

We come to a slow stop, crunching over the barren earth, and step out of the car. Around us, all of the others halt too, the air filled with the sound of hundreds of rumbling engines. It's typically scorching, despite the earliness of the hour, but the heat doesn't bother me. I stand and stare, waiting for the others to join us.

When they do, it's Athena I see first. She emerges

from the lead vehicle, and our top ranking leaders quickly gather together in the sand.

Drake, Jackson, Cyra, Markus. All move quickly towards her as she comes to them. I follow behind, watching the car she got out of, my eyes set on the shadow within. Seconds later, the shadow moves and emerges from the jeep, and a bright smile attempts to escape its constraints and rise up on my face.

I keep my cool, however, as the others meet and greet and start to talk furiously in their huddle. I barely hear them, watching Velia as her eyes sweep across and find mine. I wander towards her, and she comes towards me, and in a moment of liberation I let myself go, forget the world and all the terrible things in it, and scoop her up into my arms.

I hug her tight, and then give in to the inescapable urge to kiss her right there and then, at the heart of the two convoys. Under the burning sun, without saying a word, I do what I've wanted to do since she left, departing with that kiss that has lingered in my mind ever since.

Now, I deliver a second, and by the time I've regained any semblance of control, I look over to see that the others are looking at us with amusement in their eyes. I immediately remember myself and feel a twinge of embarrassment creeping up through me.

Then, I feel something else: Velia's hands on the back of my neck and head. She pulls me straight back in and kisses me again, and as she does, the many now watching around us begin to clap and cheer.

"OK you lovebirds," says Drake, stepping towards us. "It's time to get moving…"

The rest come over and greet Velia, my mother in particular drawing her into a hug and looking upon her in a fresh light, like the daughter she never had. And as they do, Athena comes to me and offers me a brief embrace.

"The war is calling us, Theo," she says. "Are you ready to answer it?"

"Of course," I say defiantly. "I was born ready…"

She smiles at my bravado as Drake's voice rises up again.

"OK, back to the cars," he shouts out. "We have a long way still to go."

As we all begin moving back to our respective vehicles, I see my mother still in conversation with Velia. When they split, my mother moves towards Athena's car, and Velia comes towards mine.

"Your mum says she wants to chat with Athena," she says. "So…I guess I'm with you."

The wink from Cyra suggests it's more about giving Velia and me some time together than anything else. I'm happy for it, and as we climb back into the cars and the combined convoy begins moving across the wasteland, I get to learn exactly what's happened with Velia since her departure.

By the sounds of it, they've been spending their

time moving across from town to town, trying to drum up support. At first, they gained little traction - those in the West have generally remained undisturbed by the actions of Eden and the regions, and even Petram, for a long time now.

However, this war isn't like any other, and if our enemy can't be stopped now, the fires of destruction will begin to spread to all corners of the nation, and perhaps even beyond.

"Athena was brilliant," Velia tells me. "She made some rousing speeches, got the people revved up. They've been under the thumb of the Baron for a long time. She made them realise that this was their chance for revenge, their chance to make a difference."

She asks, too, what's been going on back in Petram, and I have to bend the truth to keep from revealing too much. The most notable events have centred around AK1, whose true identity still remains a secret to all but a few. As we grow closer to the battlefield of war, however, it's going to be harder to maintain the subterfuge.

Much of her interest, however, is naturally on her sister. I tell her that Vesuvia has been missing her terribly, but that her leg is continuing to recover well. With so many departing the city, though, her loneliness and isolation is only going to get worse. Leeta now appears to be her only remaining friend.

Thankfully, I quickly learn that that's not going to be the case.

"Our mother is going to stay with her," says Velia.

"She's heading to the city now, with many others."

"Oh, that's great," I say, knowing just how desperate Vesuvia is right now, particularly after the sudden departure of Ajax.

"We'll all be together again soon," she says. "We've just got to get this war out of the way first."

She brings a tone of lightness to the conversation as we rumble on through the dirt, although I can tell it's more of a shield to her own pain than anything else. It's the right attitude, though. At this time, there's little point in stewing on such things. It's crucial that we're able to keep our heads in the game, and in that regard, knowing that her mother and sister are safely back in Petram is probably a good thing.

I have no such luck. More or less every person I care about is heading into the arena of war, and there's no knowing if any of us will come out of it alive. But in much the same way, it's a useless thing to be dwelling on the fear of death and loss. That's all part of the game, and is something I have little to no control over.

We make good progress as the day grinds on, the fall of night not halting our progress. We spare little time to stop and rest, the convoy only occasionally coming to a halt to allow people to switch over behind the wheel, or take a bathroom break. As the night descends, the convoy continues, moving slower under cover of darkness but refusing to quit.

In the back seat of one of the leading jeeps, I try to get some sleep as my body grows weary. And behind my eyelids, the sight of death and destruction grows more pronounced, more clear, our proximity to the chaos spreading through the regions bringing out more distinct and lucid visions.

The same will be happening for all of us Watchers, our minds growing busy with blood and fire. And despite the horrors I see, I know it can only be a good thing. That when we finally reach Fort Warden, we'll be able to better hunt for sight of a Seeker, or of some larger troop movement passing across the lands.

Through the night we drive, on and on as I'm rocked about in the back, the endless sound of engines creating a mechanic chorus through the silent wasteland. And soon, the light starts to appear on the horizon again, signalling the coming of a new day. The low reds turn to oranges and then brighten into yellows as the sun bursts from below the earth, bringing the world to light and life.

I look upon it all, and see some remains of Knight's Wall ahead, and my weary mind awakens with the knowledge that we're nearing our final destination. Just beyond the wall it lies, the vast military camp that will be our new home, our new base of operations from which the result of this war will be decided.

And only half an hour later, it grows in full force before me, the place I visited many months ago to witness the funeral of General Richter. Then, it was filled only with military personnel, lined up like statues to say farewell to their great leader.

Now, the base spreads far and wide beyond its own walls, figures crawling across the desert like ants. Thousands of soldiers from the Eden and Petram armies, and many more from The Guardians of Liberty, have all begun to gather here, combining their strength for the final surge.

Thousands have already been lost to the fighting, but so many more still remain. And looking upon the sight, I feel a fresh hope that, while we've been losing many battles, the war is still to be won.

And that Fort Warden is the final staging point to determine whether, in days or weeks or months time, we'll be facing victory or defeat.

19
A Special Purpose

That day rushes past quickly.

When the convoy grinds to a stop at the extremity of the base, we quickly set about our business. Immediately, the primary leaders and military commanders – Generals Trent and Proctor, Drake, Markus, Jackson, Athena – all move off to work out how best to integrate our new forces. With the camp growing so large, they'll need to be housed, fed, and watered, with the base's own security needing to be bolstered.

Already, as I enter, I can see that a significant number of gun placements, turrets, artillery weapons, and so on, have been distributed around the extremity of the camp, defending it from all angles to the East, North and South. And with more brought along by our convoy, the base's defensive capabilities are only going to be developed further.

That, however, is not for me to worry about. After being shown to our own accommodation, fairly centrally located within the base, our minds quickly turn to the fate of Link and Ajax, Ellie and me in particular. So far, no word has come from them directly. A visit to the communications centre, however, informs us that, while they still haven't gotten in touch, reports have come in that suggest that they're already hard at work.

"We have word that some enemy lines of attack have been halted," says a rather nervous technician, surprised perhaps to have legends like Cyra and Ellie descend upon his little office from nowhere.

"Where?" asks Ellie quickly.

"Lignum, ma'am," says the man. "Reports are coming in that Link is decimating the enemy, just like the Seekers have been doing to us."

A proud smile emerges on my face as I listen, thinking of Ajax out there with his dad, cutting down the enemy, giving them a taste of their own medicine.

Good on you, AJ, I think to myself.

When Cyra asks if they've encountered a Seeker, however, we get no confirmation on that.

"We haven't had any new sightings of the Seekers for a day or two," says the man. "With our forces retreating, things have gone quiet on that front."

"OK, good job. Keep searching," says Cyra as if she's talking to a Watcher.

I feel a sudden urge to get straight back into a jeep and go join them, to get stuck into the action myself. Cyra cautions against such thought, however, and reminds me in private that we both need to set our minds to AK1 and little else right now.

"Our connections with him will grow stronger now," she tells me as we sit in my basic room, fitted with nothing but a single bed and sink and little bedside table. "I can already feel it. Let your mind be fed with thoughts of him, and perhaps the other Seekers will find their way inside too."

Her orders bring me back down to earth, and remind me that I'm probably going to be just as much of a prisoner here as I was in Petram. So close now to the fighting, the itch inside me grows stronger: a desire to join my best friend, fight by his side, defend our home and country and the people within it from the spreading tyranny of Baron Reinhold.

But once more, I need to be reminded that my part in this isn't quite so easy to define or determine. I'm not just a regular soldier, waiting to be called up and sent out to battle with a thousand others. And while I can play a significant role out there, my presence here can be just as profitable. All I need is a quiet space and my own mind, and I can determine the fate of hundreds, thousands, or even millions.

That is the way of the Watchers.

The camp is just as chaotic as Petram, possibly even more so. For many weeks, there's been an almost constant buzz in the air, a hustle and bustle that accompanies such times. Back in Petram, however, most of those present were civilians, those drawn back from the war, hiding from it rather than facing it head on.

Here, almost every soul is a combatant in one way or another. Whether a General giving orders, a technician hunting information, or a soldier preparing to join the front lines, the majority here will play their part, big or small, in the battles to come.

Right now, with soldiers and militia men and women still coming in from around the regions, and with our new forces from Petram and the West arriving, it's all particularly turbulent. It will no doubt take several days to work out who's doing what, where any particular soldier should be, where they'll stay, what troop they'll move into, and so on. That will keep the top military officials busy for a little while, leaving us slightly exposed should the enemy be deciding to launch a surprise attack.

To that end, the remaining Watchers that Athena has trained are set up in their own private quarters, tasked with nothing but searching for visions. All across the country, too, we have spies hidden in old towns and bunkers, watching and waiting around the main concentration of enemy forces on the coast in the towns of Piscator and Mercator.

Skilled in the art of stealth and secrecy, they will help to make sure that we don't get any nasty surprises, waking one day to find the enemy on our dootstep. Right now, from their reports, it would appear that the enemy ranks are still swelling as ours have, many across the regions still joining them under duress or otherwise.

These spies, however, are only able to get so close. Already, many have been picked off, pushing the others back. Now, they wait at a distance, doing little but giving us an early alarm when the main armies of the Baron choose to move out.

Those tasked with infiltrating the enemy ranks properly, however, continue to stay dark.

"We haven't had contact from any of them," Jackson tells me that first night when he arrives at our accommodation. "We have to work on the suspicion that they're not going to be of any use to us."

His words come out weary and matter of factly. There's no deflation in his voice regarding the suspected fate of his men. After hearing of the deaths of two of his brothers, little can hurt him now.

Thankfully, his remaining brother and parents are being sent straight to Petram. With my grandparents old and my remaining paternal uncle injured, there's little sense in keeping them here. The same goes for others who will only be a burden, the injured shipped back to the city of stone just as they were two decades ago.

Here, we will maintain nothing but a fighting force capable of doing what it must to disable the Baron's chaotic and senseless assault on this country. Truly, the man is insane, his devotion to the long deceased Augustus Knight now responsible for the deaths of tens of thousands in the space of only weeks and months.

Should he continue his reign of terror, who's to know how many will end up succumbing to his sword. And for many others who don't, the world will once more revert to the sort of tyrannical rule that saw Knight himself rise to the summit of the nation and stay there for so long.

Here, in Fort Warden at the edge of the regions, stands the last bastion of hope for this country. While sporadic fighting continues across vast swathes of the nation, this is where the action is. This is where the fate of our time will be determined, where the good people will come together in the face of annihilation and stand as one in defiance of a tyrant.

Right at the heart of it, I turn my mind that night to AK1 once more. Turning my thoughts to him, and him alone, and leaving the likes of Velia behind, I find myself in my room with no distractions, searching for visions as I so often have.

And just as the world here is chaotic, so are the images that rush into my mind. I wade through all the fire and death, looking for him, clinging onto the growing connection that links us. I know, too, that my mother will be doing the same, her own mind even more attuned than mine to such things, her connection with this clone much stronger.

But despite that, this remains my role, and I throw myself into it, seeking him out. Working my way through the pain, the horrors, the faces of fear as they look upon their death, the wailing and screaming of men and women as their bodies are torn up by bullets and shrapnel, or cremated where they stand by surging flame.

It's more pronounced that ever, more difficult to witness. Sometimes I have no control over what I see, and how long I spend in a particular vision.

Watching a mother shield her infant from an oncoming barrage of enemy fire. Seeing entire families cowering in exploding houses, unable to flee the war as it quickly crept up onto them. All such things enter my mind, playing out like I'm right there with them. I have to watch them all, fight to stay asleep, to stay in the vision, when all I want to do is turn away.

Other Watchers aren't able to witness these relentless horrors. They find themselves waking in the night, drenched in sweat, their minds stretched too far by the terrible things they witness. Others, however, will do what must be done, growing cold to such images as they pass through their heads each night.

But here, with war raging, everything is more extreme. Only those like Link or Ellie or Athena, who had to contend with such things the last time, have experience of this. And above all of them is Cyra, her powers exceeding the rest, her hatred of death built upon having to see it in more detail than anyone else.

I have inherited such a terrible power, such a debilitating curse. And when all this is over, if I find myself still standing, maybe I'll turn away from such power, just as she did. I feel foolish for ever doubting her, for ever criticising her for choosing a simple life. And even after suffering as she did, here she is again, doing what must be done.

Never have I been more proud to call myself her son.

And that night, as I watch the world suffer like never before, I begin to see fresh images come to me. Before my eyes, a lab materialises, stretching away into the distance. It's not like before, not like the old dilapidated lap in the Baron's compound. No…this one is brand new, modern and vast, fitted with high tech equipment and machinery like I saw in Professor Lane's facility.

In the grand space, I see a shape; that of a man, cloaked in finery. His back is to me, but I remember his silhouette. It's the form of the man directing of all of this. The form of Baron Reinhold, staring into the distance beyond.

My mind begins to weaken, the vision cracking. I try to stay in it, searching harder for any sight of where he might be. Even in the vision, I can feel my heart bursting, pulsing harder and harder as my breathing grows fast. The world before me begins to break up, before slowly solidifying again as I hold my focus with one final push.

Suddenly, my eyes flash forward, moving deeper into the room, closer to the back of the Baron. And over his shoulder, I can see the sight of tubes, just like before, all lined up against the wall. But these are empty, yet to be filled, row upon row stretching out into the distance.

Dozens of them. Hundreds. An army of clones waiting to be manufactured.

And then, my eyes drift down to the front, and a large machine just ahead of the tubes. The Baron stares upon it, and it begins to clear before my eyes.

There, sitting within the machine, surrounded by equipment, a shape appears. His face comes into focus, and I see the grey-blue eyes and murky hair, the thin lips and sallow skin.

It's the face of AK1.

But on his head isn't the usual hood. I see a helmet, hovering on the top of his dome, wires sprouting out of it and connecting to the surrounding equipment.

And before I wake, a final thought enters my own head.

This is his special purpose.

This is why he's so important.

They're going to use him to give life to these clones…

20

Diversion

When my eyes open up in the darkness of my new accommodation, it takes a moment for me to remember where I am.

I'm immediately out of bed and feeling for my clothes on the floor, and wonder for a second why it's so much warmer than it's been for a while. The floor feels odd too, and it isn't until my eyes grow accustomed to the light that I get a feel for the shape of the claustrophobic little room.

I feel my way straight for the door and flick on the light switch. Then I'm back to my bed and scooping my watch from my bedside table to find out the time. It's earlier than I thought, dawn still a way off and the camp outside largely silent.

I move towards the only window in the room, however, and see that it's still fairly busy outside. Many soldiers remain on patrol, vigilantly watching the extremities of the base. Here at Fort Warden, the night doesn't give way to inactivity as it does elsewhere.

Fully clothed, I quickly leave my room and try to recall where my parents are. Then, I remember that we all have our own rooms, this particular block only housing single beds. I take a guess, and knock at the room across the hall, and after a couple more efforts hear the sound of footsteps.

The door opens, and my father stands before me, clothed himself and with the light on in the room. I can't quite work out whether he hasn't yet gone to bed or has already woken for the day. Neither would surprise me.

"Theo…what's up?" he asks quickly.

Any interruption of this kind can only really signal one thing. He'll know that I've seen something important.

"We need to talk," I say hurriedly. "All of us."

"Cyra and Drake?"

I nod, the look in my eyes calling for quick action.

"OK, I'll fetch them. Wait in your room."

I return to my little room, and a few minutes later hear the sound of movement outside. The door opens, and Jackson peers in.

"This way, Theo," he says.

I follow him out and down the corridor, where we go through a door and into a small, simple office. Already awaiting us are my mother and grandfather, their eyes bright as they watch me enter. It looks as though neither have only just been woken. That, like Jackson, they were already awake and busy.

"OK, Theo," begins Drake as Jackson shuts the door tight. "What have you seen?"

I come straight out with it without delay.

"I think I know what AK1's special purpose is," I say immediately.

They all look to each other and then back to me, waiting for me to continue, to offer some further explanation.

"They're using him as a donor," I say. "Like, a host of some kind. I think the Baron is planning on creating more clones, building some sort of army…"

"An army," says Jackson. "But it'll take years for them to develop. Even if they have accelerated growth, they won't be any use in this war."

"Maybe it's not for this war," I counter. "Maybe he just wants to spread Knight's genes all over the country, maybe the world. The man's insane, he worships Knight like he's a God…"

"And he's playing God right now," adds Cyra. "He's looking to secure the future with Augustus' progeny right at the heart of it. He wants him to live forever, and if he defeats us, he'll have the means to do it."

"How did you see this?" asks Jackson. "Explain it to us in detail."

I do as I'm told, taking the three of them through everything, step by step. From the old lab, to the sight of the Baron, to the image of AK1 hooked up to that machine. And behind him, the many tubes just waiting to breed more of him.

And, now that I think of it, more of my mother too.

"So the Baron was there?" asks Jackson. "In this facility?"

I nod.

"Then we have some hint of his location. We need to find this place and shut it down at its source. We're no longer just fighting for our future, but for that of generations to come. Four clones is bad enough. An army of them will never be defeated."

"Well, perhaps all of this is a smokescreen," says Cyra. "Perhaps destroying Eden and clearing that stretch of coastline has cleared the path for this. Maybe Lord Kendrik or another member of the Cabal has been building a base there in secret, just like before, somewhere where his full strength is gathered…"

My mother is interrupted. Not by another voice, but by a sound. We all turn to Drake as he sighs deep, staring at the ground and shaking his head. So far, he's stayed conspicuously silent.

"You know something, Drake…" asks Jackson.

Slowly, he begins to nod, before lifting his eyes to ours.

"I know where they are," he says.

"What! Where!"

"You're right, Cyra," he says quietly, "about there being a secret facility. Only, it wasn't a member of the Cabal who built it…it was Aeneas…and me."

The room is buried in a brief silence. We look upon Drake, impatiently waiting for him to proceed.

"For years, Aeneas and I had been trying to rebuild the Watchers in secret," he continues eventually. "You're all well aware of that by now. With the Senate overruling us, we looked to Athena to develop her own followers without their knowledge. But that wasn't all. We also began development of a research and training facility on the coast, built into the cliffs at a quiet stretch of land between Piscator and Mercator..."

"Drake...I can't believe I'm hearing this," interrupts Jackson. "You abused your power, and went against the orders of the Senate? What compelled you to do such a thing?"

"Necessity, Jackson," says Drake, his eyes beginning to firm up. "We were growing weak, and defenceless. It was only a matter of time before something like this happened. Aeneas and I were merely trying to safeguard the country from future threats. We never expected something this drastic to happen."

"And now this facility is going to be used to create an army of clones," says Jackson. "I can't believe..."

Cyra's voice cuts in, shutting her husband down.

"This isn't a time for throwing blame, Jack," she says firmly. She turns back to Drake. "Dad, you say that this facility was for research and training?"

"Yes, it was intended to be a state of the art base for developing and training Watchers," he says. "Aeneas and I were pushing a new vote through the Senate, and were gathering a lot of support to reinstate the Watcher program. We were merely preparing for that."

"And by *developing*, you mean what, exactly?" asks Cyra. "Please don't tell me you were looking into cloning technology."

Drake's eyes screw up, and his head shakes vigorously. "God no, Cyra. We were merely attempting to design better ways of discovering Watchers, and more efficient methods of opening their pathways and advancing their powers."

"Jeez, Drake! What if the Seekers are using these new methods?" says my father.

"Settle down, Jackson," says Drake, clearly getting a little irritated by the interrogation. "The research hasn't yet been completed. By the looks of it, the Baron has gotten wind of this facility and is merely using it as a base from which to develop his clones. What Aeneas and I were building was entirely different."

"And who else knew about it?" asks Cyra.

"Not many," says Drake. "It was a top secret project that was being built under the guise of a power station on the surface. The real work, though, was being done below ground."

"But…someone like Lord Kendrik, with all his sway, could have heard about it?"

"Oh, it's entirely possible that one of the Baron's many supporters heard, or were even directly involved. None of us knew how deep his roots went into our own government. But this is a positive, and an opportunity. We know where he's hiding, and we know what he's planning."

"And what about AK1," says Jackson. "If he's there, then that means we'll have to get past him first. Cyra, have you seen anything new?"

"I know he's stationary," she says. "He's not on the warpath like the others are. And he's still just as confused as ever."

"And do you think he knows about his role in all this?"

"He didn't know when I met him," I say. "Maybe he's learned since."

"I don't think so," says Cyra. "He still seems conflicted."

"But anyway," I add. "Do we want to take him on? I'm not sure that's right…"

I glance over at my mum as my dad does a little half roll of his eyes.

"Why is that, Theo?" he asks accusingly. "In fact, don't answer, because I already know, and this is exactly the problem. You two are invested in this boy now because you feel this connection. But he remains our enemy and that won't change. If he's in the way, he needs to be taken out."

He looks to Drake, keen on hearing his opinion.

"Jackson may be right," says my grandfather. "If we can catch AK1 alone, then our combined strength will be enough to overpower him."

"But Link's not here…nor is Ajax," I argue.

"Regardless, with Athena and the three of us in this room, not to mention Velia and a few of Athena's trainees, we have enough strength…"

"To kill him?" I ask. "This is half mum, remember."

"No, Theo," says Jackson loudly. "This boy has nothing to do with your mother. For goodness sake, Cyra has been built by her experiences, not the genes in her body. All they have done is give her this power that she never wanted. This boy isn't your brother. He is a science experiment, nothing more."

His voice rings around the room a few times. I see my mother's eyes drop. Drake looks upon her with a hint of sadness. Jackson appears to immediately regret his words, or at least the way he delivered them. More quietly now, he speaks again, calming his voice.

"We have to remember that we're trying to win a war here. We're trying to save millions of lives. Not just those living now, but many generations yet to get a chance of a normal life. If anyone stands in the way of that, they are our enemy. That is a fact, Theo. You must understand it?"

I sigh deeply and begin nodding.

"I do," I say quietly. "Of course I do. I just…hope there's another way."

"So do I, son. But if there isn't, then we have no choice…*you* have no choice. We may have to count on you to do what must be done. You have to be willing to take that step when the time comes."

"We don't yet know what will happen," adds Drake. "We don't yet have the full picture. What we do have is a vague plan that needs to be developed. We know that the Baron has taken that stretch of coastline as his base, filling the cities of Mercator and Piscator with his soldiers. They are fortresses now, and the space in between is likely to be crawling. Getting through won't be easy."

"Then…how will we get there?" I ask.

I see a light begin to shine in my grandfather's eyes, a plan beginning to form. On the wall, the black window brightens, yet another dawn beginning to rise. I never thought I'd witness so many. I never thought I'd live on so little sleep.

But right now, my mind is alert. And so are my eyes. And so are those of all the people in this room.

And quietly, Drake turns to us all once more.

"A diversion," he whispers, nodding. "What we need, is a diversion…"

21

A White Lie

Drake doesn't offer any further explanation before the meeting ends. I'm used to his cryptic ways, and so, it would appear, are my parents. We all share knowing looks as he leaves the room, my father making a move to follow.

Left now with only my mum, she comes over to me and takes a closer look at my face.

"You look tired, Theo," she says, giving me some sort of facial appraisal. "You should get some more sleep."

"More sleep? How can I with all this going on? What did grandfather mean by a diversion?"

She shrugs her shoulders and shakes her head.

"You know what he's like. Let him figure something out. We'll be caught up soon enough."

"But…"

"No buts. We need you strong. Try to block everything out for now and get some proper rest. Think of home, of the woods, of something relaxing. Then you'll drop off."

I try to offer another counter argument, but am quickly shut down again. In the end, she actively leads me back to my room and threatens to tuck me in like she did when I was a child, unless I get in bed myself.

"Fine…I'll do it," I say. "Jeez…"

She smiles warmly as I climb under the sheets, feeling as if I'm nothing but a kid again. It's strange how mothers can do that to you. I mean, I'm out here in the centre of a war, and yet she's trying to tuck me like I'm an eight year old.

When she finally leaves me alone, I spend the first few minutes thinking I'll never drop off. After five minutes are up, however, I'm beginning to feel drowsy. As my eyes shut, and fresh sights of carnage begin to creep into my head, I open them wide again and resolve to stay awake.

Then, I follow my mother's advice and begin thinking of home, of Lignum, of the quiet woods and babbling brooks. Immediately, thoughts of Ajax and Link appear before me again, and in my mind's eye I can almost see them, dashing through the forests and little woodland towns, cutting down the enemy as they continue to ravage our homeland.

It's not a vision, just part of my imagination putting images in my head. Images that make me smile. Images that I'd like to be a part of.

In the early days, it was hard determining what was what. Dreams and fantasies and proper visions were all muddled up. Now, they're distinctive, each carrying a unique feel that I've grown accustomed to.

And this is nothing but a fantasy. Something I hope and pray is happening. That the brutal and ferocious father and son combo is wreaking the same havoc as the Seekers, spreading fear through the enemy ranks.

Let them have it, I think with a smile. *Give them a taste of their own damn medicine.*

In the end, my mind tumbles away and I imagine something more calming. Just a scene in the woods, sitting down by the lake near my house, watching the animals drink at the water's edge. The birds whistle in my ears, and the insects buzz around me, and through cracks in the overhanging foliage, shards of warm light spread down to the forest floor.

It's a familiar image, and a relaxing one. What was once a place where I felt like a prisoner is now the one place I truly want to see again. I just have to hope that there's enough left when all this is over.

And there, sitting by the water's edge, I feel a presence beside me. But it's not Ajax, my confidant, by best friend, by brother in arms.

Instead, the soft face of Velia appears, her hazel eyes shining, her lips curved up in a rare and beautiful smile. I move in to kiss her, something that feels so natural now, and run my fingers through her silky brown hair.

It feels so real to me, a moment of peace in my mind amid all the violence. I watch her lips now as they open, her voice coming out quiet and weak in my ears.

Slowly, her words form, and all I hear is my name.

"Theo…Theo," she says, looking right at me.

And slowly, my eyes open, and no longer do I see the trees and lake and bright green foliage. All that is gone, replaced by a cold and lifeless room, the walls functional and grey and dull.

But one thing remains the same: Velia, staring down at me with those same hazel eyes, that same brown hair and soft skin.

"Theo…Theo…wake up," she says as my mind brings itself out of the peaceful dream.

"Hey," I croak.

"There's a meeting," she says. "Your dad told me to come get you."

The fog continues to clear and I sit up. I look to the window to see that the world is fully lit, the sun high in the sky. I must have been sleeping a while.

"A meeting?" I mumble.

"Yes, Theo," she says, laughing, "a meeting. Now come on, get up!"

She hurries me out of bed before I realise I'm wearing only shorts and nothing else. As I begin pulling on my clothes, I catch her watching.

"Do you mind waiting outside," I say jokingly.

"Do you mind if I don't?" she responds with a cheeky grin.

I shrug as I pull on my trousers, before dragging a t-shirt over my top half. She gives up the pretence of trying to avert her eyes, looking on admiringly at my frame. The look in her eyes causes a stir in me that I quickly try to keep at bay.

Soon enough, however, we're marching quickly from the room and heading towards the primary command centre in the middle of the base. Inside it's a hive of activity, intelligence officers shuffling here and there, other technicians and soldiers going about their work. We go straight towards the main control room, where we find all of the usual suspects waiting for us inside.

Unlike the war room in Petram, this place is all high tech and filled with screens and computers. In the centre, a large table sits, with a hologram of the mainland shining out from it. All across it, little figures hover, signifying towns and military units spread across the land. Areas of fighting are depicted too, with the various areas now taken by the Baron lit in red, and our own strongholds still in blue. The amount of red on the map is disconcerting.

When we walk in, a discussion is already raging. With so many of our soldiers and militia converging here at Fort Warden, organising them is proving to be a logistical challenge.

"More keep coming," says General Proctor. "Efficient fighting forces are based on good organisation. These men and women are from all over the place, and many have no official military experience…"

"We need to do the best we can with what we

have, General," says Drake. "Yes, it's not ideal, but we need you and General Trent to form a working army, and we need it done quick."

"How quick?" enquires General Trent.

"As quickly as you can manage," says Drake. He looks over at Jackson and nods, gesturing for him to take over.

"I have just gotten word from one of my spies who have successfully managed to infiltrate the enemy encampment," starts my father. "The word is that they are planning to strike right at the heart of us, sending a full assault here at Fort Warden. We need to be ready for when the strike comes."

"How does your man know this?" asks General Proctor. "Why would such information be given to a captive?"

"He isn't a captive, General. He has managed to infiltrate their reserve forces, made up of men and women from across the regions who were unhappy with our government. He is a master infiltrator, and has convinced them of his worth with his soldiery skills. It's taken him several days to get word to me, but he's convinced that an attack is imminent."

"And what else does he say?" asks Markus. "Do we have numbers? What is the scene like over on the coast?"

"Numbers are huge, well over ten thousand from what he can gauge. Yet many of these are reservists who, like our own Guardians, have little military experience. The Baron is having to deal with the same problems as we are, putting together an army from a number of disparate forces. We are not alone on that front."

"And regarding what's happening at the coast?"

"Mercator and Piscator are his staging area, as well as our own abandoned military bases along the coast. Between the two cities, huge camps have been set up for those defecting to the Baron, the poor souls who were given the option of silver or lead. They are being contained there for now."

"This seems a little rash," says General Proctor. "Why would he come after us now with all he's got?"

"Because he knows we're gathering our full strength," announces Drake. "We are pulling together numbers to rival his, and he'll be well aware by now that Link and Ajax are causing havoc to his forces in Lignum. His response will be to wipe us out in one stroke before we grow too strong."

I see some doubt behind the eyes of the two decorated Generals. Yet within the faces of Drake, and Jackson, I see resolve. I see the form of the plan we concocted only hours ago starting to take shape. Drake's next words solidify that thought.

"We cannot allow the Baron to strike at us again," he says boldly. "We are getting onto the front foot, and we need to take advantage. I suggest that we gather our own force now, and do to him what he intends to do to us."

General Proctor's face is a picture. His grizzled visage crinkles up like a piece of paper, and his face tells of someone who'll take some selling on the idea.

"Drake, that is madness," he says when he's finally able to find his words. "You want to send our army right into the hornet's nest?! It sounds like you've lost your damn mind, man!"

"I've lost nothing," says Drake calmly. "A sudden siege now will derail all of the Baron's plans. He's had us on the back foot for months now. Finally, we're subverting his expectations, doing things he doesn't expect. We need to attack as soon as possible."

Another brief silence lays itself out in the room. And now I know what Drake was thinking when he spoke of a diversion…

Send in the army. Divert the Baron's attention. And in all the chaos, we can strike right at his heart.

Once more, General Proctor speaks up, growing more irate by the minute.

"You cannot seriously believe that a siege will work?!" he says. "Not with what we're working with…"

"We have little choice," cuts in Drake. "We have it on good authority that the Baron, and the Cabal, are holed up in the area. If we strike now we can take them out in one, as they attempted to do to many of us on Eden. We need to be *brave*, General, at a time like this."

General Proctor's face curls into a snarl at the veiled insult. As he prepares a retort, however, the more level-headed General Trent steps in.

"Where exactly are they holed up, Drake?" he asks coolly.

"In a research facility built into the cliffs between Piscator and Mercator. Theo has had a vision of the place. We need to act upon it before the enemy get wind that we know of their location."

At the mention of my name, all eyes swing down to me. I didn't really want to be included in this debate. Instead, I'm forced to offer an explanation of what I've seen, although make sure to once more leave out any unnecessary details about AK1, merely referring to him as 'one of the Seekers'.

The idea of more clones being developed has some effect on General Trent, his face loosening to the idea. General Proctor, however, remains unconvinced.

"So you're basing all of this on the visions of a boy?" he asks.

"A vision is a vision, General Proctor," says Drake firmly. "It matters not who has it. Theo has proven himself essential to our cause many times already. I urge you to remember that before you open your mouth again."

I look fondly on my grandfather as he spits fire. It's enough to force the old General into silence. Markus steps forward to act mediator, his presence always calming during such encounters.

"OK, lets cool our tongues," he says. "All concerns are valid, and General Proctor has some points. However, I have witnessed the wonderful things Watchers can do time and again, and I would trust Theo as much as any of them. The point here is that we have few cards to play. We don't have a great deal of choice, ladies and gentlemen. An all out assault might be our only option."

More quietly now, General Proctor's voice rises. It's a growl, but a low one, his anger simmering but kept in check.

"Then we retreat to Petram," he says. "We give up the regions and return to our way of life. This side of the wall has always been drawing us into conflict. Forget the regions. Let them wither and die."

Now it's other eyes I see flash with anger. Cyra's. Ellie's. Jackson's. Even General Trent looks upon his military counterpart with a look of disdain. Athena's scowl remains as it always is. Velia doesn't quite know where to look.

"I never figured you for a coward, General Proctor," says Drake, looking upon the old war veteran with disappointment.

"I'm not a coward!" counters the man, growing hysterical once more. "I am merely being a realist here. I will refuse to take my men to battle to see them all slaughtered. If this is your chosen path, you can do it without the Petram army….I won't…"

As his voice rises up, and his eyes begin to blare, the most static person in the room suddenly fires into action.

With the speed of a sniping snake, Athena's fist swipes across General Proctor's face, sending him tumbling straight to the ground. His voice is wiped out and shut down immediately. His eyes roll for a second in their sockets before going blank.

For a moment, everyone looks at Athena in amazement. Then, she merely growls: "I never liked him anyway."

"Athena…" starts General Trent, the only man in the room not smiling at the sight of the coward at our feet. "What are you doing…"

"I'm sorry, General Trent," she says. "But we have no time for such division here. He was talking mutiny, and we don't take that lightly over in the Deadlands."

"But…his army…"

"Are not loyal to him alone," she says. "We have a ready made replacement right here who they'll follow anywhere."

Her eyes stare at Markus, her dear friend.

"I will lead them," he says, standing tall and proud. "It's been a while since I was at the head of such a force. I'll be proud to go to war with you all again."

I feel a bustling energy begin to build in the room. Eyes shine bright. Faces stiffen with thoughts of grand battles and war. Old friends and allies look to each other, as they did so long ago, knowing that the final act is coming.

And standing next to me, I feel Velia's hand clasp

to mine, her fingers gripping tight.

Drake's voice rises again, his eyes set on the hologram, on the huge concentration of red along the Eastern coast.

"Then it's decided," his voice booms. "Gather your forces, every last person you can muster…and get them ready to march to war."

As the room disperses, I find myself saddling up to my father, catching a word in private.

"Did you really hear from one of your men?" I ask, peering closely into his eyes, searching for the truth.

"Of course," he answers innocently.

I continue to stare, and begin shaking my head.

"You don't have to lie to me, dad. I can see it in your face. None of your spies got inside, did they? You have no idea if the Baron's marching on us or not…"

His eyes dart left and right, a sure sign of shiftiness.

"OK, Theo," he says, keeping his voice low. "I have a man on the inside, that much is true. But he said nothing of any attack by the Baron's army."

"Dad!"

"Son, listen to me carefully. Drake and I came to this decision together, OK. We need to create a diversion so that we can get into the research facility and distract the Seekers. If we can do that, then we might have a chance, and we needed everyone on side."

"So you just lied?" I ask blankly.

"It's a white lie," he retorts. "It's quite possible that the Baron is going to attack anyway."

"Nice try," I say. "And I guess you want me to keep this secret too?"

"If you wouldn't mind," he says, patting me on the shoulder.

I shake my head as he smiles and wanders off, not a minute to be wasted now as the army prepares to march on again.

More lies. More secrets.

Truth be told, I'm as fed up with those as I am this war.

22
The Drums of War

The camp is brimming and broiling, the scorching sun a relentless tormentor that many here will be happy to escape. All over the place, bodies rush and gather, the many different forces and battalions organised with a haste hitherto unseen across these lands. There's no time to lose, no time to waste. In only days we'll be moving out again. Fort Warden has become nothing but a stop off point on the way to war.

No one expected such a thing. As the hours pass following that fateful meeting in the command centre, word spreads around the base that we'll be seeking war out, rather than waiting for it to come to us.

I know that many will consider it a foolish choice, or not understand the purpose. Many others will take a little time to digest the thought of their impending death, but will rise up tall and unyielding when the time comes. Some, however, will lick their lips at the thought, desperate to seek revenge for the many losses they've suffered: friends and relatives, homes and towns, people and places they hold dear and will never forget.

But whatever the people think, they will not turn

away from this decision. They will not mutiny as General Proctor threatened to do. They will not run and hide. They will face their fears head on, knowing that this is our only chance of victory.

The dissident General himself, however, will not be taking part. Kept to a cell in a lonely corner of the base, he'll have to sit and wait for news of our victory or defeat. And should we win, he'll have to face up to the consequences of his cowardice. Either way, his day is done.

Across the base, I see the thousands of soldiers and wonder how many will come out alive. Little do they know we have no real chance of victory by strength of numbers alone. That the well fortified cities of Piscator and Mercator, lying in partial ruin after the attacks many weeks ago, cannot possibly be taken by the force we can muster.

They will not know, and they cannot know, that their main role here is diversionary. That the only way of defeating the Baron is by taking out the top leaders of his Cabal, and eliminating the living superweapons he has at his disposal.

I look upon them, and see bravery beyond compare. Unable to see bullets coming. Unable to sense an approaching explosion, or a wall of fire surging down an alley. Unable to do much but count on good fortune and luck as they charge down on the enemy. These men and women have no gifts like I do, and yet they'll lay down their lives for the cause.

I find it humbling to see them as they prepare for

the final march. It reminds me that, while I'll be facing death myself, so much may lie in my hands and those of the Watchers by my side.

As that day passes and the next emerges, thoughts turns to Link and Ajax. Ellie, who's been spending much of her time in the communications centre, comes to us with a brightness on her face that has been absent since they left.

"I spoke with Link!" she says with glee. "They've been clearing the woods in Lignum, and have gathered a bit of a following…"

"You mean soldiers?" asks Jackson.

"Yes, soldiers and Guardians they've saved. They've been fighting alongside them, giving them support. I told him about the assault. He's ready and waiting for orders."

"That's awesome!" says Velia, in a rare show of excitement. "How many do they have?"

"He didn't say. It's hardly an army, but every little helps."

"And did he say anything about the Seekers?" asks Jackson. "They haven't encountered one have they?"

"No, they haven't," says Ellie with a touch of relief. "Maybe the Baron doesn't want to risk them against my boys!"

"But there have been sightings," adds Cyra. "A technician told me about one being seen in Agricola. And I had a vision of another up the Northern coast. It sounds like they're dispersed."

"Then now's the perfect time to attack!" says Velia. "Go right there while they're not at home."

"We're doing all we can to prepare the army," says Jackson. "But I suspect that they'll be back home as soon as they get wind that we're on the warpath. They'll have enough warning of that."

"Unless we go now?" says Velia, getting a bit ahead of herself. "Why don't we strike now, all of us Watchers?"

"Because it's too risky," counters Cyra in an attempt to calm her. "If we go, and then fail, then we miss our shot. We have one chance to create this diversion, to do this right. Don't worry, honey, you'll get your chance to fight soon."

I see Velia's eyes bristling, desperate for action. The same are seen on most faces, a bubbling sense of anticipating growing by the hour. There's a desperation, whether through fear or nerves or a burning desire to fight, to get things moving as quickly as possible. However one feels about going to battle, no one likes the wait.

In many ways, that's the worst part of all...

Yet we cannot push things forward too much, and we cannot rush things. It's not only organising the soldiers that's important, but taking stock of what artillery and long range weaponry we have, mobile units that we can use to bombard the enemy from a distance.

On top of that, battle plans need to be drawn up, strategies determined. There was never a plan for this, and when so many lives are at stake, it's essential that we take the necessary time to establish a firm blueprint to follow.

As the hours turn to days, and the base continues to morph and ready itself for war, further meetings are held by the top military commanders to devise a plan of attack. The worry, of course, is that the Baron will use innocents as a deterrent, a concern given credence by fresh information given by Jackson's inside man.

By his account, many civilians remain encamped in the cities, caught in the net by the Baron's men. Launching an assault, therefore, will bring their lives into the balance, rather than giving us the opportunity to fight directly with the Baron's mercenary army.

Drake, as he often has, reiterates the point that innocent people will always be caught in the crossfire. That holding these people hostage cannot deter us from our course of action.

It's Markus who makes the point that our mere presence on the Baron's doorstep might be sufficient to yield the results we're after.

Drake, however, counters that claim.

"We need to engage them in battle," he says. "In both cities, and right along the coast, we have to draw the attention of the enemy. The more chaos we can create, the easier it will be for us to infiltrate the research facility and strike at the Baron before he knows what's coming."

I know that many of us don't enjoy the idea of further innocent lives being lost to this senseless violence. But the simple fact remains that we have no choice, that the Baron has forced our hand, and that many more will be killed should we fail.

It takes three full days for the army to be properly mobilised and organised. Three days of hectic activity as they're kitted out with weapons and armour and ordered into units. Three days of planning and designing a battle plan that will have us come at them from all angles.

The information leaked to us from Jackson's inside man turns out to be more than useful. On top of that, the various spies we have around the area are ordered to get as close as possible to the enemy camps without detection, to feed back intelligence on the fortifications they have, and the possible weak points present along their lines.

As the information is gathered, the holographic map within the command centre begins to grow more detailed. More red appears along the coast, the Baron's strongholds given better shape as we learn of their set up and defensive capabilities. Ways into the research facility are considered closely, with various different plans being proposed.

In the end, a straight line of attack through the camps appears to be the only option. With the coastline defended well from the North by way of the city of Mercator, and the South by way of Piscator, the middle ground, covering many miles, between the two seems to offer the best opportunity to enter without detection. There, it will be chaotic, with tens of thousands of refugees from across the regions gathered in large camps, just like we had down in the valleys below Petram.

"It's as if they're filling that space in order to protect the coast," suggests Jackson. "To offer a barrier of bodies to the cliffs and the entrance to the research facility."

"There will be gaps in their lines," says Drake. "There's no way they can cover a space of so many miles. The cliff entrance will be heavily protected, and any attempt to get there aerially will be impossible. In a plane, our powers count for nothing. We must advance on foot and enter via the mainland side."

As the only person who knows the layout to the research facility, Drake takes some time to bring us up to speed on the design. By the sounds of it, it's all built into the cliffside and cut back into the rock, where there's a secret entrance for incoming aircraft. However, on the land above, a small base has been built to offer an alternative entrance.

"It was built in the form of a small power station," says Drake, "in order to conceal what was going on below. That is going to be our only way in."

Exactly what's going on around this power station, however, is impossible to know. Most likely, the Baron will have plenty of security there, with the huge camps covering the last swathe of land beyond it, all peppered with towns and settlements that have been modified to act as temporary bases for the Baron's reserve forces. Exactly what we'll find when we get there we can't determine. Our spies cannot get close enough, and Jackson's inside man is largely contained to a certain camp towards the South on the outskirts of Piscator.

An argument is put forth from General Trent to wait a little longer, to gather more intel and form a more concrete plan. As a fairly risk averse man, it's not surprising to hear him offer that suggestion. But while we can all understand his viewpoint, he's unanimously shot down.

"We have to go, and we have to go now," concludes Drake. "We will leave tomorrow evening, when the night falls, to give us a head start. There is no going back now."

The remainder of the day is given over to putting the finishing touches to our plan. All over the base, soldiers and Guardians, all gathered here from the farthest reaches of the regions and Deadlands, count down the hours and minutes as the drums of war begin to beat inexorably in their heads.

For those with loved ones, the final night is provided to say goodbye. Many will have already seen family members and dear friends either killed or captured by the Baron and his men. Others will have loved ones here with them, ready to give it their all as part of the assault. Perhaps they'll be fighting side by side in the same battalions, charged with attacking the same portion of the enemy lines. Or maybe they'll be separated, their experience or expertise giving them a different role elsewhere.

Whatever the case, now may be the final time they

get to say goodbye.

For me, the evening is spent with Velia. Alone in my room, we sit up against the wall on the bed, sometimes speaking in low tones and sometimes letting the silence speak for us. Occasionally, our hands lock together and I let the soft touch of her skin give me strength. But we don't kiss, and we don't hug, knowing that such things will only weaken us, only serve to distract us from what we have to do.

And sitting next to her, the hours pass, and I find myself drifting off to sleep, happy in her company despite it all. And with her next to me, my mind remains calm and at ease, no visions coming to me. Across the lands, the world takes a long, final breath, preparing for the plunge. Right now, a growing silence pervades all, a time for reflection before the lands explode once more with the roar of battle.

And this one will be unlike anything seen for a hundred years. A final encounter that will determine the fates of millions.

The long night is fast approaching.

The battle for the future is on.

23
The Deep Breath

The convoy we've gathered puts the one that travelled across the Deadlands to shame. Then, we were coming with our forces from the West and those that remained in the valleys below Petram. Now, the largest parts of our Eden and Petram armies have been gathered for the fight, along with The Guardians of Liberty ready to provide their support.

The soldiers are easy to determine purely by sight. The forces of Eden and Petram have their own distinct uniforms, while the Guardians remain a hodgepodge of militiamen and women from all over the regions. Those from the West, like The Guardians, display their amateur status as soldiers by wearing their native desert clothes. They will mostly act in reserve forces, tasked with attacking the enemy lines known to be less well guarded.

Beyond the base, the enormous gathering of vehicles is a sight to behold. Artillery vehicles, mobile command centres, tanks and armoured personnel carriers, jeeps fitted with gun turrets, large trucks used to ferry men. Many are specific military vehicles, those that will form the front line. Many others, however, are modified desert cars and trucks, used by those across the Deadlands and by The Guardians in order to protect their lands.

There are hundreds of them, perhaps even thousands. From my vantage point at the edge of the camp, I can barely believe the scale. Standing beside me, Velia looks on in wonder.

"I grew up thinking the world was so small," she whispers. "I never knew such a force could be assembled…"

Neither did I.

And yet, the numbers of the Baron may be even greater, with many more of his men still spread out across the regions. Gathering a full force takes time, time that we don't have. And, like him, we still have many thousands dispersed all over the lands, fighting in little towns and villages, through the woods and hills. Truly, this civil war has found itself into every corner of these lands. And now, the centrepiece of it all is going to erupt, like a giant volcano that dominates the world, ready to spew its lava onto all.

Before we leave, and before all of the gathered souls climb into cars and trucks and jeeps and tanks, Drake stands above everyone and speaks a few words.

Climbing to the summit of the wall surrounding the base, and looking upon all those within it, and all those gathered outside, he holds a voice amplifier to his mouth and looks down over the gathered thousands.

"Today, we go to war," he starts, his voice booming and echoing through the lands. "I know that many of you have seen fighting already. That all our homes and regions and places we hold dear have been exposed to the terrors of conflict. But until this point, nothing has matched this day. Nothing is as important as what we are about to attempt."

His hand swings out to the East, to no man's land, and the regions beyond, and the coast a long way beyond that.

"Out there our enemy huddles. They control much of the world we once thought was safe. They have sprung up from the ground and taken a grip of this nation that refuses to weaken. In the hours and days to come, we will beat their grip into submission. We will tear off their hand if we need to. All of us are fighting for our futures: not only our own, but those of our children, and their children, and the countless generations that follow.

"Baron Reinhold wants to take this county back to a terrible time. He wants to destroy all that we've built, and revert to the systems of control that shacked us all for so long. You all know now that it is the world of Augustus Knight that he wants to restore, a world many of you will remember. If we fail, our country will never recover. The future is counting on us to be victorious. It is counting on you!"

His words bring a roar from the throng, thousands of voices gathering as one. Over their calls, his own voice rises, calling out louder and louder.

"Think of the loves ones you've lost. Think of those you want to see safe, to live long and happy in a free world. We are fighting for our world, for our regions and homes. But mostly, we fight for our families and friends, for the person stood next to you now. Look at them, and know that they will do everything to see it done. And you must do the same.

"Now climb into your cars and jeeps and APCs. Set your eyes on the East. We drive to war. We drive to victory!"

The roars reach a crescendo as Drake raises his arms and soaks it up for a moment, before descending back down the ground.

"Your grandfather's a great speaker!" remarks Velia over the din.

I look on him proudly. "He's a great man."

Then, to the vehicles we go, thousands of men and women all moving to their assigned convoys. We begin as one, grinding down the large tracks that lead through no man's land, the night now falling fast and turning the world black.

But around us, the sound of engines is constant and loud, an endless grumbling that spreads far into the distance across the lands. And in the air too, attack helicopters float, giving us fair warning of any enemy battlements down below. And planes fly, shooting across the night sky, ready to set off the bombing raids that will aim to take out the more heavily guarded enemy positions.

What military might we have has been gathered here as one. Dozens of heavily fortified tanks and artillery units capable of bombarding the cities from many miles away. Aircraft that can sweep in and out at terrifying speeds. Helicopters that can snipe and shoot as they hover above us, like angels on our shoulders.

And yet, the enemy will have the same. With the fighting breaking out so quickly all those weeks ago, we had little time to protect all of our military provisions and armaments. Military bases were raided and overcome as the soldiers marched out to protect the people. Armoured vehicles and aircraft that belonged to our forces were stolen and added to the enemy's swelling ranks. Before Eden fell, the aircraft in the hangers there were stolen too, with the military commanders who defected to the Baron making sure their own men and vehicles were available for war.

Whatever we have, the Baron may have more. These terrible machines capable of ending so many lives in a single moment. A dropped bomb that cripples a building. A missile that plummets into the heart of an oncoming troop of soldiers. A tank or artillery shell that can do untold damage in the blink of an eye.

All these terrible weapons that we have at our disposal, the enemy has too. Battle will rage on the lands and in the skies, the heavens and earth turning to turmoil. Protective measures will no doubt be deployed, blocking shells and missiles, cutting aircraft down from the air. Like a simple hand-to-hand fight, punch will be followed by counter punch, attack by defence.

But as the fight wears on, one side will weaken. One side will administer the finishing blow, knocking the enemy to the floor, and standing over them, victorious.

Such is the case in war.

Through the night, the convoy rumbles, the enemy no doubt preparing for our arrival. We have no real hope of surprising them or catching them truly off guard. Who's to say whether one of the Seekers hasn't already seen us coming? And, even if they haven't, the Baron's many lookouts and spies and little troops of men spread across the land will quickly pick up on our movements.

We have to expect that. Just as we have hidden agents moving in secret around and near the coastline, so must he have his own men watching over Fort Warden and gauging our strength. He would be a fool not to do so, and truly the man has proven himself to be anything but a fool so far.

What he may not know, however, are our numbers. Until dawn comes and he's able to accurately estimate the size of our force, he can't know exactly what's coming his way. Nor can he know our battle plans, unless of course he has spies right in our midst. It's a thought that's crossed our minds, of course, but one that we cannot possibly spend any time or energy in contemplating.

Even so, the true nature of our plan has been kept from the main army. Even some of the high ranking commanders are unaware of our real intentions. As far as most are aware, the mission is the battle itself. For the few on the inside, however, the true purpose of this enormous assault is purely diversionary. Winning by strength of arms is an unlikely feat. Only by taking out the leaders will the rest of the army crumble and fall.

My thoughts stray here and there as we cross the lands and the hours pass by. I'll get no sleep. I can't imagine that many will. My mind rumbles like the convoy with endless thoughts, moving one way and then the other, never settling for long.

With Velia sitting next to me, my mind falls on her quite often. I think of a life beyond this war, a life with her. Hunting in the woods. Sitting by the lake. Enjoying life's simple pleasures with no worries or concerns to distract us. I imagine living as my parents do, with Link and Ellie so close by. The same could happen again, all of us living in the same area. Maybe Ajax and I could build our own home, live nearby our parents with the twins. Their mother, perhaps, could come too, move to the verdant woods from her harsh home in the West.

It's a fantasy that may never come true, but one that finds its way into my thoughts as the warm light of dawn starts to spread across the lands. The fresh colours tear the daydream from my mind, however, the coast growing ever closer as we pass old towns and villages that have so recently been abandoned, many of them in a rush. All over, signs of recent fighting remain, fires still burning in some places, the sight of red blood an ever present under the early morning sun.

It's a good thing for the people to see. It will help to supply them with a fresh determination, a fresh hatred for the people who have stolen our lands, stolen so many lives, taken the liberty from the people with such wanton carnage.

Such sights will cover much of our nation, and will only grow worse if we should fail. For those tired or frightened or doubting the assault, seeing the lands like this will cement in their minds the duty they're here to perform.

With the sun rising, the convoy comes to a large midsection along a major superhighway, cutting across the earth. What was once filled with hovercars and trucks and buses is now empty, old husks of burnt and destroyed vehicles littering the sides of the road.

Here, the convoy will diverge, our forces separating for the coordinated assault across the coast. We'll see how the Baron likes it. Not so long ago, he was sending his troops into New Atlantis, and Piscator, and Mercator, as well as many others. Now, it's the two major coastal cities that we're about to bombard.

At the head of the convoy, the various leaders gather. I watch from the backseat of an armoured jeep alongside Velia as Drake, Jackson, Cyra, Ellie, Athena, Markus, and General Trent pull together, along with several other top end military commanders.

This will be the final goodbye before the assault,

the final chance to share information before we go our separate ways.

To Piscator in the South, Markus will travel with the main Petram and Deadlands army, supported by some of The Guardians. To the North, General Trent will take his Eden army and strike at Mercator. Jackson will lead the remaining forces, made up of Guardians and those from the West, with Athena at their head and Ellie in support, moving through the hills and woods and the large patch of land linking the two cities. Within those lands, the enormous camps of the enemy are situated, many of them holding civilians, but many others with the reserve forces of the Baron.

Drake, Cyra, Velia and I will accompany Jackson and Athena. Disguised as one of them, and wearing regular desert clothes, we will try to get as close to the entrance to the research facility as possible without letting our identities become known. Hidden amid the sprawling battle, perhaps the Seekers won't see us coming, their visions muddied by the many conflicts happening down the coast.

We have other Watchers with us, Athena's two finest warriors fighting alongside her forces from the West. Elsewhere, a few more of her trainees will join Markus and the Eden army led by General Trent. While Markus will no doubt want to fight on the front lines, however, General Trent will remain back at the mobile command post, directing matters from the rear.

Having a few Watchers, whilst of limited ability, will be useful in the fighting. If they don't encounter any of the Seekers, their abilities should give them some advantage. Should that occur, they may well act as diversions themselves, drawing the Seekers to their locations. The more we can distract them, the better it will be for our primary mission.

The only ones missing from all of this are Link and Ajax, moving up from the South. The last we heard from them was hours ago, when they'd already encountered a force of the Baron's men in the lands known as the Graveyard. According to Link, there were snipers and little troops of mercenaries there, hidden amid the rubble and crumbling buildings. Their progress was slowed and some of their men were killed. Since then, we've heard nothing.

When Jackson gets back into the jeep, however, he has an update for us.

"Link and Ajax are still working their way through the Graveyard, but they're not far from Piscator now. They will link up with Markus when he arrives."

"But what about us?" I say. "We need them…"

"We cannot count on them, Theo," says my father. "If they are slowed by the fighting, there's nothing we can do. The mission will progress regardless. We have no choice."

As he speaks, the growling and grumbling of engines fills the air once more, and the convoy begins to diverge and spread apart. At the main crossroads, the huge tanks and artillery units and APCs, and the smaller jeeps and modified cars and motorbikes begin to separate, some moving South and some North, the two main armies heading to war.

But ahead is where we set our sights, straight towards the coast and right between the two cities. Along with many hundreds of other willing warriors, we begin driving onwards again, edging ever closer to the lands crawling with the enemy.

We have our orders, and now it's time to see them through.

The final battle is about to begin.

24

The Plunge

As the morning sunshine blasts its warming rays down from above, the first sounds of battle reach my ears.

From the left and right, far in the distance, the booming of explosions filters through the air towards us, several miles away in each direction. Already, the bombardment of the two cities has begun, our artillery units and tanks firing projectiles from range as our infantry units begin to move in.

From the sky, planes also rush, pulsing through the air with sonic booms as they shatter the sound barrier. Mere moments later, they shower the extremities of the cities below with bombs, weakening their defences. Despite being far from the immediate action, the world is quickly engulfed by the chorus of battle.

As the two cities begin their defence, firing back with their own missiles and explosive shells and all manner of other weapons I don't understand, our forces gather in the hills leading down towards a valley below.

By now, we've had to leave our cars and jeeps behind and continue on foot, the coast several miles away and no roads suitable for the passing of such a convoy. Driving single file through these lands would make us vulnerable, creating a bottleneck that would be easy to defend.

Instead, we will work now as a series of infantry units, some lightly armed with automatic rifles, and others with heavy weapons used to apply support from the rear. Other heavy duty explosive weapons are also at hand, with many of us carrying the multi faceted guns capable of firing automatic machine gun rounds, shotgun shells, armour piercing rounds, explosive devices, and incendiary devices too.

With Athena at the head of some of the Western troops, and Jackson leading The Guardians, we begin creeping forward through the sparsely wooded hills, many keen eyes looking for any spies hidden around us. So far, no one has been alerted to our presence, the valley below growing closer and clearer. Soon enough, we're at the edge of the hillside, searching through the shrubs at the sight of a large encampment below.

It appears to be loosely constructed, extending out from a solid town that once stood here. By the looks of things, this is a forward base for reserve forces, although there may be some civilian refugees in there as well. The count of soldiers is impossible to determine, but the many buildings in the town itself, and the array of tents and corrugated iron huts in the camp beyond, suggest there are several hundred here at least.

A quick conference begins between our commanders as we shuffle a little way down the hill and out of sight.

"We could go round?" suggests Ellie. "Flank it…"

"We might find a larger force if we do that. We can expect to find camps like this regularly positioned through the area," says Jackson.

"What does you inside man say?" asks Drake.

"He won't have been this far North. His camp was nearer to the South, outside Piscator."

"Then we send out scouts immediately to feed back to us," says Drake.

Quickly, several scouts are ordered to spread further to the North and South, making sure to keep out of sight among the woods and scattered urban areas.

The world continues to boom and burst all around us, the orchestra of war building to a grand finish with the whistling of missiles and the rushing of aircraft, the booming of artillery and the endless chatter of machinegun fire.

After half an hour, word is coming in from our scouts, suggesting that there are few passable areas that are going to be any more simple than this. To the North, a much vaster camp spreads out over an area of open plains, appearing to be more heavily guarded. To the South, where the larger city of Pisctor and its suburbs spreads out, a base of armoured vehicles sits in wait, preparing to grind out to greet our army.

"We go straight on then," says Drake. "Jackson, I need you to take your force around that area of wood and come at the camp from the North side."

"Another diversion?" asks Jackson.

"Yes. Draw their eye and the rest of us will move in with Athena's forces and try to slip past. We have no time to wait here for Link. We will use the Watchers we have and cut a line straight for the power station."

He talks to all of us, directing the orders. Jackson takes them on board and then looks to Cyra and me.

"Keep each other safe," he says, drawing both of us into a hug. "I love you both dearly. I'll see you after…"

None of us allow our eyes to soften or grow weak. With the briefest of kisses for Cyra, and a firm shake of my shoulder, he steels his eyes and then begins moving off, whispering orders to his men as they disappear.

The rest of us wait for the sound of battle to commence once again, for my father's assault to begin. How I'd like to go with him, fight alongside him, protect him. How I hate all of this, with everyone I care about constantly under threat. It's not my own safety I care for, but that of my parents and friends, that of Velia.

Beside me now, I look at her eyes and see that same steel that filled my father's. It's a look that urges the same from me, forces all thoughts from my head except a single one: we need to get to the power station, get inside, and end this thing as soon as we can.

Then, suddenly, from down in the camp, a rattling sounds, dozens of weapons all firing at once. It comes from our own troop, spread out to flank the enemy from many angles, quickly joined by voices and calls of alarm as the war comes to this calm suburb of the grand, sprawling battleground that covers so much of the coastline.

No longer is it calm. Now, it has entered right into the chaos as the reserve forces of the Baron organise their defence. Moving forward, our brave men and women come, dragging all eyes and ears across the area to them.

Then, leading us on, Drake and Athena begin moving, along with Cyra and Velia and me and Ellie and the several hundred Westerners we command. Moving out of the hills and into the valley, we spread quickly around the edge, entering into the urban jungle below that peppers these lands all the way to the coast.

Dressed as they are, our strike force of Watchers are hidden, just several of a force of many, sneaking forward as the battle rages on across the other end of the base. As we move in, however, it becomes quickly evident that it wasn't going to be that easy.

With a shout of alarm, a fresh troop of enemy soldiers appear around a building, and my abilities sudden blaze to life. Bullets come clattering, and explosions sound as charges are set off, and fire begins sweeping through in their wake. Immediately, our soldiers fire back, dispersing down streets within the solid section of the camp, officially joining the war once more.

Of my close allies, only Ellie stands without the ability to see into the Void. And yet, despite that, she's a proficient soldier and leader, and immediately joins the fray. As we move through, I notice Cyra staying close to her, watching over her for any stray bullet or unseen attack. The rest of us Watchers, including Athena's students, do the same as we advance, shielding those we can from death with our powers and the bulletproof bodysuits that lie concealed beneath our clothes.

Before the battle, we discussed the idea of trying to keep our abilities hidden if possible, trying to not be too overt with them, to not alert the enemy to our presence until we were right on their doorstep. I recall one particular thing Drake said that I didn't much like, but which didn't come as a surprise either.

"Even if you have to let someone die to keep your identity hidden, do it," he'd said. "If the few have to die to save the many, then so be it. Our mission must succeed."

I understood it, and we all agreed to it. But here, now, it seems almost impossible to follow through. Urged on by the pulsing of my heart and the steady beat of battle, I find myself saving anyone I can, cutting down any enemy foolish enough to cross my path.

But in the heat of it all, no one can possibly know. Anyone who might see me coming is quickly dispatched, and before too long we're advancing quickly through the camp and escaping to its extremities at the rear, leaving Jackson and his troop to maintain the fighting behind.

Before us now, the lands are undulating and crisscrossed with roads and tracks linking the cities of Piscator and Mercator. Some hills rise up a little higher, little portions of woodland are visible, and everywhere, small hamlets and villages and larger towns dot the landscape.

But beyond all of that, only a few miles away, the coast awaits, so close we can smell the sea, that pungent salty aroma that sweeps right up my nose.

Along with our troop, we continue the advance, moving onwards and leaving my father behind. In the depths of the enemy's territory now, attack can come from anywhere. Duly, as we reach what appears to be an abandoned town, a fresh force of mercenaries arrive, pouring towards us from the South. They come on foot and in jeeps and with larger weapons, alerted to our presence.

But all over, with our thousands of troops closing in on the cities and towns, our plan is surely working. Their forces are being stretched to the left and right, and then drawn right here into the centre as they get wind of another attack.

Through the streets we go, unwilling to have our progress halted now. It's easy enough for our troop of Watchers, continually advancing without facing any competition that can do much more than slow us. But for the rest it's not the same, their presence doing nothing but holding us back.

Gathering in a building, as our soldiers fight outside, we quickly determine a route forward.

"We're going right to the coast," says Drake. "There's no sense is being coy anymore. The Baron knows we're coming…"

"Go," says Ellie. "I'll hold the fort here, and do what I can with our troops to keep them back."

"You might be overrun," says Cyra. "There's no way I'm leaving you behind."

"Cy, you have a bigger role here than me. All of you do. If you don't go now, all of this might be for nothing anyway."

As his radio crackles, Drake moves off outside of the house, casually stepping into the warzone as he picks up the communication. I watch for a moment as he stands in the open street, occasionally moving to the left or right, or ducking low to avoid a stray bullet. I see him shake his head and grit his teeth before he comes storming back in.

"What's the matter?" asks Cyra quickly.

"Link and Ajax are caught up in the fighting in Piscator," he says. "There's no way they're going to get here any time soon." He turns to Ellie. "Ellie, there's no sense in you being here now. You're too deep behind enemy lines and will have no chance without our protection. Return to Jackson's troop and hold the fort at the front line."

"Are you sure, Drake? I don't mind staying…"

"I'm sure. There's little else that anyone can do now. Just one last favour…"

"Of course. Anything."

"Give us some covering fire to shield our exit. The fighting is quite concentrated out there. We'll move out and flank around the town. Once we're through, begin your retreat, and try to get them to follow you."

"One final diversion?" she asks with a grin.

He smiles back at her and nods. "Make it count."

With that, the orders are quickly passed down the line to the rest of the Western troops and their commanders. The fighting continues to escalate, more mercenaries called to the battle. And under the cover of a brutal barrage of fire, our small force of Watchers begin moving to the far boundary of the town, the gunfire growing weaker in our ears as we go.

Drake, Cyra, Athena and her two Watchers, Velia, and me.

Now it's down to us.

25

Rise of Evil

The sky is no longer warm and blue. The sun no longer burns down from above.

Smoke pours from the cities to the North and South, poisonous fumes filling the air and spreading wide on the wind. Plumes and columns, large and small, rise up to the heavens, joining the growing blanket. A covering of man-made smog that blots out the light and casts the world below into shadow.

I've never witnessed such a thing. The battles I've fought up until now have been mere skirmishes compared to this. The prelude to the main course, the final act. Mile upon mile of coastline, filled with huge cities and towns and military bases, all drawn into a simultaneous fight for survival.

A fight for the future.

Everywhere, booms and colossal explosions continue to pulse up through my body, the ground shaking and sending shockwaves from miles away. I can only imagine how many people are being killed out there, how many buildings are being blown apart.

Above us, in the air, aircraft continue to whiz past, the battle for the skies raging. As we rush across a patch of open land towards another town, one gets shot down by a missile, one of our own crashing right down in front of us.

We all see it early enough, and hold our ground, watching in wonder and horror as the jet comes hurtling to the floor before us. It explodes on impact, blazing a trail of fire across the scorched earth, its pilot unable to eject before being swallowed up in the crash. There's nothing we can do to help him.

So we continue straight on, the fighting in the towns and camps behind now growing a little quieter. Back there, Ellie and the Westerners continue the fight, luring the larger troop of the enemy towards Jackson and The Guardians as they retreat.

The lure worked. Now, we move forward unopposed, moving into another small town that sits silent among the plains. Down the central street we run, the lands beyond becoming visible through gaps between low slung and formulaic buildings, used for housing those who work in the larger cities of Piscator and Mercator to the South and North.

Ahead, the sight of the ending of the earth appears, the low cliffs that signal the beginning of the ocean. And right there, across rail tracks and roads and a patch of clear earth, a small power station awaits, partially hidden behind low walls and gates. An otherwise nondescript place that hides a sinister purpose beneath it.

We stop for a moment and set our eyes upon the

target.

"That's it," says Drake. "We go straight in, right for the front gate. Watch each other's backs. They'll be waiting for us."

We all nod and grip tighter at our weapons, and with the need for secrecy no longer relevant, shed our cloaks and desert gear. First to do so is Drake, tossing his to the ground and leaving him more appropriately dressed in a black bodysuit, capable of repelling all but the most deadly of attacks.

The rest of us follow suit, leaving us all dressed in black, fully armed and armoured. On my belt, the extendable sword once given to me by Athena sits tight, with my bear claw necklace hanging to my chest for good luck. Cyra looks upon it with a knowing eye.

"Didn't I confiscate that?" she asks, with a small but accusatory smile.

Then, she moves towards me and, for a split second amid the madness of war, becomes my mother again.

"I'm so proud of you, Theo," she whispers, quiet enough for no one else to hear. Her lips dart to my forehead, and her palms clasp to my cheeks. "Now let's finish this…together."

As one, we turn towards the stretch of land and the power station beyond. Around us, the beating drum of war continues to sound, off in the distance in almost every direction. But here, all is quiet and still, our path ahead seemingly open.

"This doesn't seem right," says Athena, peering forward with her sleek eyes. "It's a trap…"

Her words give us cause to suddenly doubt our next move.

"Trap or not, we have no choice," says Drake. "Expect fierce competition behind those walls."

He's right. We've come this far, and there's nowhere else to go. No doubt the Baron will be fully protected. No doubt he knows we're coming right for him.

And we'd better not disappoint him…

Led again by Drake, and with the rest of us in formation behind, we step out of the confines of the small town and begin working our way across the open fields. I feel suddenly exposed out in the open, and centre my mind on any incoming threats. But nothing comes forth, nothing is apparent.

We rush quickly, darting low and with our weapons and minds primed. I couldn't hope to be among such safe company, every single one of us capable of seeing far into the Void, watching for any and all threats that may come.

Across the fields we go, crossing roads and old tracks and railway lines, some still used today, others relics of the past and long fallen into disuse. Soon, the smell of the sea grows stronger, the scent appearing amid the stench of smoke and the toxic fumes being belched up from the burning world around us.

And between the booms and roars and thundering

sound of explosions, the casual swishing of waves can be heard, crashing against the rocks right at the base of the cliffs ahead.

My eyes scan the walls to the power station closely. They're not high and manned by guards, but meant for nothing but to keep out trespassers, their tops covered in barbed wire and electric fencing. The gate, too, is a simple structure. Not the sort you'd get at a fortress or military base, but that which you'd expect to find at a place like this that no one would ever think to infiltrate.

I suppose that was the thinking when Drake and Aeneas Stein devised this place. Make it appear just like a small power station, and no one will take any notice. Turns out, that works well for us, the place under-guarded by any serious fixed weaponry.

Reaching the gate, we see no defensive machine gun turrets or missile launchers, the entrance to the power station awaiting us ahead. Narrowing our focus further, we move through the gate and into the space beyond, entering a central square between large buildings and warehouses, Drake leading us towards our primary target.

Half way in, however, Drake and Athena stop in motion. Their sudden paralysis trickles back to the rest of us, each of us turning static, our limbs fixing to stone.

"Get ready…" whispers Athena, her weapon lifting to the left and pointing at the entrance to a building.

Drake's goes right, and suddenly we're all turning

with our backs to one another, knowing what's coming.

I see it all now as well, only moments after my mentor. The world filling with gunfire, coming at us from all sides. We've walked into a deathtrap. Athena was right. We've been lured right in.

As the white wisps of bullets fill the air, the world begins to roar. And suddenly, from behind doors and on the tops of buildings, soldiers appear, firing at us from cover.

Over the sudden din, Drake roars: "SPREAD OUT! TAKE THEM DOWN!"

Caught in the web of bullets, my first thought goes to avoiding death rather than inflicting it. I duck and weave through the hailstorm of lead, just as my comrades begin to return fire. With precision and skill, several of the enemy fall instantly, unable to see their death coming as we move around their bullets, aim, fire, and then continue to weave and dance.

It's a beautiful ballet of death. We move around the central square, drawing their fire apart, giving each other space to move as dozens of soldiers empty their magazines at us. Bullets fizz into the earth at our feet and the buildings around us, but none enter our own flesh. Those that try mostly ping and bounce straight off our suits, unable to find a way through the almost impenetrable cloth.

Using the many tools on our multi faceted guns, we send explosive shells and fire at those hidden out of sight. When they upgrade their attack, we're forced to spread wider, avoiding the grenades and rockets launched in our direction. Before long, the entire square is decimated, many of the buildings around it crumbling and on fire.

An untold number of mercenaries lie amid the rubble.

All of our people remain standing.

More enemies come, however, flooding from inside the buildings that remain intact. The fight goes on, and as it does, I feel my mind beginning to weaken with a sudden and unstoppable vision. It's so close, so near, as if it's a mix between a vision and my own sight into the Void. And amid the battle, I can do nothing but be drawn into it, falling into the dark pit.

I see the world below us, the lab that's drawn us here. I see the machine, the chair, the shape of a body sitting inside it, the helmet atop its head. I see the wires going into the helmet, the computer screen around it filled with data and glowing with pale colour. And the wires, bursting with light, flashing white and shallow blue as electrical currents flow down them.

My mind twists and turns, and I feel the force of a bullet clattering into my arm, bouncing off my suit. It breaks me momentarily from the spell of the vision, and I see flashes of the battle again. I hear Drake shouting, his voice muddied, calling for me to be protected. But not just me, my mother too.

"Protect Theo…protect Cyra!" he calls.

I look through the blur and see that Cyra too is in the throes of a vision. Her eyes have gone white as bullets begin bouncing against her bodysuit, her life just as vulnerable as mine as Athena bounds towards her and Drake and Velia come at me.

Then, my mind sinks again into the vision, and the battlefield around me goes blank. Once more, the lab appears, and I feel the presence of many people in the room, standing around the machine, watching as it does its work.

But there's a presence that feels stronger, more powerful than all the others. One I've never felt before, bubbling under the surface as it rises up and takes form.

I don't understand it, can't make it all out, as the vision blurs and fades before my eyes. With my heart racing, I feel the world taking shape around me again, and find myself lying beside my mother inside a building, hidden out of sight as the others protect us outside. Only Drake kneels above us, trying to wake us from our stupor.

My eyes flicker and open, and I turn to see that Cyra remains locked inside her mind. Drake's eyes widen and come to me, shaking my shoulders.

"What did you see, Theo?! What's happening?!" he shouts.

I shake my head, barely understanding what I saw myself.

"I…I don't know. It's happening, right now… it's happening," I gasp. "I saw the lab and the same machine. But, it was different from before…"

I make no sense, my words coming out all jumbled. Drake turns back to Cyra and continues to try to wrest her from her own mind.

"Cyra, Cyra, wake up!" he calls.

Shaking her violently, her eyes suddenly open, flashing wide like a ventriloquist dummy.

"Cyra!" calls Drake again. "Cyra, what have you seen?!"

Her eyes stare for a second, making eye contact with nothing but the empty space before her. Drake shakes her again, and draws her blue eyes to his.

"What have you seen Cyra!" he calls again.

"It's him…" she whispers. "He's back…"

"Who?!" asks Drake loudly. "Who is back?!"

My mother shakes her head, and scrunches up her eyes, as the battle outside continues to rage.

"Knight," she says, the word coming between sharp breaths. "His mind…his consciousness. That's what the machine is for. They're going to put his mind into the clone's body…they're bringing Augustus back to life…"

26
The Final Fight

With the world outside us in turmoil, a short silence descends as my mother and grandfather stare at each other. For a second, Drake's lips move but no words come out. And then, finally, he speaks.

"That was the special purpose for AK1 all along," he whispers. "It's not to give life to these clones. It's to become the second coming of Augustus Knight. His body is just a vessel…"

"Then we have to stop this!" I shout. "We have to get down there *now!*"

We all stand to our feet, my mother still looking a little dazed. I ask her if she's all right, and she nods her head quickly and tries to shake the cobwebs from her mind.

We move towards the door, and outside see that most of the mercenaries have now been dispatched, Athena, her two students, and Velia doing a great job of stymying the attack.

Athena and Velia come rushing over, leaving the others to mop up the remaining mercenaries.

"What is it? What's wrong?" asks Athena.

"It's hard to explain," says Drake. "We need to get

into the facility right away."

At that moment, a fresh feeling of dread engulfs us all. We all feel it at once, and all of our eyes turn quickly towards the other end of the square, near the entrance to the facility.

As we turn and look, a cry spreads out across the air, and we look to see that the source is one of Athena's Watchers, kneeling in the earth, his neck cut open and pouring blood.

Standing behind him, a cloaked figure awaits us, deadly dagger in hand, hood slung back and hanging down his neck.

One of the Seekers has come.

Nearby, I hear a roar from the other Watcher. Seeing his friend on his knees, he charges straight in and attacks. The Seeker casually swallows the man up in his limbs, wrapping his arms around the man's neck.

"NO!" shouts Athena.

It's too late. A loud crack fills the air as the Seeker twists the Watcher's neck, turning his head backwards. And with a twisted smile, he drops him to the floor, joining his comrade, two noble warriors side by side in death.

Drake shuffles straight to Athena's side and lays his hand on her arm. I can see her staring at her men, brimming with fury and hatred, her entire body quivering and ready to strike.

Drake turns back to us.

"We have to get down there, now," he whispers harshly.

Still staring, Athena speaks. Her voice is low, full of suppressed rage, a strange calm to it. "Go," she says. "I can take care of this."

"No," says Cyra, stepping in. "We fight together."

"There's no time," says Athena, refusing to take her eyes off the Seeker. "All of you, go…NOW."

Drake nods at us.

"She's right…"

"NO," says Cyra again."

"We have no choice!" says Drake. "Now come…"

"I'll stay."

All eyes turn to the petite frame of Velia, fire pouring from her own eyes. She moves up next to Athena.

"I'll fight with you, Athena," she says. "I'll stay."

Now it's my turn to signal my doubts.

"Velia, you might…"

She turns to me with a weak smile.

"I'll be fine, Theo," she says.

I pour in towards her, and rush my lips onto hers.

"I…I…"

"I know, Theo. Now go, I'll be fine with Athena."

I stand with her hands in mine, refusing for a moment to let go. Her eyes tell me it'll all be OK, that we have to all play our part in this now. Slowly, her fingers slip from mine, and she turns back to her foe, and together with Athena, they begin walking at the smirking Seeker, standing above the two dead Watchers.

For a moment, I just stand, unable to move, as they advance on the clone. Wanting to help. Wanting to fight. Wanting to stay and protect the girl I'm falling for.

But I know that I can't. I know that, below us, even greater threats await. And I know, too, that with only my mother, and grandfather remaining, the odds are against us all.

With Drake calling for me to follow, I tear my eyes from Velia, just as their battle begins, and start to rush towards the building, straight at the entrance that will lead us into the depths of the cliffs.

Refusing to look back, I enter into the blackness, the three of us charging straight down a narrow corridor. With Drake leading us, we dart this way and that, through rooms and doors and towards the lifts that will take us down.

Knowing the lift might be rigged, we choose to take the stairs instead, rushing down flight after flight as we descend into the rock. It's quiet now, the sounds from the war above muted by the layers of earth above us, the air growing close and humid before we reach the base and Drake's eyes guide us to a door.

Through we go, the air suddenly cool once more as we enter into the air conditioned facility. Looking left and right and straight ahead, corridors stretch into the fading light, the walls slick and clean and white.

"This way," calls Drake, urging us to follow as he takes the middle passage, leading us straight on.

We move along the corridor, past numerous rooms originally intended for the housing, training, and development of Watchers. But now, this place has been infected with an evil purpose, a purpose to grow an army of clones in the image of Augustus Knight. A purpose to bring the very man back from the dead, infuse his cloned body with his own mind.

And should they succeed, Knight will once again sit at the summit of the world, commanding a force of his own clones. Destined to live forever, with the capacity to spread his own mind and body far and wide, he'll never be defeated.

Now, right now, is our only chance.

So on we rush, unencumbered by any guards or other opposition, the soldiers stationed here drawn up to the fight above. The place is vast, spreading deep into the cliffside, tunnels and corridors leading to various rooms and large chambers to the left and right.

But our step isn't halted, our path led by Drake, one of the few men who knows this facility well. Through the maze of labs and research rooms and corridors we go, eventually arriving at a door marked 'Training Bay 1'.

We pass through the security door, and beyond I

see a vast open space that instantly reminds me of the Grid. Inside, the lights blaze from above, flickering every so often. The power appears to be unstable, surges of current flowing across the ceiling.

"It must be the machine," hisses Drake. "They're using it now..."

His words bring us back into a quick step. We charge straight onwards, panting hard now. My legs begin to burn, my heart rate climbing fast. At the back of the hall, a further door leads us on towards a series of large laboratories and training areas, places where the new breed of Watchers were set to live and eat and train and socialise. Places where they'd test their strength and see their powers unleashed by the new technologies devised by our scientists.

Now, that purpose is no more. Instead, the place has been given over to the development of a clone army of the enemy instead. In the darkest, most distant part of the facility, the latest experiment of the Baron is being put into play.

Augustus Knight is coming back to life.

The lights on the walls continue to flicker, the energy being drawn from all quarters of this place to the machine in which AK1 sits. My mind turns to him now. Surely he doesn't know what's happening? Surely the true purpose of his existence has been kept from him?

Is it just him who's going to gain Knight's consciousness? Will all of them receive the same, giving Knight total power and control over all of his forms?

I think of the connection my mother has with AK1, the same as me, only much stronger. These clones all appear connected, fighting as one organism, one being. As if they have a telepathic link to communicate, to act as one. A link, perhaps, that Cyra and I have been able to tap into…

If Knight controls all his clones, all his forms, his influence would spread far and wide. This country would never recover, never be free. And maybe the entire world would fall under his rule, leaving the fate of humankind under his thumb for the rest of time…

We reach a final door, deep now in the facility, as Drake turns to us with a scowl.

"The primary labs are beyond this door," he says. His eyes scan his beloved daughter's face, then do the same to mine. "We are a family, and we fight as a family," he says, his voice quiet now. "And…if we have to die to stop this, then we die as a family too."

He quickly pulls us into a hug, and I grip tight at them both.

"I love you both, and always will," whispers Drake. "Now, be strong…let's finish this."

He releases us, and I see my mother's eyes shining with a gloss of tears as she looks at me. With a couple of blinks, she washes away the emotion, and her eyes emerge once more with a steady stare as she turns to the door.

Drake opens it up, and before my eyes the wide open lab from my visions appears. Stretching away into the distance, and filled with equipment and machinery, we draw our gazes straight up to the far end.

Stepping in, we see the many tubes lined up at the rear, and the machine before them with the shadow sitting within. And around it, a grouping of people who have seen to this dastardly plan: the Baron, the Cabal, the scientists who have lent their brains to the task.

We move in, and all eyes begin to rise up to us. Mine turn to the Baron, dressed in his fine maroon cloak, the rest of them exquisitely adorned in their regalia as they bring in this momentous occasion.

I stare at the Baron, and see that he's well protected. To his sides stand two Seekers, dressed in their usual cloaks, their hoods hanging over their heads. But in the flashing light, I can make out their faces, their eyes, as we advance into the pit.

I look closely at one, and see the shape of his jaw, the slight difference in his frame, the light blue mixed in with the grey of the eyes. And then I realise...

It isn't AK1 in the machine at all.

It's another Seeker, the top of his head hidden within a helmet, wires coiling out of it and into the machine around him. They buzz with blue and white energy, the room vibrating as the machine hums and cracks, all those around it looking on nervously to see if it works.

Then, the Baron's voice fills the room, everyone turning to the three of us, standing in a line before them, slowly raising up our weapons.

"Well well, how wonderful for you all to make it…" he says, no fear in him at all as I guide the tip of my gun right at his heart.

I look at AK1, standing to his side, and see his eyes widening a little behind his hood, staring at me and then to Cyra. The Baron casually lifts up his hand, and extends his index finger right at us.

"Take them," he growls. "And take them alive…there's someone I dearly want them to meet."

And with those words, the remaining Seeker, and AK1, begin walking slowly towards us.

The final fight is on.

27

Friend or Foe

With a roar from Drake, we open fire.

Immediately, the two Seekers begin to quicken their pace, dodging round our bullets as they advance. Behind them, the Baron and his allies take cover, but only briefly. Because within seconds, a barrier rises up from the ground, protecting those behind from the oncoming barrage of bullets.

Closed off, we're unable to inflict any damage on the men and women at the head of this plot, or the vulnerable Seeker sitting in the machine. Still, we all click to explosive rounds and send them right at the transparent wall, trying to break through and destroy the terrible machine behind it.

The rounds explode into swirls of fire and smoke, covering our view of the world beyond. But when the dust clears, the room behind remains unscathed, the barrier impossible to penetrate with the firepower at our disposal.

I turn my attention back to the two clones coming towards us, and aim my fire at the one who carries Knight's genes alone. We all do the same, trying to cut him down as AK1 drops a little behind, his pace slowing a touch. As I shoot, and watch the other

Seeker weaving towards us, I note the continued look of confusion in AK1's eyes, the conflict still raging within as he sets his eyes on Cyra, half of what he is belonging to her.

From the back of the hall, the rest watch, now safe behind their barrier. I hear the Baron's voice booming over a speaker, filling the room loudly as it looks to overcome the echoing gunfire.

"TAKE THEM. TAKE THEM ALIVE! AK1...FIGHT!"

AK1's inactivity has been noticed. The other Seeker is almost upon us now, our fire only slowing him but nothing more. I see him draw his hood back as he comes, his fists clenching and preparing for battle. To my right, Cyra and Drake drop their guns to the floor, and I see knives drawn out for the attack as the three of them come together.

Beside them, AK1 advances on me. With the others engaging in hand-to-hand combat, I drop my own weapon and lift up my fists. I leave my extendable dagger in my belt, once more standing face to face with the boy I met only weeks ago, the boy who has been in my thoughts ever since.

He marches towards me, and after a moment's hesitation, and another booming order from the Baron, begins to send his fists at the vulnerable parts of my body. I see the attacks coming, and send my own back, and we enter into a rhythmic dance as we attack and defend, block and weave.

I focus hard, and enter into a narrow state of consciousness, seeing and hearing and feeling only him. The rest of the room begins to blur, the fate of my mother and grandfather unknown as they battle the other Seeker. And in that state, I spar evenly with the clone I've spent so much time with in my mind, the boy I'm yet to truly call my foe.

I can sense him holding back, his own mind still torn. I notice his eyes glancing beyond our fight, outside of the bubble I'm focusing on. I know he's looking to my mother, their connection perhaps as strong as his is with the other Seekers. And here, now, so close to each other, his mind is being ripped apart, drawn in two conflicting directions.

The Baron calls out again, his voice now louder than ever with no gunfire filling the air. Each time his words rumble through my body, I see AK1's eyes flinch and blink, a snarl rising up on his lips as he turns his full attention back to me.

His creator's words bring a fresh ferocity to him, his supressed rage beginning to bubble up once more. His hands begin to surge and dart quicker, his body looming closer as I try to avoid a sudden and devastating barrage.

"GOOD," I hear the Baron call. "BRING THEM TO ME…"

His raging fists force me onto the back foot. I stumble and begin to retreat, loosening my focus just a touch to gauge my surroundings. I know I need to lure him from this room, get him away from the booming tones of the Baron, this voice that seems to hypnotise him.

My eyes search the nearest wall, and I see a door

marked 'Storage'. I turn my eyes back on AK1 as his mind begins to set on the task, the side dominated by Knight fighting to the fore. I focus again as he attacks, just starting to bring his full force to bear.

Suddenly, as I near the door, I turn and rush towards it, as if trying to escape. I hear him clattering after me, his footsteps beating down like a drum from behind. I reach the handle and twist, and the door opens inwards just as AK1's body hits my back, driving me to the floor and into a room filled with shelving.

The door swings shut on metallic hinges as we hit the shelves, sending dozens of beakers and tubes and flasks down on top of us. Many are made of glass, shattering as they reach the floor, splintering into a thousands pieces as the ground becomes littered with little shards and fragments.

I dart deeper, and watch AK1's eyes blink again as the Baron's voice fades away, hidden behind the door and the sound of breaking glass. As I rush into the darkness, I bump into more shelves, sending down more utensils, the room growing louder as AK1 continues to pursue me.

With the Baron's hold on him fading, I turn and see his eyes soften a little, that conflict once more growing as the two sides of him do battle. He slows his step as I reach the back wall, trapped and cornered, a sudden silence dawning between us.

"Do you know what that machine is doing?" I ask him, panting hard as he looms towards me.

He stops, his own chest heaving, his eyes staring wildly at me.

For a second, he hesitates, as if doubting his words, before saying: "It's making us stronger…it's releasing our full potential. We'll be the most powerful Watchers ever!"

"Yes, you're right," I say. "You'll be the most powerful…but it won't be *you*."

His eyes smoulder, his own scepticism growing.

"What does that mean?!" he shouts. "It WILL be me!"

"No, it won't," I say calmly, breathlessly. I watch as his fists clench again, that rage inside him boiling up. "The Baron isn't trying to release your power…he's trying to *replace* you…"

He steps forwards, prowling at me like an enraged beast. Just as he did before, when we met alone in that abandoned town, his hands grip at my collar, and he pushes me hard against the wall.

"What do you know!" he shouts. "You know nothing about this!"

"I do, AK! I know everything! He isn't releasing your power in that machine…not any of you. He's just using your body as a vessel. If you sit down in that machine, you'll *never* wake up. You're going to be replaced by Augustus Knight's consciousness! If you let him use you, then you'll die. Everything you know will be gone…"

He slams me against the wall once, twice, three times. Each time getting harder, more forceful.

"YOU'RE LYING!" he bellows. "YOU'RE TRYING TO TRICK ME!"

I take a grip of his hands, and grit my teeth, and summon all my strength to tear his fingers from my collar and neck. I push hard, and he stumbles backwards away from me as my own eyes begin to smoulder and light with a bright blaze.

"I'M NOT LYING!" I shout, grimacing. I raise my finger and point it towards the door at the end of the room. "If you go back out there, if you let him put you in that machine…then your mind will be gone forever. Your body will remain, but nothing more. You've been lied to and deceived your entire life. Don't be fooled by this."

He steps towards me again, brimming and bristling with a nervous, febrile energy.

My voice once more calls out, halting him in his tracks.

"Cyra is out there now," I say. "Half of you has come from her, and you know that. You have a connection that you can't deny…there's a large part of you that doesn't believe in any of this."

Breathing hard, he stands before me, stuck to the spot, not knowing what to do.

"If you want to live, you only have one choice…you have to help us," I continue, calming my voice and staring him right in the eye. "You've been manipulated your whole life, and I can't imagine what you've been through. But today, all that can change. *You* can change it…"

I step towards him, away from the wall, as his eyes dip down to look upon his hands. They're scarred and calloused. The hands of a fighter. The hands of a warrior.

The hands of a slave.

I look upon my own, and see a similar story, both of our fates bringing us to this moment. I know, now, that my part in this was always to do with him, that our roles were entwined.

Tentatively, I reach forward, and lay my hand on his shoulder. His eyes rise up to mine, softer now, calmer.

"You're my brother," I say. "Help me. Help us. Don't let yourself be killed by a lie."

He stares back for a moment, standing at the same height as me, the two of us similar in so many ways. Drawn from different places. Born for different purposes.

But now here, together, determining the fates of millions.

Slowly, without speaking, he starts to nod.

And I see the blue in his eyes begin to brighten.

28
Reawakening

My hands are bound behind my back. By body is bowed and beaten.

I'm walked back through the door and into the vast room, my heart racing as I search for my mother and grandfather. I see them in the centre of the wide, open lab, both of them on their knees, their own wrists bound tight behind them.

In front of them, their conqueror stands, the Seeker having disabled them both. Across his face I see signs that his victory didn't come easy, several slashing cuts dribbling blood from his cheeks and neck. So close, but not close enough.

There's a dusty and smoky smell in the room, the walls and floor and ceiling pocketed with gunfire. It's hard to make much out until we step a little closer, and my family's eyes turn to me.

I look to my mother, and see a mixture of relief and sadness. Relief that I haven't been killed. Sadness that that's the fate that now faces us all.

I'm pushed towards them by AK1 and thrust harshly down by my mother's side, Drake to her right and me to her left. None of us speak as we look forward through the clearing dust.

Ahead, I see a third Seeker, his own face battered and bruised and spilling blood from various points. Immediately, my mind turns to Velia, my heart racing once more.

Then, through the dust, I see her, propped up against the side of the wall with Athena alongside. I try to stand, but feel AK1's hand holding me down.

"It's OK," whispers my mother. I turn to look at her as she offers a weak smile, still trying to comfort me, even in defeat. "Velia and Athena are OK. The Baron wanted them alive as well. They're just unconscious."

"Are you sure…"

She nods, but her eyes are hooded. She knows, now, that we're all going to die anyway. What's the point in living just a few more minutes?

As we kneel there, the booming voice of the Baron once more rumbles around the room. This time, however, it's not coming from the speakers, but directly from his mouth as he wanders towards us.

"Well, the timing of this couldn't be more perfect," he says, smiling as he emerges through the cloud of lingering smoke.

As he comes, the room continues to clear, air conditioning units sucking out the mist. As it does so, the sight ahead appears again as it was before: the machine with the final Seeker inside it; the electric currents running up wires into his head; the scientists and members of the Cabal, gathered round. Now, though, the bulletproof barrier has been removed, opening the room up once more.

Our eyes turn back on the Baron, standing before it all.

"I hope you enjoy the show," he says, smiling.

Behind him, the Seeker in the chair moves for the first time. The sudden twitch draws a gasp from the crowd, Lord Kendrik and Count Lopez among them, the rest of the Cabal all in attendance. They peer in closer as one of the lead scientists calls out.

"He's coming out, Baron Reinhold! This is it…"

The Baron's smirk turns to one of pure joy, his eyes elated as he turns and storms back to the machine. Hovering by it's side, he watches on intently along with all the others as the electric currents flying along the wires grow more wild, sparks starting to spit and bursts from the machine.

For a few seconds, I pray that it's going to explode, this crazy experiment failing before their eyes. Some of them appear to fear the same, stepping back a little, their eyes showing concern. But not the Baron's. He merely gazes on in wonder, staring at the face of the young clone of Augustus Knight, as his old consciousness is fed into his body piece by piece.

By my side, my mother stares without moving, her face blank and empty. Drake's face is a deep scowl, his eyes growing smaller by the second.

The room continues to buzz as the lights flicker harshly once again, the machine humming louder as the Seeker twitches harder. Then, as it builds to a crescendo, suddenly the lights fade, and the wires go cold, and the clone's body falls still and silent once again, a little cloud of smoke drifting from the top of his helmet.

All goes quiet for a moment, and the entire room falls to a temporary darkness. And then, gradually, the lights blaze to life again, and everyone blinks and shields their eyes from the sudden glare.

I squint, and slowly open my eyes, allowing the harsh light to flow inside. And as the room ahead clears, I look upon the face of the Seeker again.

And now, his eyes are open.

No one breathes for a moment. The most profound silence I've ever witnessed descends upon the room. All eyes stare at the clone, his eyes slowly taking things in, moving around the room as if seeing it all for the first time.

Because he is.

Then, the Baron speaks, his voice strangely delicate and bristling with emotion.

"Master…" he whispers.

The Seeker's eyes turn to his, and stare again for a few seconds. Then, I see a smile creep up his face, and hear a voice come from his throat, now imbued with a strange new tone, a strange new calm.

"Reinhold," he says, scanning the Baron's face. "Oh, how you've aged…"

The Baron's face glows with a spreading smile, his eyes watering.

"Augustus…it's really you…it really worked…"

The man in the chair nods. No longer a Seeker. No longer just a clone. A new body, young and strong, and now occupied by a new mind.

Augustus Knight lives again.

The rest of the Cabal look upon him in awe, dropping to their knees and bowing down. Knight slowly lifts up his hands and removes the helmet from his head, before standing up to his full height. He looks to his hands and clenches his fists, and I see his eyes lighting with a red fire.

Then, as he stands there, I watch as his chin lifts and his eyes stare forward, locking straight onto my mother.

They stare for a few seconds, and then a smile builds up on Knight's lips. He steps forwards as the Baron hurries to his side, walking a pace or two behind him with a slight bow to his motion. The rest of the Cabal and the scientists stay back, hardly believing what they're seeing.

"It's my gift for you, Augustus," comes the Baron's voice. "A gift to welcome you back. I give you…Cyra Drayton, and her father, Drake."

"And the boy?" says Knight, swinging his eyes at me. Then he shakes his head, and smiles again, and answers his own question. "Her son…" he whispers. "Three generations of the Draytons. A wonderful gift indeed, Reinhold."

The Baron's eyes threaten to spill with tears, his entire body shaking with an uncontained joy. How long he must have had this plan. How long he must have waited for this moment.

They must have plotted this together, right from the beginning, right before Knight even died. A failsafe in case he ever perished, his consciousness kept safe with the Baron and ready to be uploaded to a new form as soon as they had the means.

Knight continues to come forwards, staring once more at Cyra.

"Well, Cyra, you're not a *girl* anymore, are you?" he says.

My mother's eyes stare at him dispassionately. She doesn't speak.

"I can only assume that it was *you* who led to my death?" he asks.

Again, she doesn't answer. It takes the Baron to fill in the blanks.

"It was her, yes," he says. "She collaborated with Priscilla and Emerson Graves to poison you, master."

"Ah, of course, the Graves. I suspect the death of their son, Theo, forced them to turn against me. Strange that I didn't see it all coming…"

The mention of my namesake causes certain people to look at me. Theo Graves, the boy my mother was Paired with. The boy whose parents were Councillors, right at the side of Knight. Councillors who could no longer continue to support his ideology. In the end, they helped to take him down, defeat him before he could do any more damage.

That, of course, was when his life ended, right there in the centre of Eden. I suppose his current consciousness has no memory of such a thing. He must have been uploading it regularly, the Baron keeping it safe. But once he'd died, any fresh memories he'd made were lost.

Now, my mother speaks, her voice cutting out from her throat.

"It's a shame you don't remember it, Augustus," she says coldly. "You don't remember the poison weakening you…the feel of cold steel as Priscilla and Emerson stabbed you in the chest…as *I* sent the blade right into your evil heart. Oh, it's one of my favourite memories…" she says lustily.

She glares at him hard, but his eyes only lighten with a touch of laughter.

"Oh Cyra, just as charming as you always were. I've really missed our little chats."

"And how much do you remember?" growls Drake, his voice entering the room.

Knight's eyes sweep to his, and look upon him for a few moments.

"The famous and heroic Drake Drayton," he says loudly. "We never actually met, did we Drake?"

Drake stares at him coldly, just like my mother

"To answer your question, I remember everything up until the day I died," continues Knight. "I was never willing to allow my life to end with the destruction of my body. My loyal scientists and subjects devised a machine to hold my consciousness and memory. I merely needed to upload it each day, and wait for them to bring me back. And what a fine job they've done," he says, raising his hands to clap.

As he does so, the others join in, the members of the Cabal now having risen to their feet. The Baron looks up at his master sheepishly as Knight offers him a nod of respect, before doing the same to several of the scientists in the background. Then, he marches over to them, and sets about thanking them each individually, before moving across and greeting the members of the Cabal after his long hiatus.

As he does so, I turn to look at AK1, watching proceedings with a strange look on his face. The other Seekers, too, stand by with a rare awkwardness, not quite knowing what's going on. When Knight returns, he finally acknowledges their presence, standing like statues to the side of Drake.

"Ah, and these must be my wonderful clones," he says, moving towards them.

They stare at him, seeing their brother, their doppelganger, moving towards them now, so different from before. I can see them trying to work it all through in their minds, unable to catch up on what's going on.

But they've been bred to do what they're told, not to question. Bred for chaos and war, their minds simple mechanisms. And now, their final task has become clear, to give themselves up for another, to spread Knight's mind far and wide across the world.

For a moment, the new Knight looks upon them, before smiling and returning to stand in front of us.

"For so long I'd go through that awful gene therapy to keep me looking young," he says, laughing. "It doesn't look like I'll need to do that anymore."

All his subservient slaves laugh, their voices echoing as one around the room. Only when he stops do they do so as well, following his every move. He turns back to the Baron.

"So, Reinhold, what have I missed? It looks like plenty of time has passed, going by your completion and that of our guests…"

"Yes, um…twenty years, master," says the Baron. "It took longer than we thought to develop the clones, and to master the process of accelerated growth…"

"Oh, don't sound so worried, Reinhold. You took your time and did things right. I can't ask of anything more."

As he speaks, a rare shudder sounds from above, rippling down through the rocks. Knight's eyes rise up, as a sprinkling of dust trickles down from the ceiling.

"Something I should know, Reinhold?" he asks, raising his eyebrows.

Once again, the Baron answers with a nervous cadence to his voice.

"We are at war, master," he says, gulping. "It was all necessary to get everything done…but things are all under control. The enemy army has attacked us along the coast, but they're no match for us. The world is yours again…"

Knight takes in a long breath, a little smile sitting on his smug face. For him, twenty years must have gone past like the clipping of a finger. With his consciousness in stasis, the final day of the War of the Regions, just before his death, must seem like yesterday. As if he's merely awoken from a long sleep, his memory only lacking the terrible recollection of his death.

Now, reborn and waking in a fresh body, the happenings of the last twenty years are irrelevant to him. Twenty years gone, passed by in the blink of an eye. I can barely get my head around it.

"I can only assume that Aeneas Stein and the Graves are now departed?" Knight asks.

"Yes, master," says the Baron. "Many of those who rebelled against you are gone, barring those before you. And we can dispatch them now, if you wish?"

Knight shakes his head, and once more steps a little closer to us, still kneeling at his feet. His eyes settle on Cyra again, before sweeping across and inspecting me.

"You have your mother's likeness, boy," he says to me. "And her strength…I can feel it in you. You're a powerful young man. Tell me, what is your name?"

"Theo," I say sharply.

His face erupts into another budding smile.

"Ah…Theo! Isn't that just wonderful. And I suppose Jackson Kane is your father?"

I don't answer this time, but I don't need to.

"Of course he is," he says, laughing. He turns back to my mother. "I'm happy that you two ended up together, Cyra. Truly, I am."

Standing to my left above me, I feel AK1 shift uncomfortably as he watches things unfold. The movement draws up Knight's eyes, staring upon the mixed clone for the first time.

"Well…" he says, "with all that's been going on, I must have missed *you*."

"Master, this is…" starts the Baron.

"Oh, I know who it is," cuts in Knight. "Such strength," he whispers, looking upon the clone longingly. "I'll look forward to getting inside *your* head…"

I see AK1's eyes bulge a touch at Knight's words, and notice the slightest heave of his chest. His nostrils flare ever so slightly, but he maintains his composure, just staring ahead as he's been trained to do.

Knight looks at him for a little longer, admiring the job, before stepping back again.

"So, what shall we do with them all, master?" asks the Baron.

Knight enjoys another moment of silence, soaking it all up, his grey eyes growing colder and deeper as he considers things.

"Well," he says, "seeing as Cyra took it upon herself to kill me, I suppose I'd better get some revenge."

My heart thuds suddenly at his words.

"Go ahead," says my mother defiantly. "You were always a coward…go ahead…"

"NO," I shout, my voice breaking into the room.

"Don't," calls Drake, unable to hold back.

Knight revels in our pain, watching on with a smirk.

"No…no, perhaps you're both right," he says smoothly. "You know, I'd like to chat with Cyra a bit more, there's so much we need to catch up on. And, well, I'd like to see her suffer a little more too…"

His hand rises up and points at the two Seekers standing to the right of Drake.

"You two…draw out your knives."

The Seekers do as ordered, immediately pulling knives from their belts.

"Good. Now, Cyra, it's time you watched your loved ones die…"

My mother's eyes flare, and she shouts out. "NO…don't! Kill me…"

"Oh no, that would be too easy, wouldn't it."

His fingers draw the two Seekers forwards. One moves behind Drake, the other behind me.

"NO, AUGUSTUS! PLEASE, NO…." shouts Cyra.

Her words only draw a larger smile up Knight's face. I turn to my mother, whose eyes stream with tears, her head shaking and shivering.

"No…no…" she says weakly, staring right at me.

"On three," says Knight, calling to the two Seekers, "cut right through their throats."

"No…" sobs my mother.

"Not the boy!" calls Drake fiercely, drawing my mother's eyes. "Kill me…but not the boy!"

I look at him, and then at her again, and then across at Knight as he says: "One…"

My eyes flow to the other side of the room, where Velia remains up against the wall, unconscious, Athena beside her.

"I love you dad," cries Cyra. "I love you so much, Theo…"

She squints her eyes tight as Knight says: "Two…"

I shut my eyes, as the Seeker's blade descends before my throat, my body calm, my focus pure.

I feel my entire form brimming with energy, with power, with a surge of strength. I hold myself firm, my concentration complete, and just before Knight calls out 'three', my own voice fills the room.

"NOW!"

In one movement, I rip apart the fake binds that wrap around my wrists, and AK1 surges forward, knocking the Seeker's blade away from my throat.

We stand, side by side, staring upon our foes.

And together, we go to work…

29
Fallen Hero

Drake is the first to react to the change of dynamic in the room.

With the Seeker's blade to his throat, he cocks his head back and leaps to his feet, knocking his executioner away. Immediately, I pull the extendable sword from my belt, click on the button once, and feel the blade come surging forth. As I do so, I glide right past my mother, swiping across the binds on his wrists, releasing her as I reach my grandfather and do the same.

It all happens in a flash, the two Seekers unable to react, still staring at AK1, their leader, in wonder. They stand back for a moment, not knowing what to do. And then, their new leader's voice erupts in a roar.

"KILL THEM ALL!" shouts Knight.

What happens next is a blur, a burst of activity that sets the entire room into sudden motion.

Drake turns straight on the Seeker behind him, his body burning and brimming as he pours straight in. Cyra, too, her hands now free, appears reborn as she launches herself at the Seeker who was set to kill me, charging at him like a woman possessed.

Standing ahead of us all, Knight watches on with his eyes burning bright. He looks to his hands, and clenches his fists tight, and I feel a power I've never felt radiate out through his body. His mind itself, so old, so wise, has imbued his new form with a strength that perhaps not even AK1 can match.

I can see that he senses it too, his eyes widening as Knight smoulders and pulses with energy.

"Help your family," growls AK1, looking on. "They cannot win alone."

"And you?"

"I was born for war, Theo. Leave this to me."

His words are cool and calm, no doubt in them now, no conflict bubbling inside him. He stares at Knight, who stares back at both of us, no smile on his face now. This is business, and nothing more.

Then, from nowhere, AK1 charges towards him, and Knights steps forwards too, and the two titans clash in a blast of power that spreads right through the room. I watch for a second in awe at the speed of their limbs, slashing and clawing as they enter into a brutal ballet.

And across the room, the Baron's voice booms once more, calling for AK1 to submit, to see sense. I look in his eyes, however, and see the voice having no impact now, only serving instead to intensify and enhance the crinkle of anger across his visage.

And then, as they continue to battle, I turn to my mother and grandfather, and add my own body to the fray.

In I go, my dagger still in hand, ready to swipe and cut at my enemy. Already, blades have been drawn up by the Seekers and my allies, glinting under the light, flashing with sparks as they clash against each other. I come straight forward, and fight the Seeker my mother faces, my own focus narrowing to him and him alone, my body brimming and overflowing with power and energy.

Across Cyra's bodysuit, little white lines appear, places where the Seeker has attempted to cut her, the material doing enough to keep him at bay. His own armour has similar markings, and his face is deeply bruised and bloodied. I know, looking upon him, that he's the one who fought and defeated Athena and Velia. Clearly, he didn't get off lightly in that fight.

He appears a little weary, though, as we pour forward, my added strength giving us the upper hand. I've never seen my mother fight like this, with such control and concentration, her anger guided down a tunnel right at the clone in front of her.

As we push him back, he moves towards his brother, battling with Drake, drawing together to fight as one. We close in around them, and I note the fury in my grandfather's eyes, his old body giving everything it has, emptying the tank one final time.

A little way away, the pulsing battle between Knight and AK1 rages on, my attention unable to steer away from them. I lift my eyes to them for just a moment, and see them embroiled in hectic battle, still using only their fists in combat.

My momentary lapse presents an opportunity for the Seekers. One hunts me down amid the tumble of limbs and I'm too late to see the knife come at me, surging towards my neck. As the Seeker's blade nears, however, Cyra's hand rises from below, knocking him off his stride, and sending the blade only grazing across the top of my neck below the chin, one of the few places on my body that remains exposed.

The graze is enough to slice through my skin, the cut only shallow. Blood begins to dribble, but not pour, and I quickly re-enter the fight.

More cuts are administered, some only minor, others a little deeper. Both sides find their bodies being peppered with injuries, but none hinder any of us.

Then, suddenly, from behind, I sense a new presence coming forward. I turn and watch as Knight comes in, AK1 knocked back onto the ground and struggling to his feet. He looks a little dazed, shaking the cobwebs from his head with a roar as he grinds to his feet.

Knight's eyes pulse hard, staring straight at Cyra. His hand draws up with a devilish knife, flashing silver under the light. I can see it all happening now, see him moving in to strike her down, his hatred for her spewing from every pour.

Her back is turned from him, still fighting with the Seeker. I make a move to call out a warning, but I'm distracted enough to not see the other Seeker's fist coming. It clatters into my face and I stumble back, the world blurring a little. Cyra launches herself back in at the same clone, Knight looming behind her.

The world turns slow now, everyone's motion seeming to grow muddy. Step by step, Knight comes, his blade ready to press right through my mother's back, right into her heart, just like she did to him all those years ago.

I call out '*no*' just as he comes, his blade guiding right at her, all his force levied behind it. My muted bellow is enough to draw my mother's eye, but not at the threat looming at her rear. She looks to me instead, her eyes narrowing, as I try to move forward again.

I'm too late.

The blade comes in, no one able to stop it, cutting through bodysuit and flesh alike, surging deep.

But it's not my mother's body that takes the hit.

It's my grandfather's.

Stepping right before Knight's knife, he accepts the blade for his own. It pieces his armour, his flesh, his bone, the tip unstoppable as it penetrates right through to his heart.

I watch in horror as the blade appears out of his back, cutting him right through. My mother turns, and sees her father right behind her, staring face to face with the devil, his body skewered by the longer dagger.

Now, it's her who stands distracted. The Seeker presses in on her, his own knife coming, and I rush on and knock him back, pummelling him to the floor. For a moment, Knight's knife stays locked into Drake's body, his eyes quickly fading, his light going out. And then, with a slow and callous motion, Knight pulls the blade out, and Drake's body tumbles to the floor, right at my mother's feet.

A short lull hits the room. All seem to stop for a moment, the Seekers stepping back to Knight's sides, AK1 moving across to ours. We stand, face to face, three on three, with the body of my grandfather between us.

And for several long moments, Cyra just looks at him, staring at his face, watching as his eyes go dull and the blood seeps from his body. She kneels down as his eyes flash on her, weak, fading, his body broken. Her hand strokes his head, as he tries to whisper a final word, blood bubbling around his lips.

But he can't. No words come, his life slipping away. She knows there's nothing she can do. And as his eyes go blank, and her fingers slide over them, closing them forever, Knight's voice spreads across the narrow gap between us.

"Don't worry, Cyra...you'll be with him again soon."

A trickle of enjoyment flows from his mouth, the hum of joy in his voice. As if he wanted to kill Drake and not Cyra. As if he wants, now, to cut me down before he does the same to her. As if he wants to watch her suffer, basking in the terrible picture of pain on her face.

"I love you, dad," I hear my mother whisper, ignoring Knight, looking upon her father one final time.

My heart breaks at the sight, tears welling behind my eyes. I blink hard and turn my pain to anger, as my mother stands up once again. On her face, I see the same metamorphosis, her agony transforming to hate, her emotion giving her strength.

And, inside me, the same force rises. My focus turns back to the enemy, waiting for us to engage, each of them smiling now as they watch us.

"Let's finish this," comes my mother's voice, whispering from the side as she stares forward as I do. "For Drake…"

And then, with a burst, her body explodes forward.

And AK1 and I follow.

30
Deja Vu

My mother goes straight for Knight, moving with a pace that he doesn't seem to expect. I move alongside her, joining to her right, as AK1 moves to her left. At the back of the room, the Baron now hides with the rest of the Cabal, locked behind the transparent barrier once more, calling out over and over for AK1 to stop.

He doesn't listen.

Fighting as a three, we engage with Knight and the Seekers, slashing with our fists and blades, working as one as they once did. I see them now, struggling a little to keep us at bay, the two Seekers growing weary and tired, not moving as one, as a single being, as they have before.

Now, shorn of their leader, the telepathic link between them has been weakened. Knight, with his new mind, hasn't been able to develop such a skill, unable to direct their actions and battle together in a coherent fashion.

Instead, it's us who are the more natural, flowing around each other, hooking and stabbing and darting at the enemy, coiling them into a ball of fury as we duck and weave and warn each other of any errant attacks we might miss.

I've never fought like this, never had such a link while battling with others. The connection with AK1 grows, my mind somehow picking up where he's going to attack next, my limbs acting accordingly to best strike at the enemy.

We move around the room, using any tools and equipment that we pass by, scooping them up and battering them down. We begin to unsettle them, wear them down, only Knight himself appearing to battle with the same assurance that you'd expect from these clones. He stands above us all, knocking us back as we advance, attempting to cut us down with the blade that saw to the end of my grandfather, still dripping with his blood.

But I see it all too early now. And so does Cyra. And so does AK1. Feeding each other with our own abilities, our own sight into the Void, we all see any attack early enough to step away from it, around it, anything that might get near nothing but a glancing blow that rattles off our bodysuits.

I note the rising anger in Knight's eyes as he comes forward, his throat blaring out with a roar of rage. The other Seekers seem cowed by him, their connection now growing opaque and shrouded, a veil falling over the link that once drew them together.

I can see it in their faces now, and it gives me further hope, hope which spreads from me to my mother, and on to AK1. They look upon him as he fights them, quelled by the change in him, by the turn to our side, unable to figure it all out.

Only weapons of war and chaos, their minds can't grasp all of this. All their lives they've done nothing but follow orders, incapable of forming their own independent thoughts. Only AK1, guiding them, leading them, has parted from the vice that surrounded him for so long, battling out of the darkness to see the light.

His focus is pure and deep, and together we begin to overpower the two clones. Soon, I'm circling round the back of one as my mother attacks the front, and my extendable dagger is surging right at him and finding its way into his flesh.

I feel it enter him and a flash of pity crosses my thoughts. I drive it deeper and hear him roar in pain, the dagger slowing as I push it through his spine. Suddenly, his body goes stiff, and his roaring stops, and to the floor he falls, his spinal chord severed.

He's dead.

I feel no joy at his parting. He never made a decision in his life. He never had a choice. Lying before me, with a face locked in pain, I grit my teeth with anger at what I've been forced to do. And my eyes flash on the Baron, standing behind his barrier, quivering in fear as I search him out.

This is your fault, I think, my eyes on fire. *You are to blame for all of this…*

Watching the death of his brother, the other Seeker's eyes blare, and he comes at me furiously. Knight, too, shows a new emotion. There's no smile or snigger to his visage now. It's been beaten back and broken down. It's not even anger and fury that sets his eyes aflame. Those fires have been doused, replaced by a look that sets my own face rising with pleasure.

Fear.

That's what I see in him now. I can feel it too, spreading out from him, his eyes widening as he looks upon the departed clone, his body twisted in agony on the floor.

I only get to see him momentarily, though, before the other Seeker reaches me. My eyes aren't on him, but I see him coming all the same. I feel every move of his body, every beat of his heart. As the sight of Cyra and AK1 flows down the connection into my mind, I note every move he makes before he even considers making it.

And as he comes at me, with his own focus lost, his own fury immeasurable, I know he's not long for this world. I know, now, that there's nothing he can do to me.

As the murderer of his brother, his attention turns to me, and me alone. The dam of his rage has been breached. There's nothing controlled about him now. All his power, all his strength, sparks out of him in all directions, every little move he makes so visible to my new senses.

I have no trouble dodging around his attacks, no problem avoiding the probing strikes of his knife. As AK1 continues to hold Knight at bay, watching on unable to help, Cyra sweeps round this time to administer the killing blow.

I hear Knight bellow as he stands there, impotent, watching as his final Seeker feels the sting of my mother's blade. Once more, I feel no joy at seeing the tip come through the front of his neck, at the sudden shock and pain that fills his eyes as Cyra comes at him from behind.

When his body crumbles to the floor, right to the side of the other Seeker, and the crimson pool gathers between them, I feel only pity and sorrow. Across the room, the Baron and his cowardly allies have fallen silent. They stare wide-eyed at us, nowhere to run, nowhere to hide. Never could they have expected the day to go like this.

And now, standing between them and us, only one man remains. Augustus Knight, in his new body, gathers his composure once again, and pulls himself up to his full height.

"You've grown strong, Cyra," he says, looking at my mother. I can hear the deflation in his voice, as his eyes sweep across the three of us. Yet still, some defiance remains. "Do you think you're strong enough?"

My mother shakes her head.

"Me?" she asks. "No, Augustus. I was never strong enough for you." Her eyes turn to me, and then to AK1, the two of us flanking her. "But these two…that's a different story."

Knight's eyes fall into further darkness as they set on AK1. He stares at him for a moment, a look of disgust rising up on his face.

"Weak…" he hisses. "Traitor…"

His words cause a stir in his half clone. AK1's eyes widen with anger, that same unsuppressed, incandescent rage that constantly simmers beneath the surface of all of these clones. I can feel him about to pounce, about to surge, but Cyra's hand sweeps out in front of him.

"It's OK," she says, calmly. "His words are empty. Like his heart. Like his soul."

"Heart and soul," cackles Knight. "There's no such thing."

Cyra smiles at him. "You really are the same as ever, Augustus," she says. "But you won't share the same fate as your old body. No…that's not enough for you."

Suddenly, I feel her move forward before she even does so, and AK1 and I are dragged along for the ride. We push forward as a three, driving in as Knight's eyes open once more with that element of fear.

Fear that his life is about to end. Fear that his rule will be so short. Fear that his legacy will be wiped out right here, right now.

He gathers himself just in time as we strike together. We dart in with our fists, circling him, coming from all sides, his own blade slashing and stabbing at us. Our knives deflect the attacks, but his movements remain quick, using the last of his energy as we close in like a pack of sharks.

I can see it coming now, see the end in sight. His movements begin to slow, our attacks finding their range, nibbling at him, beating at his body. Little cuts dig into his flesh, the tips of our knives drawing blood. Fists hit hard at his limbs, at his face, bursting teeth from his gums and splitting his lips.

His body becomes soaked in blood, dribbling from his face and cheeks, from a dozen wounds across his flesh. Little by little, we cut him down and watch as he sinks to his knees, his arms slowly dropping to his sides.

I see AK1 move around his back, hovering behind him with his knife. He looks at Cyra, standing right in front of him, waiting for the order from his new leader. She shakes her head and he steps back a touch, as Knight's lips dribble with blood, and his grey eyes sink deeper into his skull.

"Well, Augustus, isn't this familiar," oozes my mother's voice. "You won't remember this, of course, but you died just like this twenty years ago. On your knees, defeated before me…"

His eyes rise up to her, the final flicker of fire behind them.

"Then finish it," he says, goading her. "End it all forever."

She looks at him for a good long while, and then shakes her head.

"Oh no, Augustus. I said you wouldn't share the same fate as before. That isn't enough, not for you."

His eyes simmer with fear once again.

"Then what?" he asks, trying to prevent his voice from quivering.

"Oh, don't be afraid," she whispers. "You'll find out soon…"

And with that, she nods at AK1, who steps forward and swings his heavy fist across Knight's head.

And there before us, our enemy lies, defeated once more.

31
Brother

Silence swamps us all. Knight's new body lies before us, breathing lightly, his eyes closed, blood trickling to the floor from many little wounds.

My mother looks at him for a moment, just staring at his beaten form. Then, slowly, she turns to me, and draws me into a long hug.

"We did it, mum," I say. "We did it."

She nods at me, and finally her cool begins to break and thaw, a tear running from her eye. She turns to her father's body, and once more her face becomes etched with pain.

"You should be proud of him," I whisper. "Without him, none of this would have happened."

"I…I know," she says weakly. "I am proud. I'm so proud of you both."

She draws me into another hug, and gently kisses my cheek, before releasing me once more. We turn to AK1, an energy still bristling around him, standing guard over Knight's unconscious, bloodied frame.

"How can we ever thank you?" my mother asks, moving closer towards him.

"You…don't have to," he answers. "I've done

terrible things."

"And wonderful things," says Cyra quickly. "You saved us all."

He nods, but doesn't answer. All this must be so alien to him, so new, a fresh part of his own consciousness beginning to wake. He turns to the Baron, who continues to cower with his cohort behind the see-through wall. And once again, a fury builds in his eyes.

"What about him?" he asks. "I'll happily kill them all…"

"No," says Cyra, moving over to him, laying a hand on his shoulder. "There's been enough death today. Come with me, both of you."

We begin walking over to the Baron, still locked behind his wall with the rest of the scientists and decorated luminaries who saw to the resurrection of evil. Above us, the war continues to rage, the occasional shudder through the ceiling reminding me that those I care about above remain locked in combat.

As we reach the barrier, my mother turns to me.

"Theo, I trust your special dagger can cut through that?"

I nod, and immediately send the blade deep into the barrier, cutting straight through it. Those behind it whimper with fear as I open up a doorway.

Before us, the Baron stands, his eyes locked in anguish as he stares ahead at Knight's body. His lips seem to move, whispering to himself, unable to compute what's just happened.

"Baron Reinhold," says my mother loudly, drawing his eye. "Send word to your people immediately to end the fighting."

It seems to take a while for her words to sink in, his mind a mess, his eyes swollen and small.

"You heard her!" I shout, stepping forward menacingly.

My movement makes him half jump and yelp, his hands shaking as they rise up in surrender.

"OK...OK..." he whispers. "I'll...do anything you say..."

We stand and watch as he fumbles with his communicator, his voice rushing as he sends out word to the various commanders out in the field. Soon enough, all of his people have been alerted and ordered to stand down.

Above, the muted sounds of war quieten, the Baron's voice squeaking into the room.

"What are you going to do with me?" he whimpers.

We all look upon him in disgust, his face stricken, his eyes red. Before him, his God lied defeated. There's nothing left for him now.

"There are so many people who want to kill you, Baron Reinhold," fumes Cyra. "Three of them stand before you now. But I won't deprive the many others of the sight."

He whimpers in fear again, nothing but a weeping

child, as Cyra's fist flashes across his face and his eyes switch to the back of his skull. He crumbles to the floor, as Cyra takes his leg and begins dragging him out into the room. We add our strength, and slide him right beside Knight.

"Lie with your fallen God," bites Cyra, as we set about binding their hands.

Now, my mind turns to Velia, and Athena, so nearly forgotten amidst it all. She lurches right back into my head, and I rush over to her to see if she's OK. I cut the binds on her wrists, as Cyra does the same with Athena, before slowly stroking her hair and drawing her back from her sleep.

One side of her face is badly bruised, but other than that she appears to be OK. Slowly, her eyes open, and set their focus on me.

"Theo…" she whispers.

"It's me," I say. "It's all OK now."

She sits up, and her eyes take in the room.

"What…what happened here?"

I smile as wide as I have in a while, and draw her into a soft kiss.

"It's a long story," I say.

As Athena is roused from her sleep, her own questions begin to tumble. Most of all, their eyes fall upon the bundle of bodies in the middle of the room: the Seeker, who they have no idea is actually Knight; the Baron, lying bound beside him; the other two clones, heaped together in a pool of blood;

and AK1, standing above them, no longer our enemy but fondest ally.

Then, to Drake's body their gazes drift, Athena's face in particular crinkling in pain.

"Is he…" she starts, looking to Cyra.

My mother nods, and a fresh tear drifts down her cheek as Athena pulls her into a long hug.

I sit back against the wall, exhausted and drained, and feel Velia lay her head against my shoulder. So many questions must lie on the tip of her tongue, so much to tell. And even now, there's so much still to do.

But as she lies there, she asks only one thing.

"Is it over?" comes her voice, sweet and soft.

I stroke her hair again, and pull her a little closer.

"It's over," I say. "It's all over..."

We stay sitting there for a little while, as Athena rises and sets about communicating with our allies. I wait for word of my father, of my friends, and watch Athena as she paces from side to side, gathering up intel. Cyra, meanwhile, moves over to Drake's body, sitting beside him, finally able to mourn in peace.

Soon, Athena brings word that my father is safe, and that Ellie is with him. And Link and Ajax, too, have both survived, battling to get here but, in the end, unable to do so.

"They're coming here now," says Athena, informing us of the more important events taking

315

place outside.

She doesn't overload us though, drained as we are. I can sense that she knows where the line is drawn, that we've been through enough for one day. So she doesn't tell us of the thousands of brave men and women we've lost. She doesn't tell us how close we were coming to defeat. She doesn't tell us, either, that Markus has been killed, lost to the fighting in Piscator. It's not until later that day that I learn of such things.

Sitting there, with Velia in my arms, I look upon AK1, still standing like a statue above Knight. There's a growing awkwardness to his face, not quite knowing what to do next, just staring at the ground at his feet.

I call out his name, and his eyes venture towards mine.

"Come sit here," I say.

He hesitates for a moment, before moving over to the wall and sitting a few paces away from me. All upright and firm, like he's never been taught how to relax.

Velia's half closed eyes open up as he comes, her gaze following him.

"Velia, meet AK1," I say.

She frowns, still confused as to why this Seeker has joined our cause.

"Um, hi…" she says.

AK1 hardly knows where to look. He glances at

her, but nothing more, and doesn't utter a word.

Then, she whispers harshly into my ear: "What's going on, Theo?"

I smile at her, and take a long breath.

"He's my brother," I say. "He's family…"

She still looks confused, her eyes turning to him again, inspecting him more closely. And then, I see her eyes change as the truth dawns.

"I understand," she says. "I understand it all now."

I look to the boy who saved us, and our eyes lock for a moment, the blue in his continuing to grow brighter.

"Brother," I whisper, staring at him.

Slowly, he nods.

"Brother," he says.

The minutes drift by, and soon enough the room begins to fill as our allies make it down to join us. I leave AK1 where he is, but promise to stay near him, promise I'll be back, as I dart forward to meet my father, covered in dust and soot and spattered blood.

As a family we hug, drawn together through the crowd of bodies, Jackson taking up Cyra's frame as she sobs into his chest, his eyes growing hooded as they look down upon Drake's body.

More people come, and my eyes search for Ajax, my best friend, my closest ally. He emerges as my father did, covered in the carnage of war, stepping into the vast room alongside Link. The two towering heroes gaze upon it all, and I can only imagine what things might have been like were they in here with us, and Athena and Velia too.

In the end, we managed alone, just my family fighting off the darkness. And now, they'll all learn of a new member, AK1's identity no longer to be shrouded in mystery and doubt, his name to be spoken, not as a threat or enemy, but as a hero, as a saviour to us all.

I greet Ajax with a long hug as more people come, and the Baron and the Cabal and the newly embodied Knight are all gathered up and taken away. Through the lands above, the dust will not settle for many days, many weeks. It may even be months before people can consider moving on.

And down here, right now, this is where it all starts. This is the first block placed at the foundation of a new world. Here, right now, we will come together and begin the process of growth once more.

The lost will be mourned. The heroes will be praised. The towns will be rebuilt and the lands resewn.

Here, in this lab, where the fate of the world has been decided, the future will be reset.

And it's a future that we can call our own.

A future that we can determine.

32
A New World

Never did I expect to attend so many funerals. Never did I expect to see so much death.

It all started with that of Troy, Master of Petram, so many months ago. Now, the new Master is dead too. But it's not his death that lingers in my mind most of all, it's that of Drake, my grandfather, a hero without equal.

So close were the two men that they're sent on their way together. Once more, I find myself out on the plateau of Petram, hardly able to hold back the tears as I stand before the plinth, the bodies of Drake and Markus atop it.

My father stands before them, issuing a touching eulogy to two men he knew so well. Across the plateau, and the city inside the mountain, tears are shed and silent words of prayer and thanks are whispered. The same will be happening all across the lands, from the far Western shores to the Eastern coast where both men met their ends. Tears for them, and tears for others; tens of thousands of soldiers and civilians who will were killed in the conflict.

The architect of it all has already seen his end,

answering for his crimes before the masses. No one wanted to wait for that. No one wanted to have it hanging over them. As our armies gathered on the stretch of earth between the cities of Piscator and Mercator, a stage was hastily erected.

Upon it, the Baron was set, tied up to a noose, his mouth gagged so we couldn't hear his wails and pathetic cries for mercy. Many thousands surrounded him, witnessing his end, watching from any vantage point they could find.

But only one could be given the honour of kicking away the stool.

So many wanted it, so many staking their claim. But in the end, only one person came to mind, the one who'd spent more time than any under his thumb.

It was a symbolic moment when AK1 stepped up to the stage, and looked the Baron in the eye. When he struck out with his foot, and kicked away the stool, and set the Baron swinging wildly in the air, his hands bound and neck tightly wrapped in strong rope.

As his face when red and then blue, no one uttered a word of pity. And right there, the real purpose of AK1 was revealed to the masses, this boy who had been bred for chaos, groomed to be infused with the mind of Augustus Knight.

This boy whose true purpose was to save us all.

He waits inside the mountain now, hidden away where he feels more comfortable. It isn't attention that he wants or craves, but silence and freedom. His entire life has been spent following orders, doing terrible things for the sake of a madman. Now, he's atoning for those things, desiring nothing but a quiet life away from war and terror, away from the chaos he was created to inflict.

He'll be given that, given space and time to try to find peace. After everything that's happened, it's the least he deserves.

Jackson's eulogy continues, his own place now atop this world. In the weeks and months to come, we'll all vote on a new leader to take us forward, a new President to see to the rebuilding of our lands.

I stand proud, knowing that my father will be at the front of the queue. That he will continue the proud tradition in our family, and lead us to a better future.

But for Drake, his part is over. Soon, his body will be set alight, and the ashes will be gathered. We'll spread it to the places he loved the most: his home of Agricola, where he once raised my mother; the city here, where he helped build the rebel cause; the old husk of Eden, still spiking out from the churning surf, the crumpled city so dear to him for so long.

Many places have seen his influence. Many places will miss him dearly. As will the people.

But none more than my mother, who stands beside me now, tears rolling gently down her cheeks. I take her hand in mine and squeeze tight, and we stand together and listen to Jackson speak of her father's great deeds, and the great deeds of Markus too.

He could go on forever, such were the lives the two men led. But he doesn't, bringing the service to an end as their bodies are lit to flame.

He steps down from the plinth, and we watch for a time as the stage turns to flame, and the bodies of the masters of Eden and Petram get consumed by the warming blaze.

Behind, some people begin to shuffle off, returning to their lives. But others remain, setting into a long vigil, unwilling to leave until their beloved leaders are gone, their corporeal forms fully cremated.

And with Cyra and Jackson, and Link and Ellie and Ajax, and Velia and Vesuvia and Athena and Leeta, we stand. All of us, together, side by side, waiting with our heads bowed in respect, the hours passing by like the flowing of the wind.

And only when the flames have fallen, and only embers remain, do we turn and move into the mountain, the air now growing with a bitter cold as the night descends.

Inside, the sounds of music are heard, the people turning to the celebration of their great leaders' lives. And to all those across the lands who have been lost to this war, words are spoken and memories shared, drinks sunk down throats as the people give thanks for the lives they still hold onto.

I hold Velia tight amid the throng, and pray that I never have to let go. And across from me, Ajax and Vesuvia do the same, her leg now fully healed, the four of us back together again.

We drink, and talk, and for the first time I meet Velia's mother. She draws me into a hug and kisses my cheek, and I see Velia's face light up with a beaming smile. And in that moment, as the music plays and she cuddles up close to me, I hear her whisper in my ear that she loves me.

I look at her with warm eyes and repeat the words back at her, and we kiss and dance among the people. And as we celebrate, never do we forget those we've lost, those we're here to say farewell to. Fathers and sons, mothers and daughters, brothers and sisters and distance relatives, dearest friends and colleagues. Everyone here has lost someone. Everyone here has felt the sting of grief.

But now, it's time for us all to move on.

The future depends on us to do so.

As the party continues, my mother comes to me. I'm reminded of how she did the same during Troy's funeral, passing me my first alcohol drink. Back then, the world was so different, my desire for adventure so strong. Now, I've seen enough to last a dozen lifetimes.

This time, she comes with no drink, moving through the crowd and setting her fingers and eyes to my bear claw necklace.

"Seems like a long time ago that I took this from you," she says. "I should never have doubted you, Theo."

"No, mum, you were just trying to protect me. You didn't know what was going to happen."

"Perhaps. But I need to learn to let go. I see you now…you're a man. And you're in love."

A knowing smile brightens on her face, and I feel a warmth beginning to build on my cheeks. I look to Velia, dancing with her mother and sister, and nod.

"I am…" I whisper.

"I'm so happy for you," she says, beaming. "But can I pull you away from her for a moment?"

"Of course."

"Good," she says, her words flattening a little. "Now follow me."

She leads me towards the back of the chamber, and down a long passage away from it. Winding away into the darkness, we descend through the mountain, the lights fixed to the rocky walls growing more and more sparse the deeper we go.

Soon, they stop completely, and my mum pulls out a torch to guide our way. The music above grows quieter and quieter, until it's barely audible. Eventually, as we reach passages and chambers I've never been to, it stops completely, only our footsteps now heard as they echo around us.

Eventually, we come to a final turn, and Cyra leads me onwards to a small gap in the stone. She squeezes through first, and I follow, entering into a small cave, cold and damp and dripping from above with an endless form of aural torture.

Her light shines towards the far wall, and I see a creature appear, dressed in rags and chained to the wall, his face pale as snow and covered with the early growth of a patchy beard. His black hair hangs down, lank and unwashed, his body littered with scars and cuts, his eyes shielded from the light with long, calloused fingers.

In the cold chamber, my mum's voice drifts out of her.

"Augustus," she says. "Augustus, are you awake?"

I watch on as Knight continues to squint at the light, such a rare thing for him down here.

"So this is where you've been keeping him," I say.

"Oh, this is the place," says Cyra.

Knight stirs, and his eyes open a little wider.

"You can't keep me down here forever," his voice comes out, raspy and hoarse. "Nothing can contain me!"

"Oh, I beg to differ," counters Cyra. "Do you know what day it is?"

He doesn't answer.

"Today is the day of my father's funeral, a man loved across this country. A man you killed. Oh, I think we're quite happy to keep you down here."

She hovers the light a little away from his face, shining it on the wall nearby. With the brightness doused, his eyes open wider, and he looks straight at my mother, standing above him.

"Look at me, Augustus. Look me right in the eye. I will be the last person you see. No one will come down here again. No one will save you. You will sit here, and you will think of everything you have done. You will rot here in the silence, with only your thoughts for company. Here, in the endless night, you will live, and you will die."

She takes a little step back, moving towards the gap in the stone where I stand.

"Now say goodbye to the light, Augustus. You will never know its warm glow again."

"You can't keep me here," he growls. "You can't…"

"Say goodbye," repeats Cyra slowly, moving back. "Say goodbye…"

"You can't do this to me!" he calls as she reaches me, his voice echoing down the passage behind us.

As his voice rages, my mother turns to me.

"Now come on, Theo. Let's rejoin the party."

We move through the little gap once more, and she tells me to take a grip of the rock. I note, now, that it's a boulder, capable of being rolled a little to the right. With all our might, we heave and push, and Knight's mad screams continue to rage. And bit by bit, the boulder moves, blocking the entrance and muting the calls of the devil within.

Alone in the darkness, he will face the endless night, stewing on his failure, his body still young. From a small gap in the stone above, food will be dropped, and water provided by the leak that incessantly drips to the cold, wet floor. Should he want it, he can stay alive, subsisting on the meagre rations we provide. Or should he choose to end his life by starving himself, or by battering his head on the rock walls, he can.

But live or die, he will never see the light again.

He wanted to cover the world in darkness, to spread his shadow across it.

Now, that's all he'll ever know.

But not us.

Despite the suffering we've faced, and the terrible horrors we've endured, life will go on. Many have been laid to rest, but many more are still alive, ready to fight on and rebuild our world. Better. Stronger. Fairer and more prosperous than ever before.

A new day is dawning.

And with Velia, and all my friends and family by my side, I know it will be a bright one.

THE END

To hear about the author's latest discounts and new releases, sign up to his newsletter at www.tcedgebooks.com